BUTTERFLY
KILLS

BRENDA CHAPMAN

BUTTERFLY KILLS

A **STONECHILD AND ROULEAU** MYSTERY

DUNDURN
PRESS

Publisher: Kwame Scott Fraser | Editor: Jennifer McKnight
Cover designer: Laura Boyle
Cover image: Unsplash/JR Korpa; Unsplash/ Cerqueira

Library and Archives Canada Cataloguing in Publication

Title: Butterfly kills : a Stonechild and Rouleau mystery / Brenda Chapman.
Names: Chapman, Brenda, 1955- author.
Description: 2nd edition.
Identifiers: Canadiana 20230163513 | ISBN 9781459752856 (softcover)
Classification: LCC PS8605.H36 B88 2023 | DDC C813/.6—dc23

  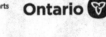

We acknowledge the support of the Canada Council for the Arts and the Ontario Arts Council for our publishing program. We also acknowledge the financial support of the Government of Ontario, through the Ontario Book Publishing Tax Credit and Ontario Creates, and the Government of Canada.

Care has been taken to trace the ownership of copyright material used in this book. The author and the publisher welcome any information enabling them to rectify any references or credits in subsequent editions.

The publisher is not responsible for websites or their content unless they are owned by the publisher.

Printed and bound in Canada.

Dundurn Press
1382 Queen Street East
Toronto, Ontario, Canada M4L 1C9
dundurn.com, @dundurnpress 𝕏 f ⌾

For all the courageous hearts.

I only ask to be free. The butterflies are free.

— Charles Dickens

1

LEAH SAMPSON COULDN'T wait for the day to end. Twelve straight hours on the phone talking students through school jitters, boyfriend troubles, and suicidal thoughts was enough to make anyone go mad. Whoever said this generation had their shit together was dreaming in Technicolor. The problems she'd worked this lot through today had left her drained. A glass of Pinot, bowl of chocolate ice cream, and soak in a hot tub were long past due.

She turned her head as Wolf skirted past her desk to flop onto the couch positioned under a line of grimy windows. Darkness pressed against the glass and she glanced at her watch. *Ten to nine.* Ten more minutes and she'd be on her way home.

She tuned back into the girl's voice droning into her ear and waited for her to take a breath. "If he threatens to hit you again, call me back," Leah said. "We'll talk further about your options. It'll be time to decide whether you want to make a change. Yes, call anytime. We're always here to help you through."

She wearily hung up and looked across at Wolf, his long legs stretched out on the floor in front of him. His eyes were closed.

"What have you got on for tonight?" he asked.

A question inside of a question. He was really asking if she'd ended the affair. Had she stopped slinking around behind his back?

She couldn't risk him finding out what she'd done. Not yet.

"I'm going home, *alone*, and putting my feet up," she said, using both hands to refasten the clip that held her long hair away from her face. "And I'll be in the library writing a paper tomorrow, so no chance of getting into trouble."

Wolf's eyes flashed open; expressive green orbs flecked with gold. They were half of the reason why he'd been nicknamed a member of the animal kingdom. The other half lay in his mane of brown hair and full beard. She could have added his animal fierceness in bed, but that was an observation she'd attempted to seal away in her memory bank. Some days with more success than others.

He nodded, a smile tugging at his lips. "I'll walk you out if you're ready."

She glanced at her watch again. Four minutes after nine. "Where the hell is Gail? She's taking over the line from me and late as usual."

"Getting a coffee. She'll be back in a few."

"I can't leave until she gets here."

"I'll wait."

With blessed kindness, the phone remained silent until Gail traipsed in at a quarter past. Leah grimaced in her direction, but Gail ignored the rebuke just as she ignored most subtleties in life. Spiky red hair, round face, and rounder body littered with cartoon character tattoos and piercings, her style was as unapologetic as her character. Yet, Leah had to admit that Gail had a way with the callers; an empathy one couldn't fake.

Gail balanced a coffee cup in one hand and a biology text and iPad under her arm. "How're our loonies doing today?" she asked. "I hope they had the grace to call you and didn't save up their anxieties for my shift."

"Nice," said Wolf, rubbing a hand through his beard. "If callers knew the sensitive face of Queen's University at the other end of the help line, they might think twice about sharing their secrets with you."

"I'm just talking about the repeat loonies who wallow in messes of their own making." Gail dropped into the swivel chair newly vacated by Leah and scattered her possessions across the desk. "Thank God for the rule never to meet any of them. Can you imagine?"

"The regulars have all phoned in this afternoon, I think," Leah said. "Some more than once." She grabbed her cellphone from the desk. "We're off then." She turned her head so that Wolf didn't see her face. He'd know she was hiding something. He had a sixth sense when it came to her and lying.

They exited their office in the limestone house sandwiched next to the student centre on University Avenue. A cool breeze had come up from the direction of Lake Ontario and the air smelled of rain, dank, fecund vegetation, and earth worms. The fall semester had only begun four weeks ago, but the student problems never took a break. Summer, fall, winter, spring — each season had its own emotional issues. Leah noticed the asphalt was wet in the circle of light under a streetlamp. She shivered in her light T-shirt and denim skirt. Late September had brought in a welcome Indian summer. It had been a hot day when she left for work that morning. She hadn't thought to bring a jacket.

Wolf walked on the road side. He told her one night in bed that they'd been taught how to treat a girl in gym class:

walk closest to the oncoming traffic, hold the door open, wear a condom. He'd taken it all to heart.

She'd been hurt at first when he ended their relationship. Hurt that he'd doubted her, then anger that finally resolved itself into acceptance. She'd been shocked when he told her the month before that he knew she was having an affair. It was exactly the wrong time for him to accuse her. He'd pressed for a name and she'd refused. Predictably, he'd made the leap that she was protecting a married man. She hadn't denied it, not even when Wolf told her they had to take a break from each other. It still made her chest constrict and her eyes burn to think he didn't want her anymore, that he could doubt her so easily. They reached a truce after a few weeks of not speaking. Now she was grateful for his brotherly presence in her life. It meant he might still come around and become something more. She just needed a bit more time.

"I've handed in my notice to Mark," he said.

She stopped walking. "I hope it wasn't because of my …"

"No," he interrupted quickly. "Our breakup had nothing to do with my decision. I just think it's time I got into the field. I've accepted a job with the Kingston Public School Board that starts next semester. I'm heading out west for a few weeks first."

She caught up to him. "Then you'll come back to Kingston." For a moment, she'd feared losing him altogether.

"For now." He turned his head sideways and grinned at her. "I'll have an office, but will travel to different schools to work with the kids."

"You'll be terrific. I'm jealous."

"When you finish next year, I can put a word in for you too."

"I'm not sure this kind of work is for me. I've had doubts lately."

"It's the first you've said."

"It's just all the pain, you know? People and their problems that never get resolved. I think they've finally worn me out."

Wolf reached an arm around her shoulders and pulled her into a hug. She let herself relax against him for a moment before pushing him away.

"I'm just thinking about it, okay? No decision yet."

"Don't do anything rash. You're good at helping people, even if the results aren't always obvious. You have empathy."

"I just can't distance myself." Some of their troubles hit too close to home. She wanted to tell him about what she'd done, but couldn't bring herself to yet. She'd crossed lines, but wouldn't drag in anybody else. Still, her actions proved she wasn't professional enough for this field of work.

Wolf looked down Sydenham Street toward the house where she had an apartment. It was dark along the road, a street lamp burned out near her driveway. "I could walk you to your door if you'd like."

"I thought you were meeting someone at the pub."

"Yeah, but they can wait."

"I'm fine, Wolf. You go."

"You sure?"

"I'll see you in a couple of days."

"Get some rest, then." He gave her a quick kiss on the cheek. She held on to his arm for a moment before he turned away. She would have liked to wrap her whole body around him and make things right. From the look in his eyes, she believed he wanted the same.

Leah walked briskly down Sydenham toward Johnson, chilled in her light clothing. At the walkway to the front door of the two-storey red brick house where she'd lived for the past two years, she stopped and looked back toward the corner. Wolf still stood in the shadows where the streets intersected, watching until she made it safely inside. Another gym class lesson well learned.

She smiled and waved at the same time he looked down to check his phone. She slowly lowered her hand. A feeling of sadness welled up unexpectedly. One day Wolf would find somebody else and this fragile friendship would slip away. Some things could never go back to what they were. It always went like that with the people who meant the most to her. *Sometimes you don't know what you've got till it's gone.*

She started up the short walkway toward the house and surveyed the apartment windows. Lights on the main floor were off, but Becky appeared to be home on the second. Leah's spirits rose a bit. It looked like there'd be some company around for the weekend.

The house was built in the 1930s when front porches and bay windows were in vogue. Leah liked the old style elegance of the structure, even if time had worn the brick and peeled the paint on the wood detailing above the windows. Her one-bedroom apartment in the basement was cozy but definitely student digs. She'd filled it with IKEA furniture and her parents' cast offs. As soon as she finished her thesis, she planned to move into a nicer place and have a yard sale. The Queen's Help Line had promised her more hours whenever she had more time to give them. It would do until she made up her mind about the future.

The front door creaked open and she entered the hallway. An envelope lay at the base of the stairs, stark white against the grey carpet. She walked over and stooped to pick it up, flipping the envelope over to read the name as she straightened. Becky must have dropped it on her way upstairs.

Leah walked up the creaky stairs to the second floor landing and knocked on Becky's door. She could hear music and Becky talking on the phone when she leaned her ear against the wood. She listened for a while to see if Becky would hang up. After a minute or so, Leah knocked a second time before bending to slip the letter under the door. She would have liked to share a glass of wine and a chat, so she lingered a while longer before giving up and heading downstairs. For some reason she didn't feel like being alone this evening.

She flicked on the light switch at the head of the basement stairs and cursed as the light remained off. It was the second time the bulb had burned out within three weeks. She'd phone the landlord as soon as she got inside and get him to check the wiring. She should have insisted last time.

She stepped carefully down the steep stairwell, the light from the landing just enough to make out the outline of the steps. A mustiness seeped up from the basement concrete floor that no amount of air freshener could disguise. She'd bought a dehumidifier that helped slightly and lit a lot of incense, but it was time to start looking at apartment ads in the *Whig Standard*. Hopefully she'd find a better place not already rented for fall term.

At the bottom of the stairs, she felt in her pocket for her keys, then slid her hand down the door to the lock. She stopped with her hand on the knob and turned her head toward the laundry room. Was that a noise she'd heard or was fatigue making her jumpy? She listened for a moment more, her heart pounding like a jackhammer. Silence filled the space and she exhaled slowly. A braver person would have gone to look, but that would not be her. She had no desire to face a rat or other vermin in the dark.

It took three fumbling tries before she unlocked the door and opened it into her apartment. She stepped inside and felt along the wall to the light switch. She smiled when the room burst into brightness. At least the wiring problem hadn't entered her inner sanctum as she'd feared it might.

She reached back with her foot to shove the door closed. Instead of clicking shut, it swung back toward her. Her first thought was that dampness had warped the wood and the lock didn't catch as it should. "Dammit," she said aloud.

She turned and took a step toward the door before her legs stopped working. Her eyes widened as her brain scrambled to make sense of what she was seeing. A person dressed entirely in black filled the opening like a character out of a slasher movie. Her first thought was how absurd they looked, but horror quickly followed. The hand she'd extended toward the door handle found her mouth. She let out a shriek.

The figure stepped inside her apartment and pushed the door shut. Their eyes stayed on hers. "Did you think this was a game?"

She shook her head but comprehension dawned. Her mind was scrambling, searching frantically for toeholds. The chance of Becky hearing her scream two floors above was remote. There was no chance of pushing past the person in the narrow hallway and even less chance to make it out the closed door without being grabbed.

"I have no idea what you want," she heard herself beg. "Please just leave." She stumbled backward, her leg banging against the wall.

The person took a step closer, leather-gloved hands reaching toward her. Leah turned to run into the living room, knowing she was trapped with no way out.

Knowing she was in very big trouble.

2

AS SOON AS he got into work Saturday morning, Jacques Rouleau dialled the long-distance number that Whelan, his former colleague on the Ottawa force, had forwarded to him the month before. It was the sixth time he'd tried in as many weeks. He'd resorted to calling at odd hours since nobody had returned his messages, even though he left his cellphone, home, and work numbers. He shifted the phone to his other hand. On the fourth ring, somebody picked up.

"Is this Shannon MacDonald? Yes? My name is Staff Sergeant Jacques Rouleau. I've left a few messages trying to track down Kala Stonechild."

"Kala's not here. Sorry I never called you back, but I had nothing to tell you."

"She hasn't been in touch?"

"No." He heard a deep intake of her breath. "Kala came back to Red Rock and got her dog after she left Ottawa and disappeared into the bush. I haven't heard from her since. It's been four months, give or take."

"I'm trying to hold the job in the Criminal Investigations Division in Kingston open for her, but I was handed a stack of resumés last week. I have to come up with a name by the end of the month."

"I don't know what to tell you. Probably go ahead and fill it with someone else."

"That might be my only option."

He sensed she wasn't telling him everything. He waited. The silence lengthened to the edge of social politeness. When she finally resumed talking, her voice was less certain, worried. "Kala wasn't in a very good frame of mind last time I saw her. I've sent her several messages on her phone, but she hasn't responded to any of them. She's never been out of touch this long before."

"She left Ottawa without much notice. Did something happen to upset her on the job?"

"It was a family matter. She didn't talk about it much."

Rouleau remembered Kala's dark, haunted eyes, her closed-off expression the last time he'd seen her. For some reason he couldn't name, he knew she needed his help. After only a few months of working together in Ottawa, he felt this irrational responsibility for her. "I'll put off filling the position as long as I can. Let's hope she gets in touch this week."

"There's no saying she'll even want to work in Kingston with you."

"I know, but something tells me she might."

"You don't really know much about her, do you, Detective?"

She was right, he didn't. It was his turn to hesitate. "I know she's a good cop and maybe could use a break," he said at last.

"Kala's not one who likes to owe anybody or have any favours done. She never gets attached. I wouldn't hold my breath about her taking that job. I'll let her know though, next time I hear from her."

"I'd appreciate it." He heard the clunk of the receiver and then the dial tone humming in his ear.

He walked away from his desk and stood in front of his office window on the second floor of the Kingston police detachment, thinking about the enigma that was Kala Stonechild. He couldn't shake the worried feeling he got every time he thought of her. She'd seemed desperate, more alone than anyone he'd ever known. He'd scoured her personnel file for clues and knew she'd been in foster care as a kid, from the age of three. She'd all but disappeared after leaving high school until she turned twenty-two. He wondered what she'd done in those five years before she started college.

The view from his office window was Division Street and a farmer's field beyond. He studied the limestone farmhouse with the purple door and the John Deere tractor parked in front of the well-maintained barn. The farm, now subdivided into treed lots with houses set back from the road, had seen more prosperous days. The owners at some point had sold off most of the property, likely staving off foreclosure. Still, he had to admire the current landlord for stubbornly clinging on to a dying way of life.

There was a knock at the door and Rouleau turned. Paul Gundersund's lanky six-foot-two-inch frame filled the doorway. He crossed to Rouleau's desk and set two mugs on the only clear surface between two stacks of folders. As he stepped back, he pushed blond hair out of his eyes. A muscle jumped where a scar marked his left cheek.

"We've got a call. Your line was busy so they put it through to me. A woman named Della Munroe says her husband raped her last night."

"Where is she now?"

"Hospital with a counsellor. The beat cop took her statement and we're to follow up."

"Is she pressing charges?"

"Not sure. They've sent someone to pick up the husband, Brian."

"Spousal rape is a bugger to prosecute."

"Yeah. He hurt her though, so we might get lucky."

Rouleau picked up his coffee and started toward the door. He reached into his pocket and pulled out his set of car keys, tossing them to Gundersund.

"You can drive."

———

Rouleau and Gundersund sat across from Della Munroe in one of the small waiting rooms. They'd been given the go-ahead from the doctor to question Della about the rape. She'd decided to press charges.

Della's eyes were luminous blue, red-rimmed from crying, still glistening with tears. She was taller than Rouleau had first thought, nearly matching his five foot ten when she stood to shake hands with him, but slender, with long, black hair and a heart-shaped face. She wore a green hospital gown and incongruously pink flip-flops with diamond sequins. Rouleau took a seat across from her. Gundersund remained standing near the door.

"Where's your husband now, Mrs. Munroe?" he asked.

"Brian's at his bakery. It's the Sunshine Bakery on Brock Street, a few blocks from the university campus. I want to apply for a restraining order this morning."

"We can get that started."

Della pressed a tissue to her right eye and inhaled a shuddering breath. "I knew it wasn't good between Brian and me for a long time, but this … I never thought he'd do something like this. We should never have gotten married."

"Your husband was abusive before?"

Her head barely inclined in response, her eyes avoiding his. "He was ... obsessive about me. He insisted we move here and now I think it was so that I was away from my family and friends ... that he wanted me isolated. I was just so stupid. But I made one friend, at least for a while. Celia Paules. She lives next door." Della raised her eyes. "He made me stop visiting her last month. I've been *such* an idiot to let him do this to me."

Rouleau nodded in Gundersund's direction for him to jot down the information.

Della bit her lip. "I just want my marriage to be over with and I want to go back to Toronto. I should never have left. Never." She'd begun rocking gently back and forth on the couch, her hands folded across her chest and wrapped around her elbows.

"You have a four-year-old son," Rouleau looked at his notes. "Tommy."

Della's eyes snapped onto his. "Tommy is coming with me. I won't let Brian near him after this." Her voice had risen to just shy of hysterical. "They've kept him in the play-room down the hall." She started to get up from her chair. "I should go see him."

Rouleau raised a hand. "He's fine, Mrs. Munroe. We've got someone watching. You'll both be protected."

Her body eased back into the chair. Her shoulders hunched in like an old woman's and she resumed rocking back and forth.

Rouleau gave her a moment, then asked, "Has he ever hurt Tommy that you know of?"

"Brian ... he's been working long hours. Sometimes his patience wears thin. Tommy's active and, well, I suppose Brian has lifted a hand from time to time. I tried to prevent it by putting Tommy to bed before Brian came home or taking him to the park. Brian shouldn't be around kids when he's tired ... or drinking."

"Last night you said that he'd been drinking, that you'd both been drinking."

"Yes. I made a nice dinner — lamb and potatoes, his favourites — and we shared a bottle of red wine. I had a glass and he had the rest. I thought he needed to unwind and I was prepared to have, you know, sex, until he got angry with me. He said I was dressing too provocatively when I went to class. We started arguing and he grabbed me. I told him that I wanted him to leave me the hell alone."

"Take your time."

"He ... he pushed me into the bedroom and ripped off my shirt. I struggled but he held me down. I kept telling him to stop." Her voice broke. "He was rougher than he's ever been. He pulled off my pants and raped me." Tears started rolling down her cheeks. She whispered, "He hurt me. I have bruises all down the inside of my thighs. It hurts to go to the bathroom."

Rouleau paused for a moment to give her time. "In your original statement you said that you took a shower when he left, is this correct?"

"Yes. I felt so dirty. He made me feel like a slut. I curled up on the bed and must have fallen asleep. This morning, I just ... I couldn't let him get away with it. I was scared to leave Tommy alone so I drove us both here. I need this to stop."

Rouleau looked at Gundersund. "I think we have enough for now. The doctor was able to get a specimen of Brian's semen. Can you follow up on that lab report?"

"Certainly." Gundersund packed up his notepad and went in search of the doctor.

Rouleau leaned forward. "Try to get some rest, Mrs. Munroe. Other officers are picking up your husband now.

We're heading back to the station when we leave here to question him."

"Then, you'll be keeping him in jail?"

"It all depends on the judge and bail. With the restraining order, he won't be coming near you or he'll be arrested."

She nodded. Her eyes and mouth relaxed for the first time. "I'm going to start making arrangements to leave Kingston. Would that be alright?"

"Yes, as long as we can reach you and you're still in Ontario. You cannot take Tommy out of the province until custody is settled. Do you know the address where you'll be staying?"

"I'll phone it in when I've confirmed. My family and I've been estranged since I married Brian. They never liked him. I lost my mother a few years ago but my dad ... well, I'm hoping enough time has gone by."

"We'll be in touch soon, Mrs. Munroe." He handed her a card with his name and phone number. "If you need us at any time, call my cell number. Call 911 if you're in danger, although we'll do our best to make sure that your husband doesn't contact you."

"I wish this had never happened. I wish I'd never defied my parents to marry him." She lowered her face into her hands and began to sob.

———

Rouleau and Gundersund entered the interview room where Brian Munroe had spent the better part of two hours. His hands covered his face and he didn't stir from this position even when Rouleau greeted his lawyer, Suzie Chen. Rouleau had met Suzie once before on a youth justice case. Her reputation was that of a legal pit bull who tenaciously defended the down and out. She sat next to Munroe, expensively decked out in a navy power suit over a grey silk shirt buttoned to her neck. Munroe hadn't dressed to impress anyone, wearing ripped jeans, a stained sweatshirt, and unlaced black runners.

"Detectives." Suzie nodded and put one hand on Munroe's forearm. She could have been a child, so petite next to the massive bulk of Brian Munroe.

Munroe finally lifted his shaved head and stared at Rouleau with baleful black eyes. He was a black man, the skin taut over high cheekbones and broad forehead. The corded veins in his neck bulged as he pressed his hands on the table and started to push himself to his feet. Rouleau thought that even with Della Munroe's height and size, she would have been no match for her husband's brute strength.

"It's okay," Suzie said, and Munroe lowered himself back into the chair. She looked at Rouleau. "Brian's instinct is to stand and shake hands, even with cops. He'll get over it."

Rouleau spoke into the tape recorder, giving the time and the names of everyone present in the room. He confirmed that Munroe knew and understood his rights. When he finished, Suzie raised her hand.

"We have a statement, if I may."

"Go ahead," Rouleau said.

"Brian Munroe denies all of the allegations put forth by his wife Della Munroe. He did not lay a hand on her, nor did he rape her."

Rouleau observed Munroe while she spoke. He was shaking his head and mumbling under his breath.

"Is that right, Brian?" Rouleau asked.

Munroe lifted his eyes to Rouleau. "Damn straight. The bitch is lying."

"Do you deny having sex with Della last night?"

"We had sex yesterday morning. Consensual sex. I should have known she was plotting something."

"Why would she do that?"

"Because I told her the day before that we should separate. She said this would be the last time, you know, for old times' sake." He hit himself on the forehead. "What was I thinking? Our entire marriage has been her playing me and me falling for it."

Suzie touched the back of his hand lying on the table. "I think we've said all we're going to say at this juncture."

"Did you spend last night at home with your wife, Brian?" Rouleau asked.

"I slept in the basement and left at close to four a.m. to start work at the bakery. I have no idea what she was up to all day yesterday."

"Have you ever hit your wife?"

Munroe shifted and his eyes dropped to the table. His neck drooped so that his chin almost touched his chest. "Once. Once I grabbed her and pushed her off me. My fingers left marks on her arm, but that was it. I never lifted a hand to her otherwise."

"What about Tommy? Have you ever hit your son?"

Munroe started to stand. "Damn that bitch all to hell." He pressed his hands on the table and the muscles in his neck and arms rippled dangerously. "Is that what she's saying? I never touched my son."

"We're done here." Suzie reached over and put her hand on his wrist. She swung her briefcase from the floor to the table, then stood and looked down at Rouleau. "Unless you plan to charge him."

"The Crown is laying sexual assault and battery charges. He'll be detained until his bail hearing this afternoon or tomorrow morning."

"I serve notice that I'll be fighting Della Munroe's absurd allegations every step of the way. This won't be the open-and-shut case you think it is."

"They never are," Rouleau said.

———

"So who do you think is lying?" Gundersund asked. He took his eyes off the road for a moment to look at Rouleau.

"My guess would be him based on the bruising. The photos in her file are brutal. No way she did that to herself. We should check with neighbours and friends to see if they observed anything nasty going on between them before this."

"Their times are off. He says they had sex in the morning and she said the evening. Is it possible to prove either way?"

"She waited to go to the hospital, so it's hard to tell exactly from the medical report."

Gundersund grimaced. "They should have separated before things got this far."

Rouleau nodded. "The problem is, they rarely ever do."

3

GAIL PANKHURST STEPPED through the main door and removed one of her ear buds. It was hot in their little office space with only two fans mounted on the ceiling, rotating on full, uselessly moving the soupy air around and around. The university funded their help line but hadn't coughed up any more money than necessary, budget restraints being the usual excuse for skimping on air conditioning. She stopped at Jucinda Rivera's desk on her way to the vacant one near the far wall.

"Hey Juicy. Are you starting shift or finishing up? I thought you had today off."

Jucinda flinched as she did every time Gail used the nickname, but she didn't comment. Gail routinely poked her with the moniker, curious to see when Jucinda would react. So far, she'd kept any displeasure from reaching her lips. Gail had made Jucinda one of several unofficial subjects for her experiments in human psychology. She was particularly interested in how her guinea pigs dealt with upset or annoyances in social settings. Jucinda wasn't alone in pretending that something that obviously bothered her wasn't a concern.

Jucinda tossed her black hair, dyed fuchsia at the tips, over her shoulder and reached for the ringing phone. "Leah was supposed to be in but couldn't make it. Mark worked this morning, but he had to leave after lunch for an appointment. I'm filling in until he gets back," Jucinda said, picking up the phone.

"Great." Gail tossed her bag under her desk and plopped into the chair. Adele was singing into her right ear and she left the other ear bud swinging loose. She could relate to the British superstar — criticized for being a little pudgy but her own woman nonetheless. Gail had learned not to give a rat's arse what people thought of her. She'd let all that go when she had Mickey Mouse tattooed onto her right bicep. She'd had Betty Boop inked the length of her forearm right after she told her parents she was gay. Every tattoo marked another step in her emancipation. She now felt completely liberated, which was good since she was running out of available skin with the exception of her face and neck. She'd promised her mother to keep those ink-free zones.

It was an hour later before both she and Jucinda were off the phones at the same time.

"Busy afternoon," Gail commented. She stood and stretched. "Would you like a cup of Earl Grey?"

"Sure," said Jucinda. She opened her desk drawer and pulled out a package of Fig Newtons. "I have these to go with it."

They decided to drink their tea and eat the cookies standing directly under the fan near the window while they got the chance to leave their phones.

"Leah never takes the day off," Gail said. "Do you know when she called in?"

"There was a voice mail message, or that's what Mark said when he phoned me to replace her. He said the odd thing was that Leah left the voice mail early Friday night right after her shift ended saying she needed a day off, especially since he'd booked the Saturday off a month ago and so missed her message until he got in Sunday afternoon. If you ask me, she could have cleared it with him before she went home instead of leaving us short-staffed today. But *no*, that would have been too much trouble for our princess Leah. Anyway, Mark should have been back by now."

"What about Wolf?"

"He's studying. He has that board exam and then has to defend his thesis. He told me they have him slated in next month. Hard to believe he's that close to a Ph.D."

"Dr. Wolf. Has a nice ring. It's too bad he and Leah broke it off."

"He can do better."

Gail looked more closely at Jucinda. Was that a blush under her swarthy colouring? If she didn't know better, she'd say Juicy had eyes for Wolf. They said the cool, detached ones often held the most secrets. Maybe Jucinda had it going on. "You don't think much of our Leah," she said in a neutral voice. She studied Jucinda's face.

"She's a ho."

Gail choked on a mouthful of tea. She wiped at the hot liquid dribbling down her chin. "Excuse me?"

Jucinda's eyes flashed righteous anger. "I don't respect that kind of woman. It's hypocritical for her to be giving advice to university kids when she's carrying on like a common whore with a married man."

"Wow. I didn't know you felt that way about her. I'm not sure I'd call her a ho, myself," said Gail. "She's more like a free spirit."

"Only if free spirit is a euphemism for loose and easy. Anyhow, Wolf is better off without her."

Gail was close enough to Jucinda to smell the sweet coconut scent of her hair when she flipped it back from her face. In the two years they'd worked together she'd always thought of Jucinda as virginal and placid, like a shallow green pond with nary a breeze stirring. Pretty, petite, and pudding-dull. This opening into the workings of Jucinda's brain was unprecedented and a wee bit disturbing. Just what did Jucinda know about Leah and why hadn't Gail picked up on it? *A married man?*

They finished their tea and returned to their desks. Gail talked a boy through his urge to quit calculus all the while keeping one curious eye on Jucinda, who'd opened a biology textbook. She read it while twirling a long strand of hair around and around in her fingers, every so often lifting her head to look toward the front entrance as if waiting for someone. Gail found her own head turning toward the door in unison.

Mark Withers sauntered in as Gail hung up the phone. Jucinda glanced over at him and said hello, but her shoulders slumped and the smile didn't stay on her face for more than a second.

So it's not Mark you're waiting for. Gail looked across at their boss, the eternal beach boy dressed in his navy shirt with wide horizontal white stripes, khaki shorts, and brown loafers, worn sockless. His hair was a tousle of sun-bleached strands, cut like Robert Redford's in that Butch Cassidy movie. You'd never know that Mark had a good ten years on the rest of them. He could have passed for early twenties.

"Hey ladies," he said. "You can head out, Jucinda. Nate will be here in a few minutes."

"Good. If Leah's away tomorrow, maybe line up Nathan or Wolf. I have an exam in the afternoon."

"No problemo. She hasn't called in so I expect her back for her shift."

Gail looked over his shoulder. Nate was coming through the door, carrying a large coffee and a box of doughnuts that he offered around. He and Mark were the only two married employees. He was also Mark's polar opposite, quiet and observant, always dressed in jeans and a shirt with the sleeves rolled up. He'd graduated the year before and worked part-time on the help line and part-time as Professor Dino Tadesco's teaching assistant. Gail found Nate the most attractive of the three men on staff, not that she was into men.

She looked over at Jucinda to see if his entrance had brightened her up. She was biting into a cruller and it was hard to read her expression, but she didn't look all aglow in Nathan's manly presence. Gail hadn't seriously thought Juicy would go for a married man anyway. That only left Wolf.

Jucinda stuffed the textbook she'd been reading into her purse and made her exit. Nate sprawled out in her desk chair and immediately took a call. Mark disappeared into his cubbyhole office to do some paperwork. He shut the door as per usual. Gail blew him a kiss that he would never receive.

Beach Boy, her pet name for Mark, had been complaining for weeks about all the forms he had to complete and the hoops he had to jump through to keep their grant. He had to defend all over again the need to have a help line when the university had face-to-face counselling available most weekdays and evenings. Even though kids needed an appointment to see a counsellor and the waiting list was getting longer by the day, the help line still had to justify its existence. *Try telling a suicidal student to book an appointment*, Gail thought. *Go ahead and tell them to hold on to their anxiety until regular office hours that don't include the weekends.* How many kids had phoned in and told their secrets and fears only because it was safe and anonymous? The help line was open seven a.m. to eleven p.m. seven days a week, and graduate psych students fielded the calls with Mark supervising and filling in as needed on the phone. They operated close to the bone, but they all believed in what they were doing. Professor Tadesco was their biggest supporter. Gail hoped he wouldn't get tired of the politics and toss in the towel. They'd done a lot of good work and the need was great for both walk-in counselling and the anonymous help line.

She answered two more calls — a first-year student who'd broken up with his girlfriend and a fourth-year in teacher's college who didn't know if she could handle problem kids — and the shift was over. Mark would answer the phone for a couple of hours and Nate would close at eleven. They only had one person on the last two hours of the night and before lunch. They used to have full shifts but Mark made the cuts when their funding dropped the year before. So far they were barely coping with the demand.

The front door opened and Wolf entered. He looked from Gail to Nate and back again. "I thought Leah was on tonight. I must have got it wrong." He walked over to Gail's desk and picked up a wizened honey doughnut on his way by. Nate had the phone to his ear and waved in Wolf's direction.

"Leah called in Friday night and said she needed the day off today," Gail said. She looked into Wolf's piercing green eyes and wondered if it was true that Leah had been sleeping around on him. She was a fool if she was, but it would explain their sudden break up. It would explain other behaviours she'd witnessed when silently observing Leah: uncharacteristic evasive responses to questions, sudden unexplained disappearances.

"Strange," Wolf said. "She never called to cancel our plans. We were meeting up with classmates at the campus pub after her shift today before everyone separates for good."

Gail tilted her head. "Maybe she got a better offer." She lobbed the line out like a hand grenade and studied Wolf's face, waiting for a crack in his armour. He didn't react one way or the other. She was momentarily disappointed. "Well, time for me to head home," she said cheerily when it was obvious he wasn't going to play ball.

"I'm going to talk to Mark. See you later." He smiled and strode across the office toward Mark's closed door. She watched him knock and disappear inside.

Most peculiar, she thought as she gathered up her books and stuffed them into her knapsack. She looked inside Beach Boy's office as she walked past on her way to the front door. He and Wolf were deep in conversation and didn't notice her leaving. *I wonder what that's all about.*

4

THE DOOR WAS answered by a woman with a baby on her hip and a two-year-old clinging to her leg. Celia Paules was dressed in a purple tank top and black shorts, her feet bare with toenails painted bubble gum pink. Brown hair hung in damp curls to her shoulders. Rouleau judged her to be midthirties despite her teenage clothing so similar to Della Munroe's. After carefully inspecting their badges, Celia invited them into a kitchen that looked like a whirling dervish had carved a path of destruction through. The heat from the day had landed squarely in this room. Her hand motioned them in the direction of the table as she turned to get a bottle of milk from the counter.

Rouleau cleaned a handful of soggy Cheerios from a chair and sat down. The two-year-old stood staring up wide-eyed at Gundersund, a thumb in his mouth and a blanket clutched in his chubby hand. The cloth diaper, his only bit of clothing, sagged dangerously.

"Sit, Gundersund," said Rouleau. "He probably thinks you're a giant from a storybook. Maybe that one at the top of the beanstalk."

"Little kids love me," said Gundersund, lowering onto a chair that looked like it might break into kindling under his weight. "They're not smart enough to fear me yet."

"Go play with your trucks," said the woman to the boy. She patted his head on the way by. He didn't have far to go. Toys littered every square foot of floor space. She shoved a pile of laundry onto the floor and sat in the chair with her back to the patio window. Cradling the baby on her lap, she popped the bottle into its mouth, then angled herself to look at them while keeping an eye on her son. "So how can I help you, detectives?"

"Della Munroe told us that she spent time over here talking to you this past year," said Rouleau.

"Della's okay, isn't she?"

"She's fine; but there's been an altercation and we're following up. How well do you know the Munroes?" Rouleau glanced at Gundersund. He took out a pen and slid his notebook from his pocket onto his leg.

"They moved in about two years ago. Della used to come for coffee."

"Used to?" Rouleau asked.

"Up until about a month ago. She said Brian didn't like her wasting time. They have a four-year-old boy, Tommy, and she was home with him in the mornings. Other than that, she takes a couple of university courses in the afternoons when Tom's in kindergarten. Brian works at the Sunshine Bakery on Brock."

"Would you say Brian and Della were happy together?"

"I thought so at first, but Della said Brian had to be into the bakery at four a.m. so it meant he was in bed by eight most nights. It was putting a strain on their relationship. Also, I don't think they had a lot of income. She complained a few times about being stuck without a car. Brian thought the courses she was taking were a waste of time and she told me he didn't want to pay for her to continue in the fall. She's working on an undergrad degree in English lit with a psych minor."

Rouleau accepted a race car that the child placed on his knee. "Any signs of violence, or did she ever say she was scared of him?"

Celia bit her lip. "Actually, she went out of her way to say everything was good at home. You know that saying: methinks she doth protest too much? One time she had bruises on her arm. When I asked about them, she laughed and told me she'd walked into the door. She said that she knew how that sounded, but Brian would never hurt her. She kept insisting. The last time I saw her, her left eye was black. She didn't say how it happened, and I didn't ask."

"Why not?"

"I didn't need to. Della finally admitted that things weren't going so well at home, but she was going to try harder to make it work. That meant stopping our coffee hour and spending more time cleaning the house. She really wasn't very good at running a house from what I saw." Celia looked around her kitchen and laughed. "Luckily, my husband doesn't care what our place looks like."

"How well did you know Brian?"

"I met him a few times, but he worked a lot. Maybe their different backgrounds put another strain on them. Della implied that race was the reason her parents disowned her."

Rouleau wasn't convinced that skin colour was a factor in the Munroes' current marital problems but filed the comment in his possibility file. "And did you form any impression about him?"

"He was quiet, an introvert, I'd say. Della's the opposite … or used to be. I wasn't sure why they ever hooked up, well, except for their obvious good looks. Brian's gorgeous, like a football player, and Della's that outgoing cheerleader type. They were living in Toronto when they met. She was in her last year of high school and he was a few years older.

She told me that he was a cook in a fast food restaurant and they saved enough to open this bakery. Della never said too much about it except that she was the one that did all the scrimping and saving; otherwise they'd still be living in some slum high rise. She got pregnant with Tommy right after they hooked up and said it was bad timing but she was always blessed to have him." Celia shifted the baby onto her shoulder and began patting on its back. "Sex doesn't carry you as far once the babies arrive if that's all that's holding your relationship together."

"The long hours Brian had to put into his business must have been difficult."

Celia nodded. "Especially with her mother dying and her father shutting her out. I just hope Della's okay. She deserves someone better than Brian. From what I saw, he needs to control and she went along with it. He never should have made her leave Toronto. She wasn't cut out to be a housewife in a town the size of Kingston. She was made for a bigger life."

———

The afternoon sun was fading when Rouleau sat across the desk from his new Chief of Police, Malcolm T. Heath. Heath was forty, younger than Rouleau by ten years, but well connected according to Gundersund. He'd used his influence to rise quickly through the force to rank of chief at an age when most were a few levels lower. It hadn't taken Rouleau long to figure out that Heath wasn't particularly involved in the day-to-day and didn't care for detailed reporting. He preferred to be told the big picture and relied on a solid media relations team with himself as spokesperson to keep the force well positioned in the community. Heath's

Achilles heel was scandal. Any whiff of a negative news story and he whipped his communications machine into a frenzy. Rouleau wondered how tenuous Heath's appointment was and whom he owed. He could live with Heath's PR obsession, however, because it didn't involve micromanaging cases. Heath left the heavy lifting to the detectives.

Heath ran a ringed hand through his greying curls and leaned back in his chair to look out the window. On their first meeting, Rouleau had been reminded of a cherub — plump cheeks and rosy complexion with curly hair that women spent serious dollars to achieve in the salon. His round, blue eyes usually focused on a point just beyond Rouleau's right shoulder. Heath would appear to have drifted off, and then surprise Rouleau with an astute observation. Rouleau was curious to know whether the Columbo routine was for real or a carefully tuned act. He'd buy it, though, if it meant the hands-off approach continued.

Heath swung his eyes toward Rouleau. "Any movement on the new hire?"

"I have someone in mind but am having trouble reaching them."

One eyebrow lifted. "Odd. Are they working now?"

Rouleau shook his head. "Kala Stonechild is on a canoe trip and out of range. I'd like to give her a few more days."

"I want to be staffed up by the end of the month." Heath glanced at his computer screen. "Any luck finding a place to live?"

"I'm still at my father's apartment. He had foot surgery four weeks ago."

"There might be vacant student housing but you won't want any part of that. I'll send your email address to a friend of mine in real estate. She should be able to come up with something suitable."

"Thanks."

"This Munroe case. You think it'll get any media play?"

"Depends if it goes to court. The Munroes could battle it out in the press."

"Keep me informed."

"Will do." Rouleau stood.

"I'll be taking a holiday next week. If something urgent comes up, let Vera know. She has my coordinates."

"You're heading out of town?"

"Fishing trip in Northern Quebec. Rainbow and lake trout, pristine lakes, and blue sky that goes on forever. It's my yearly pilgrimage to commune with nature."

Rouleau looked closer at Heath. Heath's eyes were guileless behind wire-framed reading glasses. Rouleau could picture him on a cruise or stretched out next to a pool with a martini in his hand, but definitely not tromping around the woods or sitting patiently in a boat waiting for fish to bite.

Rouleau stood to leave. Heath scribbled something on a writing pad and ripped off the top sheet. He handed it to Rouleau.

"Tell Laney Masterson that I sent you. You should have a place to call home by next weekend."

"Thanks, I'll give her a ring." Rouleau glanced down at the paper. Heath had written Laney Masterson's phone number from memory.

He stopped at Vera's desk on the way to his own office. She lifted her unusual almond-shaped eyes from the computer screen and met his. They were the warm amber colour of his ex-wife Frances's tabby cat.

"Question, Rouleau?" she asked, her eyes dropping back to her work. Her elegant fingers, loaded down with gold rings and glittering stones, flew across the keyboard. Rouleau had only seen her blond hair wound tightly into a bun at the nape of her long neck, at odds with her tight sweaters and pencil skirts that showed off her Marilyn Monroe body.

"Just wondered if the Chief goes to the same fishing hole every year."

Vera raised her eyes. He saw amusement in their golden depths. "You thinking of taking up the sport?" she asked. "You should know that he's quite protective of his secret spot." Her voice was low and suggestive.

Rouleau smiled. "Night, Vera. See you tomorrow."

She returned his smile. "Later, Rouleau."

5

ROULEAU LEFT THE station and drove slowly down Princess
Street toward downtown. Rounding the curve south past the
Division Street intersection, he took in the shops and cafés
that lined the busy street. Far in the distance he glimpsed
the sparkling blue of Lake Ontario, just past the Holiday
Inn at the bottom of Princess. Traffic was stop-and-go but
not as bad as it would be in the Ottawa core at this time
of the evening. He rolled down the window and rested his
elbow on the door frame. A hot breeze ruffled his sticky shirt
and gave the illusion of relief. The temperature had risen
over the afternoon and clung to the city like heat from a
sauna. Finally reaching Ontario Street, he hung a right. The
road paralleled the waterfront, his father's condo building
with a view of the harbour several blocks farther on. The
Royal George, where his father lived on the seventh floor,
protruded awkwardly, a green glass tower of modernity, the
last in a series of high rises that included an upscale hotel.

Rouleau pulled into the visitor parking lot and turned
off the engine. He sat for a moment, looking toward the
lake, visible over the tall grasses that lined the property. He
attempted to let go of the stresses of the day to find the reserve of patience now required. His father, a normally calm,
methodical man, had become irritated by the limitations

surgery had wrought on his body. The last few days he'd sunk into a worrisome depression, a state so foreign to him that Rouleau could barely bring himself to think about what it foreshadowed. The urge to find his own place to live was eating at him, but he wasn't sure if he should leave his father alone just yet.

Rouleau exited his car and took the elevator to the seventh floor. He used his key to enter and was surprised to hear his father's hearty laughter coming from the living room. A woman's voice joined in and Rouleau's heart lightened. His father had refused visitors, so this was a good sign.

Rouleau walked down the short hallway lined in bookcases and rounded the corner. Both faces turned to smile up at him: his father stretched out on the couch, and surprise of surprises, Kala Stonechild in a chair facing him. A black Labrador retriever lay at her feet, its alert eyes following his every movement. The dog looked friendly but on guard. Rouleau crossed to the empty easy chair and dropped into it. He reached across to squeeze Stonechild's shoulder and the dog's eyes followed him. "You're here," Rouleau said, leaning back. He grinned wryly at having stated the obvious. "So you got my messages then?"

"I did." She shrugged and her lips curved upward. The smile almost reached her eyes. Almost, but not quite. She was dressed in a white cotton blouse, gauzy and unbuttoned to just below her collarbones, and faded jeans. A turquoise, white, and red beaded belt was threaded through the loops. Her ebony hair hung in two braided pigtails to her chest. She'd taken her sandals off at the door and her bare feet were tucked underneath the coffee table.

Rouleau glanced over at his father. His blue eyes had recovered some of their brilliance. "You're looking better, Dad."

"I've had good company today," his father responded. "I hope you're about to pour us each a little of the Glenfiddich before dinner."

"Of course." Rouleau stood. "Ginger ale, Kala?" he asked. He knew she didn't touch alcohol. She nodded and he walked into the kitchen. When he returned with the drinks, Kala and his father were deep in conversation, as if they'd known each other a long time instead of a few hours.

Rouleau sat down and took a sip of the single malt. It burned pleasantly all the way down. He looked at Kala and waited for her to tell him why she was sitting in his father's apartment. She raised her eyes to his and smiled as if fully aware of his impatience for her to commit to his job offer. She took her time, letting his father finish talking about his research at the university before responding.

"I'm not sure if I'll be staying in Kingston. I've come to check out the town on my way to Ottawa. Grayson is waiting for me to join the unit again." She shrugged. "I thought I'd resign in person."

"Where would you go if not here?"

"Not sure. My old job in Red Rock is still open."

"Is that where you really want to be?"

"One place is as good as another." Again the slight lifting of her shoulders. The defiant tilt of her jaw he'd seen before. "I'm not ruling out your offer. I'm just saying that I don't know what I want to do yet."

"How did you find my father's apartment?"

"I'm a detective, remember?" she said. "You left a trail of bread crumbs as wide as Highway 417."

"I'd like you to come work for me."

"I gathered that from your phone messages."

"You'll like Kingston. It's a welcoming kind of town."

"I don't know yet if this town is for me. Honestly, I feel more at home in the North."

"The Criminal Investigations team is small, and you'd be working with another inspector named Paul Gundersund. He's good. We also have a solid in-house forensics team and cold case unit in our division. Think about it. That's all I ask."

She nodded, but her eyes were evasive. Rouleau had the uneasy feeling he'd oversold the job.

"Will you stay for supper?" his dad asked her. "Jacques will be cooking some steak with baked potatoes. We'd be delighted to have you."

"Thank you, but I really have to be going. Taiku needs a walk and I have to check in with my friend."

"Where are you staying?"

"Just west of the city but this side of Bath. My friend owns a house on the water. She's expecting me sometime today."

"At least finish your drink before you go," his father said. "It's been a long time since I had a young woman come to call."

Kala's eyes swept the room and Rouleau's eyes follow-ed behind. It was the lair of a long-time bachelor with few feminine touches. The parquet floor was typical of the apart-ment buildings built in the eighties, now in vogue again. The oak furniture was solid, functional, but not pretty. His dad kept piles of documents and textbooks on the floor and scattered across the dining room table where he worked on his computer in front of the balcony window. An anemic vine had taken over one wall, surviving God only knew how on sporadic watering and inattention. His dad's ten-speed bicycle leaned against the wall behind the couch, put out to pasture until the cast came off his foot.

"How long have you lived here?" she asked him, lifting her glass.

"I moved into an apartment near the university campus after Jacques took his first job in Ottawa. What was that, son, twenty years ago now? I moved into this condo when it was built a few years ago."

Rouleau's phone rang in his pocket. He reached for it, saying, "One minute, Dad. I should get this."

It took a few seconds to assimilate the facts from the dispatcher. A young woman had been called in dead in an apartment just off campus. He was needed on site as soon as he could get there. It was certainly murder. Gundersund would meet him there. She rhymed off the address and repeated it to be sure.

Rouleau slipped the phone back into his pocket and looked at Kala and his father. Both sets of eyes watched him expectantly, one set liquid black and the other a crystal blue. They'd overheard his side of the conversation. There was no point hiding his destination.

He stood. "A murder just off campus. I have to go."

"Should I come along, sir?" Kala asked. She'd already pushed herself to her feet. "It might help me decide to come on board."

Rouleau thought about it for a nanosecond before he nodded. Perhaps all wasn't lost with Stonechild after all. This case could very well tilt her decision in his favour.

6

KALA FOLLOWED CLOSELY behind Rouleau in her truck. Taiku sat in the passenger seat, his nose through the open window. She reached across the console and ruffled the fur on his back.

"So what do you think, boy? Is this a town you'd like to spend time in or should we keep moving?"

Taiku pulled his nose from the window and turned his head toward her, his pink tongue lolling to the side of his mouth. He stared at her as if considering her question.

Kala laughed before turning back to the road. Sometimes she thought Taiku was a human disguised as a dog. He was smarter than most people she knew and was considerably more dependable.

They were heading east, but only for a short distance before Rouleau turned north on Gore. The grey limestone houses dated back to Sir John A. Macdonald's time. It was a pretty city with mature oak trees and wide streets flanked to the south by Lake Ontario. This felt like a town you could breathe in. She was surprised to find herself looking forward to a few days at her friend's place.

Rouleau pulled left onto Sydenham and she followed a few car lengths behind. A busy scene greeted them a few blocks in. Police cars and an ambulance with red lights flashing filled the street. The target house was toward the far end of the street and they had to park and walk a short distance. Kala left Taiku locked in the truck parked under a shady oak with the window open and an order to stay. He immediately lay down on the seat, his shaggy head resting against the passenger door, his black eyes watching her walk away.

Rouleau stood waiting for her on the sidewalk next to his car. He looked tired, his eyes sadder than she remembered. The connection she felt to him was odd. Uncomfortable and uncharacteristic. She'd felt it in Ottawa the short time they worked together. It was the reason she'd detoured on a last-minute whim off the 417 to find him. She'd been surprised that he'd sought her out for this job. She hadn't decided yet whether to trust him.

Rouleau filled her in as they walked. The house was divided into apartments and rented as student housing. The woman's body was found in the basement by the upstairs tenant. Apparently there was a lot of blood. They passed a couple of beat cops in navy uniforms on their way inside the limestone house. The officers appeared to know Rouleau and let her inside only because she was with him. One cop directed them to the basement.

Rouleau introduced Paul Gundersund, who met them at the bottom of the stairs. She felt dwarfed by the size of the man. He was over six foot, close to two hundred pounds, and appeared slightly out of shape. A scar marked the left side of his face, giving him the look of a street fighter. His blue-grey eyes were surprisingly pretty for a guy with a face like his. She shook his outstretched hand, his fingers long and slender.

"It's not good, boss," he said as he led them down the dark hallway. Kala's eyes lifted to the unlit bulb hanging from the ceiling socket, obviously not working. It would have given the attacker cover as they waited, if that's what they'd done. She made out the squat shapes of a washer and dryer angled deeper into the gloom. Gundersund stopped and handed them white suits and covers for their shoes. Kala stepped into the suit and shivered as the cool dampness seeping from the basement's concrete walls wrapped itself around her bare arms. She quickly pulled the suit up over her shirt.

The apartment door stood open, the putrid smell of death getting stronger as they approached. Down the length of the hallway, the forensics team in white suits worked in the bedroom. She could see a trail of dark blood on the floor, pooled in spots, where the woman looked to have dragged herself toward the apartment door.

Kala stepped closer and saw that the blood trail detoured left. She carefully negotiated the blood splatter as she followed behind Rouleau and Gundersund into the living room. They stepped aside to make some space for her. She looked from their grim faces to the floor near the coffee table where the coroner kneeled next to a woman lying face down, one of her arms stretched in front of her as if she'd been trying to swim away using the front crawl. A purse had spewed its contents onto the carpet; a blood-covered cellphone lay near the woman's curled fingers.

Kala swallowed back the urge to gag. Congealed blood covered the woman's face and matted the long, dark hair on the back of her head. It had seeped from her body and surrounded her in sticky globs. It had spread from her midsection in a circular pool. The smell of rotting flesh and blood and feces was overpowering.

Rouleau touched Kala's shoulder and motioned her to take a few steps closer. A photographer who'd been taking pictures of the body signalled that she'd gotten enough. The coroner looked from her to Rouleau.

"I'm ready to turn the body," he said.

Rouleau's eyes swept the scene, ending with a long study of the woman. Finally, he nodded and the coroner rolled the woman onto her back, her one arm remaining awkwardly extended above her head. Kala looked past the bruising, discoloured skin and dried blood and saw that the girl had been attractive: late twenties, masses of black hair, medium height, with a muscular physique. Someone had gone to great lengths to disfigure her beauty. The coroner held up the palm of one hand.

"Her fingers are broken." He traced upward along the underside of her arm. "Cigarette burns." He turned to the photographer.

"Make sure you get close ups."

"How long …?" asked Rouleau.

"It's a guess, but I'd say twenty-four hours based on the rigor mortis. I couldn't say how long she was tortured in the bedroom, but I think it went on a while, judging by the burns and wounds. Her attacker used a knife."

Kala saw Rouleau's jaw clench. Her own felt as tight as a fist.

"Can you isolate the wound that killed her?" he asked.

The coroner pointed to her stomach where blood had stained her shirt almost black. "The assailant drove a weapon into her midsection. I can't say with complete certainty until we do the autopsy, but she almost definitely bled out from there."

They stood quietly for a moment, contemplating the strength of will it had taken for the dying woman to drag herself this far. Kala glanced at Rouleau. His eyes were hard, unflinching. She lowered hers to search for clues in the carpet and the woman who'd died while reaching for her phone.

Rouleau said, "Have you got her name?"

Gundersund nodded. "Yeah. Leah Sampson. I've got somebody checking for her next of kin. We should find out more about her within the hour."

Kala looked around the stifling living room. She already knew a lot about Leah Sampson. She was a struggling student who lived alone, although she was close to her sister and parents. Their faces smiled at her from two framed photos on a table next to the couch. Horses were a passion, judging from the other photos. Leah read murder mysteries when she should be studying. The stack of paperbacks next to her unopened textbooks was a giveaway. What secrets had she kept that were worth dying over?

"I'm going to look in the bedroom," Kala said abruptly.

"I'll come with you," Gundersund said.

Rouleau didn't turn or look away from Leah's body. "I'll stay with her until she's ready to be moved."

"Okay boss," Gundersund said.

He and Kala walked sideways down the narrow hallway, stepping on their toes past pools of congealed blood. Kala made a cursory check of the bathroom and galley kitchen off to the right. Neither room appeared to be part of the crime scene. The bedroom was another story. Three officers from Forensics noted their entry and carried on with their work. Two were dusting for prints and the other was taking samples from the chair where Leah Sampson had been tied.

Kala lifted her eyes from the pink rosebud-patterned duvet in a heap next to the bed to the one-eyed stuffed teddy bear leaning against the mirror. Silver and gold costume jewellery lay in front of the bear, scattered in shiny heaps across the top of the dresser. A silky blue housecoat hung on a hook next to the closet door. The bed was rumpled, unmade. A spray of blood crossed the sheets as if from a garden hose. Nobody had mentioned sexual assault yet, but the coroner would be looking for signs. Gundersund broke into her thoughts.

"We can't do anything here until Forensics is finished. I'm going to talk to the person who found her. Maybe they heard something. Coming?"

"Sure." Her eyes fixated on the bloody chair for a moment before she turned to follow him.

They retraced their steps down the hallway. Rouleau was still with the coroner and Leah Sampson's body. They let him know they'd be upstairs starting interviews.

"Hell of a welcome to the team," Gundersund said with his foot on the bottom step. "Rouleau speaks highly of you, by the way. He wasn't sure you'd be coming to Kingston though. Glad you changed your mind."

"I just dropped in for a visit," said Kala. She gave Gundersund a quick sideways grin. "Guess I'll be sticking around for a few days."

7

BOBBY HAMILTON SAT in a chair in front of a giant television, his face ashen in the pooled light from the table lamp. A Blue Jays game was playing on the screen with the sound off. Bobby sucked on the end of a cigarette while avoiding looking directly at Kala and Gundersund as they lowered themselves kitty corner to him on the stained green couch, the only other place to sit. Bobby had shot them a darting look when they entered the room, then fixed his unblinking eyes on the screen.

Kala sat on the edge of the couch and tried not to think about what had made it so filthy or what could be crawling underneath her. She forced down her revulsion and angled herself to get a clear view of Bobby. His shoulder-length blond hair was already giving way to baldness — the hairline had receded with a circle of thinning noticeable on top — and his eyes were pale blue in his bony face. His hollow cheeks and pointed jaw hinted at malnourishment. Someone who'd rather spend their money on drugs than food. A smell of pot hovered in the room, filming the walls and ceiling, giving silent confirmation of her assessment.

Gundersund coughed as if his throat was constricting. "So you found Leah's body," he said when he caught his breath. He coughed again and his face turned a deep red. He glared at Hamilton as the choking came to an end.

Bobby chanced a glance at him before nodding. He pulled on the cigarette like he was sucking on a straw.

"Do you mind putting that thing out?" Gundersund asked, pointing at the smoke rising from Bobby's fingers.

"What, this?" Bobby shrugged and dropped the cigarette into a beer bottle on the table next to him. It hissed and sputtered, then went out. He spread his legs wider and sunk deeper into his chair.

"You found Leah Sampson's body." Gundersund had pulled out his notebook.

"So it was her."

"Can you tell us what you saw?"

"I went downstairs to do some laundry after supper. Around eight o'clock. I smelled something stinkin' and followed it over to her apartment. I knocked but the door was open a bit so I yelled to see if she was okay."

"Did you go in?"

"No way." Bobby shook his head and looked at them for the first time. "I just looked down the hall and saw blood and combined with the smell ... I hightailed it back upstairs and called 911."

"Did you hear anything coming from Leah Sampson's apartment the last few days? Anything unusual that you can remember?"

"Like what?"

"Like noises or raised voices; anything at all unusual."

"Nope."

"Did you see anybody coming or going?"

"I'm not her bloody keeper."

Interesting choice of adjective. "What do you do for a living, Bobby?" Kala interrupted.

"I work for the city. Garbage collection."

"So you're not home during the day."

He looked in her direction, his eyes assessing her like a woman he'd just met standing on a street corner. "That's right. I leave for work around five a.m. and get home midafternoon, unless I go to the bar when I'm done."

Kala ignored the suggestion in his weasely eyes. "Did you do that last week, say on Friday after work?"

"Yup."

"You said that without thinking about it," said Gundersund.

"That's cause I go to the bar every night after work. It takes a while to get the taste of garbage out of my throat." He smiled, showing yellowish teeth. One of the bottom front ones was missing.

"We'll need details and names of the people who might have seen you," said Gundersund.

"Why? I didn't have nuttin' to do with what happened to her. I was the good corporate citizen that reported it, remember?"

"We know that," said Kala, cutting off his sudden burst of anger. "We just need to find out where everybody was."

"Yeah, right," said Bobby. "I got an idea how this works." He reached into his pocket and pulled out his wallet. He handed Gundersund a card with the phone number of his supervisor. "Wayne was at the bar with me Friday and tonight." His eyes went back to the television screen.

"Did you know Leah at all?" asked Kala.

"Nope. I keep to myself."

"Is there anything else you can tell us?" Gundersund asked.

"Such as?"

"Who might have killed Leah."

"I ain't got absolutely no idea. A guy does his civic duty and all of a sudden you're checking out his whereabouts and asking if he knew her killer. I think I'm all done talking."

"Thanks for your time," said Kala. "We appreciate your assistance." She kept her voice flat, hiding any trace of sarcasm.

Out in the hall, Gundersund snapped his notebook shut and tucked it into his pocket. "Think the guy's done time?"

"It's not a question of if, but how much and for what," Kala said, starting down the stairs.

She looked through the screen door at the bottom. A red-haired girl carrying a gym bag stood outside talking to one of the officers. As Kala reached the bottom of the stairwell, the gym bag hit the sidewalk with a *thunk* and the girl covered her mouth with both hands. Her scream filled the hallway.

Kala turned to Gundersund. "Looks like the second floor tenant just arrived home."

———

The girl's name was Becky Pringle and she'd been living in the top-floor apartment for three years, two years longer than Leah Sampson had lived in the basement. They'd walked Becky upstairs into her apartment after rescuing her from a near collapse on the front steps. Kala sat with her on the couch while she cried. Gundersund signalled to Kala before leaving the room, and she soon heard the kettle boiling. He returned with a cup of tea that he placed into Becky's shaking hands. She sipped it in choking slurps. Eventually her sobbing subsided.

"I just can't believe it. Anybody but Leah."

How many times had Kala heard these same words come out of victims' mouths? Anybody but their loved one.

"We know it's been a terrible shock, but if you can tell us about Leah, it might help us to find out who did this to her."

"This is just unbelievable," Becky repeated. "Leah and I liked to get together after work and have tea or something harder to drink. She was warm and funny. She was the kind of person who would do anything for you."

"Could you tell us where Leah worked?" asked Kala.

"She was finishing up her Master's thesis in psychology and just completed her last exam. She worked part-time at the crisis hotline on Queen's campus."

"Did she have a boyfriend?"

Becky paused. "They broke up about a month ago."

"What was his name?"

"She called him Wolf. I don't know his real name. He worked with her at the help line. I think they grew up in the same town. Do you think he …?"

"We won't jump to any conclusions. Do you know where her parents live?"

"A little town near here, but I don't know which one. Oh wait, she told me they sold their house and moved to Montreal. She was going to visit them at the end of the semester."

"Was Leah worried about anything or anybody recently?"

"Yes. No. I'm sorry. My thoughts are all jumbled. She seemed lonelier after she broke up with Wolf and distracted the last few times we talked, but I wouldn't say she was worried. She went away for a weekend last month for a break but she didn't tell me where. We haven't had a real chance to talk since she got back because of schoolwork or I would have asked her about her trip."

And now they never would. Kala could see the girl was near breaking. "Okay, Becky. That's all for now. We'll probably come back to see you again once you've had a chance to take all this in. Is there somebody you can call to come stay with you?"

"My boyfriend. He lives a few blocks over."

"Good. It's best you have someone to be with you now. This has been an awful shock."

They waited while she made the call. She spoke briefly and nodded after hanging up. "He's on his way."

Kala and Gundersund stood and headed for the door. Gundersund stopped as Kala stepped onto the landing. "Becky, how long has Bobby Hamilton lived below you?"

"About a year. Just a bit longer than Leah. She and I were hoping he'd move out so Leah could move into his apartment, but he wasn't going anywhere soon so Leah was thinking about finding another place to live. Moving on up since she'd be done school and making money." Becky's voice caught in a sob.

"I can stay until your boyfriend arrives," said Kala. She motioned at Gundersund to go on without her. "I'll meet you downstairs in a few minutes." She started back toward the girl on the couch.

8

THE DARKNESS GATHERED in the crevices and over the tree line the farther Kala drove west and away from downtown. She turned off the air conditioning and rolled the windows all the way down. The air smelled earthier and greener and she could almost see herself here for longer than a day. She drove past the limestone turrets and sand-covered walls of now-closed Kingston Penitentiary, continuing on past a drug store and single-home dwellings that lined both sides of the road. The pavement hugged Lake Ontario with stretches of beach and water shimmering through the trees in the moonlight. Taiku sat at attention next to her, taking in the view through the front windshield, his nose sniffing the air and the gusts of breeze ruffling his fur. Bonnie Raitt's bluesy "River of Tears" filled the truck cab and trailed out the windows into the passing darkness of the countryside.

Fifteen minutes from downtown, Kala glimpsed the turn-off to Old Front Road tucked inside a cove of brush and trees. "Almost there, boy," she said, and reached over to ruffle Taiku's head. She made a quick right and drove slowly down the paved road, peering at large homes behind the oak and maple trees. A few minutes down the gently curved road, she spotted the red mailbox on a white post that marked Marjory's driveway on the left. She'd visited the year before on a long weekend when she was stationed in Ottawa. It had been the first time she and Marjory had ever met. Tonight, Marjory had left the outside lights on to guide her way.

Kala parked the truck next to Marjory's Subaru and leaned over Taiku to open the passenger door.

"Out you go, boy."

She let him run down to the water and stood looking out over the lake while he snuffled through the underbrush and ran along the shoreline. The heat of the day had been broken by a breeze sweeping off the lake. Crickets chirped in the swaying sweet grass while a sprinkle of fireflies flashed in the grass near an ancient maple. The night air held the dusky scent of jasmine and roses from a garden built into the incline. Kala inhaled deeply and closed her eyes. She heard the back door open and turned in time to watch Marjory run lightly across the deck and down the steps to where she stood. Marjory enveloped her in a bear hug.

"I was starting to get worried. I thought you might have gotten lost."

"I should have phoned but I got involved in a police call."

"In my heart I knew that you could look after yourself." Marjory took a step back to look at Kala. "You're thinner than last time I saw you, but you look rested."

They linked arms and started back toward the house, a greyish-blue two storey with a red roof. Taiku bounded ahead of them. "I'm so glad you made it tonight," Marjory said. "I leave for Northern Ontario in the morning. I'm researching a court case that will take months."

Kala's heart dropped. "I was hoping we could spend some time together. When will you be back?"

"Likely not until November, and then only here for a visit. I'll be gone a year, probably longer. I'd like you to stay and house-sit for me, that is if it suits your plans."

"I'm not sure how long I'll be staying."

"When Roger called day before yesterday to tell me you were on your way, I told him that I was going to ask you to stay for a while. He said good luck with that." Marjory smiled at her.

Kala returned the smile with a shrug. "It's just that I don't know where I want to be."

A shrill whistling and the smell of marinating herbs, red wine, and beef greeted them as they stepped inside. Marjory turned. "I put the kettle on when I heard you pull in. I have stew on the stove if you're hungry."

"I'm beyond hungry. It smells delicious."

Kala fed and watered Taiku while Marjory got the food ready. The kitchen was wide and bright with pine cabinets and a large window that looked out over the water. The grey slate tiles felt cool underneath Kala's bare feet. The room's neutral colours were warmed by a woven red-and-orange rug positioned under the pine table near the sliding patio doors. Kala looked down the hallway and into the living room at the Inuit paintings on the wall above a wood fireplace. She remembered them from her last visit.

They took plates of stew, homemade dinner rolls, and a pot of tea to the back deck and settled themselves at the patio table. Marjory lit a camp lantern and candles while Kala poured the tea. Taiku flopped down at Kala's feet and stretched out with a grunt. The distant sound of waves rolling onto the shore soothed something in Kala's soul, like a faithful friend waiting to be rediscovered.

"This is so good," Kala chewed a spoonful of stew. She ate quickly, ravenous from hours in the truck and the energy used to comprehend the crime scene. The evening had gotten away on her. The nervous anticipation in the pit of her stomach when the murder call came in, the surge of adrenaline that always accompanied the first glimpse of a killer's trail had kept her from thinking about her own needs until this moment relaxing on the deck with Marjory.

"You went to see Roger?" Marjory asked.

"Yeah. We flew in and canoed Sand Lakes. It took about a month. Your dad's doing well for a guy in his seventies."

"Roger didn't tell me why you were heading back this way."

"Just tying up loose ends."

"Roger told me that you found Rosie in Ottawa."

"That's right. I was looking for her in Ottawa last year when I came to see you." Kala had forgotten that she'd told Marjory. Now she wished she hadn't because Rosie hadn't cared enough to stick around once they'd made contact. The rejection still hurt.

"You call her Lily, don't you?"

"Yeah. Rosie is Lily to me. She used to call me Sunny." Kala grinned. "Hard to believe, I know."

"Roger said she's got a daughter."

Kala nodded. "A twelve-year-old girl named Dawn. Nice kid. Lily's involved with some guy who did time for robbery. They disappeared after I made contact." She was silent, reliving the moment when she discovered them gone; the moment her dream of having a family evaporated like morning mist.

Marjory shook her head. "Lily's picked a difficult path. You must have found it hard to lose her so soon after finding her."

Kala nodded again but didn't say anything.

Marjory dropped her head and Kala knew she was deciding whether to keep going or leave the subject alone.

Her dad, Roger, wouldn't have said much, she knew that. Marjory raised her black eyes to Kala's. They were kind eyes, non-judgmental eyes, the reason Kala had returned for a visit at Roger's urging. Marjory nodded as if telling herself to let it go.

"Roger and I had that falling out when I left Birdtail Rez to follow Tommy Lightside to Winnipeg. I was just sixteen years old — thirty years ago if you can believe it. God, I thought I knew it all back then, and man, was I wrong. It took a few years but I went back home and Roger ... Dad was still there, waiting. He's why I got on track and finished high school. I never would have gotten the law degree if I'd stayed with Tommy."

"I know what you're trying to tell me," Kala said. "It's not going to happen in this case. Lily won't be looking to change her life anytime soon."

"People have a way of coming around. Lily knows you're there for her when she needs you. She still keeps in contact with Roger, if only sporadically. He's there for her too."

"I wouldn't put any money on Lily." Kala wasn't prepared to talk about her any longer.

Marjory took the hint. "So, where are you planning to go when you leave here?" she asked. She refilled their mugs with tea and settled back against the cushions.

"Back to Red Rock, although I'm not sure that's even a good idea."

"Why not?"

"It's complicated, but the man I was seeing has moved on." *Moved on back to his wife and baby.* "I just don't want to stir up what's best left alone." Kala put her fork down and leaned over to pet Taiku's head. "I guess Taiku and I'll stay here and house-sit until you finish your research up north. This might be the space I need to figure things out."

"Well now, that would be a help to me. I'll be on the road a lot these next few years and worry about leaving this place empty."

"I'll just commit to the next month if that's okay with you. I'll be here in November when you return but can't promise anything longer."

"Fair enough."

Marjory lowered her head to eat but not before Kala saw a smile turn up the corners of her lips. Kala picked up her fork and dug it into the warm stew. With a slight nod in Marjory's direction she acknowledged Marjory and Roger's small victory of manipulating her into this decision before tucking into the last of her meal.

—

An hour later, Kala settled into the back bedroom on the second floor. She'd slept here on her one previous visit and was happy to be back in this small room with its casement window and window seat looking out over the water. She propped herself up on the cushions for a while, letting the day's events settle and her mind decompress until she felt that she could sleep. Taiku appeared to also have remembered being in this room on their one and only visit. He'd immediately stretched out on the hooked rug at the foot of the bed, snorted a long sigh, and fallen asleep.

Kala reached across and opened the window as wide as it would go. The wind rushed in as if it had been lurking outside, waiting for an invitation. It blew the hair back from her face and billowed the curtains around her. It filled her nostrils and lungs. No matter how difficult her day had been, the wind always made her feel connected to something bigger than herself. It brought her a measure of peace.

She stepped back and slipped out of her clothes, then climbed naked between the crisp sheets on the double brass bed. She lay awake a while longer, listening to the waves lap onto the shore as she began to drift off to sleep. Rouleau's concerned face, strong and sure, hovered above her just out of reach as she finally let go of the day.

9

DALAL TOOK HER sister's hand and gently traced the lifeline carved into her small palm. They lay side by side in the hammock between the two fir trees, rocking gently in their cooling shade and the swaying light that slipped like liquid gold through the leaves.

"You will have a long life, Meeza, and I see two boy-friends in your future. One will be tall and rich and the other will be a poor, handsome boy who truly loves you. You will be very happy if you follow your heart."

Dalal pulled her hand away and let her arm rest across her forehead. Her long black hair was tied back with a purple silk scarf. It was desperately hot but they both wore skirts to their ankles and long-sleeved blouses.

Meeza giggled and ran her index finger along the line her sister had just traced. "Do you think I will live with you and your husband when I get married? I don't think I'd want to be in a house if you aren't there." Her eyes changed like quicksilver, from dancing stars to pools of misery.

Dalal lowered her arm and grabbed Meeza's hand firmly in hers. "Don't worry, little sister. I won't ever leave you. Besides, you are only twelve years old and we'll be living together for a long time yet."

"But you're fifteen and so much older than me."

"Fifteen in six months. I have three more years of high school before I go to college. I'll probably still have to live at home even then."

She didn't dare think about the work it was going to take to convince her father to let her study to become a nurse. Already she'd begun dropping hints. Nobody had said no to her wishes and she took this as a good sign.

"I don't like it when people leave." Meeza pouted and moved her leg away from Dalal's.

"I don't either."

They lay quietly, letting the wind rock them and trying not to think about the event that they were not allowed to talk about. Meeza began singing a song she'd learned in school and Dalal knew she'd gotten over her sadness of a moment before. The thing about Meeza was that she never held a thought or emotion for long. Dalal closed her eyes and felt her body relax. The soothing motion of the swing and the warmth of the sun even in the shade were making her drowsy. She was almost asleep when Meeza stopped her chant and poked Dalal in the side.

"I heard a car door. Daddy's home."

"We'll have to start supper."

Dalal felt the lurch of the hammock as Meeza launched herself onto the lawn. She watched Meeza race toward the back gate to head off their father before he made it to the front door. Meeza might be nearly twelve years old but she had the mind of a much younger child. The teachers had been telling her parents for years that Meeza needed to go into a special class. They'd called her a simple child with special learning needs. After her report card and a late afternoon call from the school, her parents and older brother Ghazi had huddled together like plotting generals. They'd gone for a meeting the next day and returned without saying what had happened. Dalal knew her parents wouldn't allow Meeza to bring dishonour, whether real or imagined, to the household. Sure enough, Meeza remained in the same class and was promoted at the end of the year without any more phone calls from the teacher.

Dalal reached into her pocket for her cellphone and checked her messages. *A text from Joe!* She read it quickly before erasing it and tucking the phone back into her pocket. It wasn't safe to answer him back.

Her father and Meeza came through the gate a few seconds later, Meeza holding onto his hand and skipping at his side. Her father looked sternly in Dalal's direction as if he sensed her guilt.

"Ghazi will be home from his course in half an hour and he'll be hungry. What are you doing lying there without supper started?"

Dalal jumped to her feet. "I'm sorry, Father. I'll get it going right now."

"See that you do and take Meeza with you. She needs to learn how to prepare a meal."

Dalal hurried across the lawn, but an unsettling thought made her stare at her father as she neared him and Meeza. What were her parents and Ghazi hatching now for Meeza? Were they going to send her to be a helper for another family? Dalal wouldn't put it past them. She held out her hand to Meeza as she walked by.

"Come, Meeza. You can make the rice tonight."

"Oh goody," said Meeza, clapping her hands. She leaped into the air and twirled on one foot before reaching for Dalal's hand.

Dalal turned at the door and looked at her father again. He stood tall and motionless in the full heat of the sun, watching them with laser-beam eyes. Dalal smiled in his direction, but a sudden cold tingling up her spine made her hand slip from the door knob. She banged her shoulder against the door before she managed to twist the handle open. Meeza squealed when Dalal yanked her into the kitchen away from their father's piercing stare.

The bad stuff's not over yet, Dalal thought. *And I have no idea how to stop it.*

10

ROULEAU INTRODUCED KALA to the rest of the team first thing the next morning. She shook hands with Ed Chalmers and Zach Woodhouse, then took a seat next to Gundersund. They were in a small boardroom down the hall from their offices. Kala had already been taken on a quick tour after getting a temporary building pass and signing some paperwork that made her an auxiliary officer on loan from the Ottawa force.

Rouleau watched Vera cross the room in her tight pencil skirt and six-inch heels with Kala's paperwork in hand and thanked whatever deity had brought her to the chief's door. She'd performed bureaucratic miracles all before eight thirty in the morning. Her head tilted toward him and she winked just before stepping outside and pulling the door shut behind her. Rouleau noticed that Kala had witnessed the exchange but her face remained impassive. Rouleau was happy to be a man who didn't blush easily. He looked directly at Kala. "Right. Chalmers and Woodhouse have been brought up to speed about Leah Sampson's murder. What you don't know is that we're also working on a spousal rape case, so we're spread thin this week."

"Where would you like me?" asked Kala.

"You'll be teamed with Gundersund and leading on the Sampson murder. However, Chalmers and Woodhouse might need you to help on the rape case, so be prepared to go between the two, if necessary." He broadened his gaze to include the others. "Everyone is going to have to be flexible, so keep up-to-date on both files. We'll have debriefs every morning at seven thirty. I'll be coordinating both and dealing with media, needless to say, with Heath's assistance."

"His forte," said Woodhouse. The others smiled at some inside joke. Kala guessed that the unmet chief must fancy himself a media star. The knowledge might come in handy down the road.

"Calls have been coming in. The *Whig* and the CBC are probing the murder story. We've even had calls from the *Globe* and *Post*."

What Rouleau couldn't say was that he had little faith in Ed Chalmers, who was close to retirement and dogging it. Woodhouse was in his early forties but had shown little initiative. The two men even looked alike — both balding with middle age paunches. Woodhouse was taller and wore glasses, but aside from that they could have been brothers. Around the station they were known as Lazy and Lazier.

"So, Chalmers and Woodhouse, start interviewing neighbours and co-workers — anyone who knew Brian and Della Munroe. We need evidence to back up Della's story if it's true."

"We're on it," said Chalmers.

Rouleau wished he could find faith in Chalmers's words, but failed. "Gundersund, can you sit in on the Sampson autopsy this morning?"

Gundersund nodded.

"We've located her parents in Montreal and they're on their way, and the autopsy is scheduled for right after they see her. Stonechild, I want you to check out the staff where Leah worked. Her murder could be tied into her personal life or the help line. The killer might have been a stranger, but if so, why torture her? See what you can find out and bring along Officer Marquette. He's waiting at his desk for you."

"Yes, sir."

"Check in as you go and I'll let you know next assignments."

Everyone stood and started for the door. Gundersund fell into step with Kala.

"Do you have the help line address on campus?"

"No, but it shouldn't be hard to track down."

"I'll call you when the autopsy's done to find out where you are. Can I have your cell number?"

She recited the number and he jotted it down in his notebook.

———

Gail Pankhurst lurched forward a step and dropped into the empty chair facing Jucinda and Nate sitting on the couch. Jucinda's melodramatic announcement that Leah had been murdered kept repeating in her brain like a news bulletin stuck on replay.

"I can't fucking believe it," Nate said. "No fucking way." His face was the colour of whipped meringue. He slumped back and held on to his chest as if he'd been shot.

"Well believe it," said Jucinda. "The cop in there talking to Mark and Professor Tadesco is one hundred percent certain. Plus, Leah missed her shift yesterday and again today, so that would appear to clinch it."

"Where's Wolf?" asked Gail, her head swivelling around the office. "Does he know?"

Jucinda shook her head. "Mark called him to come to the centre but didn't tell him why."

The two women exchanged looks and the expression on Jucinda's face sent a jolt through Gail's nether regions. Juicy was smiling, her lips lifted at the corners, with a smug look in her eyes as if someone had handed her a gift. Gail recalled her vitriolic condemnation of Leah the day before and her interest in Wolf. She squirmed at a sudden rush of guilt at her own part in the conversation. For God's sake, Leah might have already been dead when they were discussing her loose morals, her spirit hovering in the room, listening to herself being called a slut. Surely Juicy had nothing to do with Leah's death, but her smile was disturbing. Gail swung her eyes back toward the office.

"Who's that with Beach Boy and Tadesco?"

"It's a detective. Stonechild, I think she said her name was," Nate roused himself to respond. "And she brought along a police officer."

"Christ," Gail said. Her stomach rolled and she swallowed hard. Sweat was making her armpits wet. She was glad she'd worn a sleeveless white top that wouldn't show the dark stains.

Mark's office door opened and the detective crossed the floor in their direction. Gail looked her over: Indigenous, about their age, younger than thirty anyhow. She had long black hair tied back in a ponytail and black eyes that were drinking them in, assessing and processing. Dressed in navy slacks and a white shirt, the detective looked lean, muscular, and confident, everything Gail knew herself not to be.

"Hello, I'm Detective Stonechild," the woman said upon reaching them. "I know the news of Leah's death has come as a shock, but it would help our investigation if I could speak with each of you individually." She looked down at her notepad. "I'll start with Jucinda Rivera. Please follow me into your supervisor's office. Gail Pankhurst and then Nathan Anders will follow. Officer Marquette will stay with you. I'd appreciate it if you do not discuss anything about Leah amongst yourselves. Thanks."

Wow, no messing around. Gail felt that sick feeling back in her stomach. They were actually being interrogated, like on a police show, but this was no work of fiction.

The detective turned and Jucinda rose to follow, throwing a rolling eye glance in Gail's direction. Lucky for her, Marquette had his back turned. He was leaning against Gail's desk and pulled out his cellphone as she passed by him. Mark and the professor joined Nate on the couch.

"Well, this wasn't what I was expecting today when I got dressed for work," Gail said. Nobody smiled and she couldn't really blame them. Making light when their colleague had just been murdered was in extremely bad taste, but she had to cope somehow. Every inch of her body felt like it was burning up with fever. She even smelled rancid, fear changing her body odour to something putrid and disgusting.

A curious thought came to her as she looked at the three stooges — Tadesco, Nate, and Mark — lined up as if they were facing a firing squad. Juicy had said that Leah was sleeping around with a married man. Could it be one of these three? She studied them to see if any was more broken up than the others, but had to admit they all looked devastated. Tadesco won out in the red-eyed category though. She looked at him again.

Immaculate blue suit and open-necked shirt the colour of daffodils, tall with jet-black hair gelled back, and a Mediterranean complexion. Attractive enough if you liked the Italian-prince-slash-*GQ* look. He was the hotline's staunchest supporter and considered a socialist — a handicap the wealthier right-wing students overlooked because his psych classes were so interesting and he was such an easy marker. His wife, on the other hand, was an unpopular English prof. Medieval lit major, a horsey face, and expensive silk dresses labelled her elitist and stuck up. Rumour had it that she was cold in the sack. There might have been enough dissatisfaction in their marriage for Leah to move in on Tadesco. As Gail watched, Tadesco leaned into Mark. Gail shifted forward to hear their exchange.

"I have to get over to the president's office. He'll need to speak with media and put out a news release. A murder on campus could create mass hysteria if not handled properly," Tadesco said quietly.

Mark and Tadesco both lifted their heads to look at the officer, who was just tucking his phone into his pocket.

Mark nodded. "You've already given a statement so it should be okay."

"I just feel helpless sitting here when I know time is of the essence for keeping this contained."

Tadesco stood and strode over to talk with Marquette. Tadesco was the kind of man who strode, not walked. Gail thought he was a self-confident son of a bitch and maybe colder than his wife, if his words were anything to go by.

Marquette and Tadesco discussed his departure in low voices and then Tadesco called across the room to Mark. "I'll talk to you later. I'll be available by cellphone if you need to reach me." He broadened his look to include Nate and Gail. "We'll get through this. Stay strong, kids, and I'll be back later so we can talk."

Gail felt she should pump her fist in solidarity but instead waved a hand in his direction and wondered why his promise for a *tête-à-tête* sounded like a warning. The person he probably should be telling to keep quiet was Juicy, but she was already spilling her guts to the detective. If Tadesco was the married boyfriend and Juicy knew it, things could go badly for his marriage and career. The university was strict about enforcing its rules regarding professors fraternising with students, especially if the student was in their class. Leah had been in Tadesco's this year and last.

Gail felt a surge of excitement replace the horror and dread. She itched to get out her laptop to start a new file about the murder and the players in Leah's life. This could turn into the biggest psychological study ever and she was going to have a front-row seat. At least making this into another human experiment would take her mind off the horrible end that Leah had suffered. It might help her to make sense of the unfathomable *and* it could turn into a thesis that might get her published. What was that saying? Every cloud has a silver lining. It might sound crass, but life had to carry on and you had to make the most of whatever bounty fell your way.

11

KALA SAT IN her truck and checked the address she'd copied into her notebook when Mark Withers brought up Wolf's personnel file on his computer. She pulled out her map of Kingston from the glove compartment and traced the route with her finger. Wolf Edwards lived outside the campus, heading northwest.

She tossed the map onto the passenger seat and started the engine. If there'd been a common thread running through every interview, it had been the boyfriend Wolf and his recent split with Leah Sampson. Jucinda Rivera was the only one who'd said Leah had been sleeping around on him with a married man, but she'd stopped short of giving a name. Gail Pankhurst had admitted that Leah and Wolf dated at one time, but clammed up about their breakup.

How angry had Wolf been at Leah's infidelity? Angry enough to torture her? Men did crazy shit when women left them. Sometimes men you would never suspect of being capable of violence.

Her phone buzzed in her pocket. She slowed the truck and pulled over to the curb. Scanning the tree-lined street ahead, she counted mainly oak and maple with the odd poplar. Old trees in an old town. She held the phone to her ear.

"Yeah?" *Shit.* Gundersund. She'd forgotten all about him.

"Where are you?" he asked.

"Just finished up the interviews and am heading to see Leah's ex-boyfriend, who lives northwest of the university on Centennial Drive. He also worked at the help line until recently. Autopsy over?"

"No. The parents were late and had a hard time with their daughter's death. They were with her a while so we're about an hour behind. I just stepped out to call you. Maybe you should wait for me and we can go together. What's the guy's name?"

"They call him Wolf. Last name Edwards. Has the coroner found anything yet?"

"Says she died sometime in the early morning hours on Saturday. There are bruises all over her torso and broken ribs. The fingers on one hand are mashed. She has rope burns on her wrists and ankles where the bastard tied her to the chair. Whoever it was cut her superficially all over her body, but the knife wound in her stomach was deep and nicked her liver. She died when she bled out."

Kala let out her breath but didn't say anything. She watched a squirrel do a high wire act above the road in front of her. A cardinal flashed red in its flight between two trees. She thought about all the normal life that had been going on while Leah Sampson was strapped to a chair, being beaten and cut.

Gundersund's voice dropped. "Her crawl to the living room must have been excruciating."

She could hear the gentle in and out of his breathing in her ear. She wondered if he was waiting for her to react. If so, he was going to wait a long time. "I'll come back in after I've interviewed the ex," she said before the emptiness on the line stretched out too long. "Don't worry, I'm used to working alone."

She turned off the phone without waiting for his reply and flung it onto the map lying next to her.

———

Gundersund slipped his phone back into his pocket and thought about having a cigarette. Autopsies were stressful and being teamed with Stonechild was becoming another thing to worry about. What was she doing tracking down a prime suspect by herself, especially someone named Wolf? He could feel the beginnings of a headache starting up behind his right temple.

He'd quit the habit for two months and three days but could conjure up the taste of nicotine and the round feel of one between his fingers at will. Usually, it was enough. This autopsy was the first real test of his resolve and it was weakening. All he had to do was step outside and head to the smoking area on the north side of the building where he could easily bum one. He could feel the pull.

He looked down the hallway. Fiona was walking toward him with two coffees in her hands. The baggy green scrubs hid her slender body and the heart tattoo on her left shoulder. Her rubber-soled shoes squeaked on the waxed floor. She stopped a foot away and handed over one of the Styrofoam cups. Her fingers touched his hand longer than they needed to.

"No sugar, right?"

"You remembered."

"I remember lots of stuff when it comes to you."

Gundersund laughed to cover his discomfort. "Let's not dredge up the bad memories. As I recall, you had a long list of my failings by the time you moved out."

She tilted her head so that her blond hair swung over one shoulder. Her perfume filled the space between them. It was spicier than what she'd worn when they were together. "We had more good than bad between us." She sipped her coffee. Her blue eyes stared into his. "I'm living alone again."

"What happened to the surgeon?"

"Long gone. Why don't you come for dinner tomorrow night? I could barbeque steaks, bake some potatoes, uncork a bottle of red."

"This case will probably have me tied up." He was quite certain that taking her up on her offer was a very bad idea.

"Well, if you end up free, the invitation's always there." She pushed the door behind them open with her hip and stepped inside the autopsy room. She looked over her shoulder. "Coming? I'm cutting into her brain next."

"Well, since you put it that way."

He followed his wife through the door and realized he'd forgotten all about the cigarette, but he hadn't forgotten about the maddening Kala Stonechild. He should call Rouleau to let him know what she was up to, but that would alienate her and get their partnership off to a bad start. He'd try to finish up early here and track her down. She was turning out to be just one more woman out to make his life hell.

———

Guitar music circled the house from the backyard. Kala pushed open the gate and followed a brick path into a small patio area wrapped in flower gardens and shrubs. A man sat on a stool with his back to her, a guitar in his lap, one leather-sandaled foot crossed over the other leg. She recognized a Gordon Lightfoot song: "Railroad Trilogy." The man's brown hair was pulled back into a curly ponytail.

He was shirtless, his broad shoulders and back lean and muscled. When he turned around, Kala saw why he'd been nicknamed Wolf. The lower half of his face was bearded and his eyes were almond-shaped and a curious shade of green and gold. His hands and body went still.

"Yes? Can I help you?"

She stepped around clay flowerpots bursting with begonias and impatiens. Thyme grew between the bricks at her feet, sending up a dusky fragrance as she walked closer. "Are you Wolf Edwards?"

"I am. And who might you be?" He smiled, his face friendly, unguarded.

She pulled the ID from her pocket that Vera had typed up that very morning and watched his expression alter. "Detective Kala Stonechild. I'm here about Leah Sampson." She was now a metre from him. She stood in full sun while he sat in the shade of a blowsy willow tree that draped around him, only a short distance above his head. His brow furrowed as he read the ID and for a moment, she hesitated.

He lifted his eyes to hers. "Has she gotten herself into trouble?"

"I'm sorry to say that she's been murdered," Kala said. The words never came out soft enough, but how could they?

Wolf started to stand and then fell back. He stared at her as if seeking evidence in her eyes that she was lying. When he couldn't find any, he gripped the neck of the guitar with both hands and levered it upward, level with his chest. He began to swing it into the trunk of the willow tree but instead swung it past and into a rose bush several feet away. Kala stood stock still in front of him and waited, unfazed by his anger. She'd seen every reaction imaginable after delivering this news, from complete denial to physical illness. Without warning, he stood and kicked the stool against the trunk of the tree. One sob ripped through his throat into the silence of the garden. Kala took a step closer and put a hand onto his forearm.

"Should we go inside and sit?" she asked quietly. "I can tell you what I know."

His back straightened. He searched her face, his eyes seeking purchase. "I need to know what happened." Each word seemed ripped from his throat.

He turned abruptly and led her through a torn screen door directly into a kitchen. She took in a clean square room with a green tile floor and white cupboards. A wooden blind hung at a crooked angle over an open window. The sun streamed in through the slats. She crossed to the table, ignoring the remains of a joint in an overflowing ash tray. They sat across from each other at the pine table.

"Tell me," he said.

12

"I CAN'T SHARE much, but we believe Leah was killed late Friday night or early Saturday morning in her apartment. When was the last time you saw her?" Kala pulled a notebook and pen from her handbag and sat back, waiting for Wolf to answer.

"I walked her home after she finished her shift on Friday. I watched her go into the house where she's living. It was around nine thirty. Then I met a buddy at the campus pub. Did it happen in her apartment?"

"Yes. Did you see anybody on the street or hanging around near her building?"

Wolf shook his head. "Was somebody waiting for her? If I'd walked her to her apartment door, would she still be alive?" He moaned and dropped his head into his hands. When he lifted his eyes to hers a minute later, they were wet. "I'd like to see her."

"In time. Can I have the name and address of the buddy you met that night?"

"This is a waste of time."

"It's called crossing out possibilities."

He sighed and gave her the information while she took it down. "How did you meet Leah?"

"I don't see how this is going to be of any value."

"It will help me piece together who she was and hopefully lead to who killed her."

"From finding out when I met her?"

"It's just one piece of her life. It could lead to more avenues for us to investigate."

"High school. My parents moved to Brockville when I was seventeen and she'd grown up there. She was in grade nine and I was three years ahead. We lived on the same street and walked home together one day."

"Did you begin dating then?"

"No. I thought of her more like a little sister. In fact, she hung out with my younger sister, Amber. You know how it is in high school. A three-year age difference is a lot when it comes to dating."

"But things changed."

"I started in psychology at Queen's and saw her whenever I went home, usually at our house. She and Amber remained best friends through high school and our house was where they spent their time. Leah came to Queen's four years ago and we started going out her second year."

"You're finishing up your Ph.D. this year," Kala said.

Wolf nodded without asking how she knew. "I took a year off and travelled after my master's."

"While you were dating Leah?"

"Yeah. We'd just started going out but I'd had the trip to India planned and didn't want to miss the opportunity. I was volunteering with a children's orphanage. Leah stayed here and carried on with her studies."

Kala thought this man sounded too good to be true. "I understand that you and Leah broke up a few months ago. Could you tell me about that?"

Wolf shifted in his chair and avoided looking at her. Perhaps he'd realized for the first time how wrong this could all go. He crossed his arms across his chest and scowled.

"Leah had started up with a married man and I asked her to choose. She told me that I was insane. But Leah'd been secretive and gone one weekend without explanation. I could read guilt on her face. There was enough evidence that I knew it was true."

"Do you have a name?"

"No."

Kala searched his face. He'd answered too quickly, but she'd give him a little leeway … for now. He'd just had a major shock and perhaps hadn't fully comprehended what was at stake when it came to proving his innocence.

"Can I see Leah now?" he asked.

Kala wrote her cellphone number on a piece of paper and ripped it out of her notebook. She set the paper on the table in front on him and stood. She looked down at him. "We're currently doing an autopsy. Leah's parents are here and perhaps you should contact them about the arrangements. We'll be releasing her body once all the forensics are completed."

"Her father's here?"

"Yes. Is there something I should know?"

Wolf shook his head again and looked down at the table.

"When you're ready to tell me something of substance, I'll be ready to hear it," said Kala. She pointed to the paper. "That's my cellphone number. Call me anytime. I should also advise you not to go anywhere. We'll certainly be back to speak with you again."

She left by the back door and was stepping over the trailing vines on her way to the gate when he came outside and called to her.

"You didn't tell me how she died. I think you owe me that."

She stopped and faced him. He reminded her of too many other people who'd just found out the world as they knew it had ended. Maybe she didn't owe him anything, but the anguish on his face gave her pause. She took a few more steps and raised her hand to push open the gate. She looked over her shoulder at him.

"Leah died of a stab wound. We're following up on every lead, I promise you that."

He took a second to digest her words before nodding. He wiped his forehead and pushed the hair from his eyes, then he pulled the door shut and disappeared inside.

———

It was nearly six o'clock and Rouleau could feel his stomach rumble with hunger. He'd breakfasted on four cups of coffee and a stale doughnut and missed lunch. He decided to get through the day's reports quickly and head to his father's to cook the steaks, still wrapped in brown paper in the meat cooler from the day before. He'd gotten home too late from the murder scene to cook supper and his father had managed with a sandwich. He'd said that morning that he would wait for Rouleau to get home even if it meant a late meal.

There was a knock on his office door and Gundersund entered. The big man looked tired, the scar on his cheek sharper than usual against his pale skin. He took the seat across from Rouleau.

"Any word from Stonechild?"

"Not yet." Rouleau looked over Gundersund's shoulder. "But it looks like she's just arrived."

Rouleau watched her crossing the floor in the outer office to her desk. He raised a hand and signalled for her to come into his. She hesitated, then walked past her desk and pushed open his office door, flashing Gundersund a quick smile before taking the seat next to him.

Gundersund's eyes fixed on Rouleau as he recapped the day's progress. "We think somebody grabbed her just inside her apartment. There's no sign of a forced entry so the attacker could have been waiting in the laundry room. It's the most likely scenario."

Kala interrupted. "I spoke with Wolf Edwards, who walked her home Friday night. He watched her go up the sidewalk to the house but didn't see anybody lurking outside."

"He's the ex-boyfriend?" asked Rouleau.

"Yeah, but I got the feeling he didn't know about her death. He seemed genuinely grief-stricken. He gave me the name of a friend he met up with after he dropped Leah off. That's why I'm late. I went to check Rick Carlson out. He wasn't home so we'll have to follow up." Her eyes darted to Gundersund and then straight ahead.

Rouleau looked from Kala back to Gundersund, who sat silently, his hands still in his lap. "The door-to-door interviews haven't come up with anything else. Nobody saw or heard anything. What about the autopsy?" Rouleau asked Gundersund.

"What I told Kala this afternoon about the autopsy hasn't changed much. Leah's ribs and fingers on her right hand were smashed in addition to lots of other bruising. She was superficially cut with a knife over a good part of her body but the thrust in her stomach killed her. Fiona says we're looking for a hunting knife most likely, six-inch blade."

"Was she raped?"

"No."

"What about her co-workers?" Rouleau swung his eyes back to Kala. "Find out anything useful?"

"Hard to say. It's going to take a few visits to get all the secrets out of them."

"Well tomorrow, Kala, you'll be working with Chalmers and Woodhouse on the rape case. Gundersund can make the follow-up call to the help line."

"But …" Kala began.

Rouleau held up a hand. "I know. This is hardly the time to split you up, but the two of them need a woman's point of view. I apologize if that sounds sexist, but I assure you it's a compliment. You can move back and forth between the two files."

"The two of them already given up?" asked Gundersund, amused. "Or have they got a lead that needs chasing down?"

"They got nothing today that we didn't already have," Rouleau said. "I need some imagination on this file." He slid a folder across the desk in her direction. "A little light reading for your evening's entertainment."

"How did you guys ever get along without me?" Kala asked, reaching for it.

"Not all that well obviously," Gundersund said.

13

GUNDERSUND WATCHED STONECHILD as he packed up his desk to head home. She'd started up her computer and was now hunched over the file that Rouleau had given her. He didn't find her pretty in the regular sense of the word. *Arresting.* That was the word he'd use. High cheekbones, dark eyes with so much hidden in their depths anybody could get lost just trying to find a way in, long legs, and a toned body. She looked unapproachable; an island unto herself.

She flipped a page and set down the file, typing her password on the keyboard. Her eyes skimmed the computer screen then lifted toward him. He was leaning back in his chair, hands folded behind his head.

"Did you need something?" she asked.

"No, but I thought you might like to grab a bite to eat."

"What, now?"

"It's past suppertime, so yeah now."

"I have to read up on this rape case."

"Well, if you come eat with me, I can tell you what's in the file since I wrote everything in it." He smiled. "I can even tell you what I didn't include."

She studied him a moment longer, biting her bottom lip as she considered the offer. "I guess I could eat."

"Then let's go." Gundersund stood and waited for her to pack up her bag and shut down her computer.

"Where are you staying?" he asked as they walked out of the building.

"Heading toward Bath, on the Old Front Road."

He stopped for a second, then resumed walking as he said, "No kidding. We must be neighbours. I moved out that way about a year ago."

"I'm staying at a friend's. Marjory Littlebear."

"The land claims lawyer?"

It was Kala's turn to stop. "You know her?"

"I'm just down the road. She'd come over Sunday evenings and we'd walk my dog. I have a border collie named Minny." He watched Stonechild's face but couldn't tell if the news pleased her or not. If he had to guess, he'd bet on the side of not. "What were the odds?" he asked smiling.

Her face closed down but not before he saw the grimace. "I like my privacy," she said. "You might not find me as good a neighbour as Marjory. She's gone for a month or so."

"She told me last week she might be going North on short notice," said Gundersund. "I guess you could be her replacement, seeing as how you have a dog needs walking too."

They continued toward the parking lot. He shortened his strides to match hers. "Is that your truck?" he asked, pointing to a black Ford. When she nodded, he said, "Mine is the silver Mustang over there. We can meet up at the Merchant Tap House at the bottom of Princess Street. I can lead if you like."

"I passed by it in my travels." She glanced over to his car. "Nice wheels. What year?"

"It's second hand 2010. My pride and joy. See you in a bit then." He started to cross the parking lot but stopped and turned when she called his name. She'd opened her truck door and stood with one foot on the riser.

"My dog Taiku doesn't like other dogs much. You're better off taking those Sunday walks without us."

She slid into her front seat and slammed the door without waiting for his response.

—

The first dinner crowd shift had finished and the pub staff was regrouping for the nine o'clock rush. The hostess offered them their choice of seats. Gundersund followed Kala through the tables to the back corner in the smaller room to their right with a window overlooking Princess Street. Night had fallen and candles flickered on the tables.

They took a few minutes to read the menu and order: bangers and mash with a pint of Guinness for Gundersund; chicken burger, fries, and salad with a soda and cranberry for Stonechild.

Gundersund stretched out his legs under the table, angling them so he wasn't crowding Stonechild. He liked this bar. It didn't pretend to be anything but a place to drink. The food was basic too: no pretentious sauces or fancy presentation. Rock and roll pumped through the speakers. His kind of music. Tunes that never wore out.

"This place has a good feel," said Stonechild, as if reading his mind. She leaned back in her chair and stretched out her legs alongside his.

He nodded his agreement. "So how long have you known Rouleau?" he asked. For the first time that day, the pinched look left her face and she smiled.

"Not long. We met last winter in Ottawa when I went to work on his team. We hit it off."

Two peas in a pod as far as Gundersund could see — a twin set of loners. "I heard he was married."

"Are you digging for dirt, Officer Gundersund?" asked Kala. Her smile widened.

He grinned back. "Maybe. It's good to know who you're working with."

"Rouleau was married but now he's single. His ex-wife remarried last year but she's been ill. Rouleau doesn't talk about it." Her gaze studied him. "I found this out from my last partner in Ottawa. We're detectives after all. So how about you? Married or single?"

"Separated."

"This job is tough on relationships." He heard genuine regret in her voice.

"We're cop clichés all right," he said.

Their food arrived and they agreed to talk work after they'd eaten. Gundersund glanced across at Stonechild as she ate the food. She ate like a kid, not caring if anybody watched her devour every morsel, licking her fingers as ketchup oozed from the burger. A spot of relish dimpled her cheek. Gundersund grinned and bit into one of the sausages. The smoky taste laced with garlic, cayenne, and rosemary spread like fire across his taste buds.

Fiona had picked at the meals he'd cooked her, saying she wasn't hungry, but he knew it was vanity driving her small appetite. She'd feared growing out of her size four clothes as if her worth was tied up in a dress size. She'd hated his complacency about putting on weight and getting old. When he knew their relationship was going south, he'd started going to the gym to prove he was open to changing for her. After she'd left, he kept going, hoping it would bring her home. At some point, he'd just given up the fight and stopped working out.

Kala pushed her empty plate toward the edge of the table and sighed contentedly. "So what's the story on Chalmers and Woodhouse?"

Gundersund took one last bite of mashed potatoes and put his plate on top of hers. "Let's say they're not known for their relentless search for the truth. Rouleau was saddled with them as was the last series of inspectors in his job. Chalmers used to be good but he doesn't care anymore. Retirement is on his horizon and he's been easing into it for a while. Unfortunately, he and Woodhouse found each other. They share the same work ethic."

"Hard to get rid of somebody, even if they're not pulling their weight."

"Woodhouse and Chalmers are banking on it. I give Chalmers another year at the most before he starts in on his pension. Maybe it's not too late for Woodhouse to be re-educated once he gets a new partner."

"There are just the four of us plus Rouleau?"

"With cut backs, that's it for our investigative team. The city and region is just over a hundred and fifty thousand people and major crimes are usually low, although you wouldn't know it by this week. Murders are rare."

"What about the rape case? Della Munroe."

Gundersund nodded. "This is a university town so we get rapes. A spousal rape is an oddity."

"From what I read in the report, there's physical evidence. Do you think Brian Munroe did it?"

Gundersund silently replayed the facts before answering. "Yes, I do. She had bruising inside her thighs as well as other places and he admitted to hurting her before. He's adamantly denying the charges though. He sounded convincing, I have to say."

"Great. It's a he said/she said."

"The prosecutor should be able to make a good case. Della had a girlfriend named Celia Paules who backs up the abuse and jealousy. It sounded like Della Munroe was going to divorce him, so their kid could become the issue. Any judge in their right mind is going to give her sole custody."

Kala looked out the window, withdrawing into herself, a memory of something darkening her expression.

"It's been a long day," said Gundersund softly, sorry for whatever he'd said to make her mood change so quickly. "Why don't we go home and get some rest, because tomorrow is going to be just as long."

Kala turned her face toward him. "You're right. Thanks, Gundersund."

"For what?"

"No reason. Just thanks for inviting me to dinner and filling me in. I know you didn't need to."

"Anytime. We're partners, don't forget."

"I won't."

14

TAIKU PADDED ACROSS the deck and laid his head on Kala's knee. She dropped her hand and rubbed him behind the ears while staring through the darkness in the direction of the lake. The full moon illuminated the woods enough to see the dark outlines of trees. Above the horizon, stars punched through the black velvet sky like polished diamonds. She could smell the grass below her feet and the perfume from sweet peas climbing the trellis.

"Can't sleep either, boy?" Kala asked. She'd slept a few hours before waking disoriented, her heart pounding until she remembered where she was. After that, she hadn't been able to relax enough to drift off. The Leah Sampson crime scene had played on a loop in her head. Imagining the girl's last frantic moments was a disturbing image that kept bringing her back from the edge of sleep.

She pulled the blanket tighter around herself and closed her eyes. The breeze from the lake cooled her face and its soft buffeting soothed her. Taiku flopped down at her feet and rolled onto his side. His soulful chocolate-coloured eyes closed and Kala felt her own stresses begin to fade in rhythm to his slowed breathing.

When she next opened her eyes, streaks of pink and orange laced through an indigo sky and morning chill made her shiver under the blanket. She'd slept a few hours. Stiffness had set into her neck and shoulders and she rolled her head back and forth to work out the cricks. She looked around the deck. Taiku was gone, likely investigating the underbrush at the end of the property. He never strayed far from her and she wasn't worried. By the lightness in the sky, she judged it to be nearly five a.m.

A rustling noise in the underbrush at the other end of the yard, and her eyes caught a flash of black streaking across the yard toward the side of the house. She stood and moved quickly toward the railing.

"Taiku! Come!"

He'd disappeared in the direction of the road. Kala cursed and raced down the steps after him in her bare feet. The dew on the grass was a shock of cold on her skin. She hoisted the blanket up higher, trying not to trip as she ran. Underneath she was naked and wary of dropping her cover until she knew what had captured Taiku's attention.

She reached the edge of the house and heard Taiku's low growl. It was the threatening noise he made in his throat when danger was nearby. Kala paused. If Taiku had cornered another skunk or porcupine, she'd be best not to frighten either animal.

"Come, Taiku," she called softly as she stepped round the side of the house. She stopped. A smile spread across her face.

"You never said you had an attack dog," Gundersund said, his body motionless, caught in midstride. His white cotton shirt was strained under the tension in his muscles, as he'd readied himself for the dog to lunge. Six feet of muscular male suspended in a cartoonish pose.

"Come, Taiku," Kala said firmly.

Taiku looked from her to Gundersund and back again. His shoulders dropped and he ambled over to Kala.

"Good boy." She reached for her dog's collar and held him while Gundersund wiped the sweat from his forehead.

"Shit, Stonechild. Would your dog really have attacked?" Gundersund closed the gap between them. His eyes remained fixed on Taiku.

"He's never gone after anyone before." She shrugged. "There's always a first time. What are you doing here anyway?"

"I got an early morning wake-up call. There's been a death at Della Munroe's house and we have to get over there. I phoned you a couple of times, but when you didn't answer I came over to get you."

"I fell asleep on the deck." She followed the line of his eyes to the gap in the blanket that showed off a stretch of leg up to her thigh. She wrapped the blanket more firmly around herself. Gundersund's cheeks reddened and he looked down at the ground. She would have liked to prolong his discomfort but there wasn't time. "Did Brian kill her then?" she asked. Kala knew the odds of coming out alive when a partner turned violent. She'd lived in a few foster homes where she'd witnessed escalating abuse first-hand. This was a depressing start to the morning.

Gundersund shook his head. "Wasn't Della who died. It was Brian. He'd ignored the restraining order and broken into their house. Della cracked his head open with a hammer. We have to go interview her now at the station. Rouleau's at the scene with Woodhouse and Chalmers."

Kala shook her head in disbelief. "Nothing showed up in the reports to make this a possibility." She started back toward the house, signalling to Taiku to follow. "Man, I hate domestics. Give me a second to get dressed and I'll follow you into the station in my truck."

———

Rouleau watched while Fiona Gundersund finished her examination of Brian Munroe's gaping wound. Munroe lay in a pool of blood on the top landing outside the master bedroom. Blood splatter painted one wall and the beige carpet. The hammer that caused the damage had already been bagged and sent to the lab.

Fiona stood slowly from where she crouched next to him, her hands on the small of her back. She rolled back her shoulders before she turned to look at Rouleau. The pain on her face reminded him that she'd been off work the month before with a lower back injury. A car had sideswiped her bike on a downtown street and she'd gone for a tumble.

"Della hit him with enough force to crack his skull. If that wasn't enough, she hit him a second time. She made a real mess of his brain. The wife's confessed, I gather?" Fiona's blue eyes gave nothing away.

"She has. She's claiming self defence. She'd taken out a restraining order just yesterday morning after she charged him with rape."

"A marriage gone horribly wrong, I'd say."

"Evidently. Safe to move him?"

"Yeah. I'll be doing an autopsy first thing. You're keeping me busy this week."

"Not on purpose, believe me."

"It's unusual but not unheard of to have two murders back to back like this. Kingston isn't known for its homicides."

They started walking down the stairs together. Rouleau noted the angle of the sun slanting through the window on the landing. People would be up getting ready for work now. They'd been here close to four hours. He could use some sleep.

Fiona stopped at the bottom of the staircase and looked back up at him. Her blond ponytail had come undone and tendrils of hair fell loose. Fatigue lines on her face had deepened from the day before.

"Will Paul be working this one too?"

"He's on his way to the station to interview Della."

"I hear you finally snagged him a new partner. Word around the station is that she's attractive … and young."

"Kala Stonechild's a good cop."

"But not too good I hope." Fiona flashed him a wide smile, but her eyes were giving a different message. She turned toward the front door without waiting for him to respond.

Rouleau followed slowly. He'd been unable to avoid the stories circulating around the station about Fiona's treatment of Paul Gundersund. She'd left him the year before for a married doctor who'd also left his wife. Apparently, this hadn't been her first extramarital fling, but it was the first time she'd left home. Odds in the office pool were weighted on the side of him taking her back by Christmas. Everyone agreed that he was better off without her. By what he'd seen in Fiona's eyes, he wouldn't bet against her if she decided to reel Gundersund back in.

—

Della Munroe's hands shook as she lifted the coffee cup to her lips. She was wrapped in a blue wool blanket, sitting forward, her eyes staring at nothing. Kala nodded at the officer sitting next to Della on the couch and they exchanged places. Gundersund hung back near the doorway as he and Kala had agreed he would before entering the room.

Kala knew on paper that Della was young, but was surprised by just how young she appeared. Della's long black hair hung loose around her face, her pale skin flawless and unlined. The blue eyes she raised to Kala were red from crying but still brilliant blue. Dressed in a white T-shirt, jeans, and sparkly pink flip flops, she looked closer to a teenager than a woman approaching thirty. Della would make for a sympathetic accused if the case came to trial. Kala had doubts that it would get that far given the circumstances.

"How are you doing, Della?" Kala asked. "Is there something I can get you? Anything you need?"

"No, thanks."

"I'm sorry for what you've been through, but I need you to tell me exactly what you remember about last night and what led up to your husband's death."

"Am I under arrest?"

"No, we're just trying to find out what happened at this point. Can you take me through your evening? Take your time. I need you to know that we are recording what you say. Do you understand?"

"Yes." Della took a deep, shuddering breath and hunched deeper into the blanket. "I put Tommy to bed around seven and crawled in to read him a bedtime story. I must have fallen asleep because next thing I knew, it was ten o'clock. I got up and checked that the doors were locked and poured some milk for Mr. Paws." She smiled. "Tommy named him when we picked up the cat from the humane society." Her face crumpled and she picked up the coffee cup, letting her hair fall across her face. She raised the cup to her lips and sipped. A portion slopped onto the blanket as she lowered the cup to her lap.

"You're doing fine," said Kala. "What happened next?"

"I had something to eat, I think a muffin and milk. I'd hardly eaten since that night when Brian ... when Brian raped me. I lay down on the couch in the living room and dozed for a while. A noise woke me up. It was glass shattering in the kitchen. At first I thought I was dreaming." She stopped talking, and tucked her chin onto her chest.

"What did you do next?" Kala asked.

"I lay there for a few moments getting oriented. It was dark — I hadn't turned any lights on before I lay down — and then I saw him in the hallway." Her voice dropped to a whisper, "Brian."

"Did he see you?"

"Not at first. He started for the stairs and my first thought was Tommy. I got up and asked him what he was doing. He turned around and said he'd come to take Tommy away from me and not to try to stop him. I ran toward him and grabbed his arm, pleading with him to talk to me. He hit me across the face." Della raised her face and pushed back her hair. An ugly bruise had spread across her forehead.

"Has that been tended to by anyone?"

"It's nothing." Della let her hair swing back across her face. "I fell on my knees and landed on the floor next to the hammer. I'd been putting up a mirror at the bottom of the stairs and left the hammer beside the hall table. I don't remember picking it up, but I must have. I called to Brian to stop. We needed to talk, but he told me to go to hell. He said that he was done talking and now he and Tommy were going to disappear. He'd kill Tommy before I would see him again. I ... I panicked. I climbed the stairs after him, but he refused to stop. He was going to take Tommy and maybe kill him. I swung the hammer at Brian just to slow him down."

"You hit him twice on the back of his head."

"He … he didn't fall right away. I was scared. I don't remember hitting him a second time, but I must have. I didn't mean to hit him so hard."

Kala looked across at Gundersund. He stood leaning against the wall near the door. He nodded his head, encouraging her to continue. She detected kindness in his eyes before his face cleared of expression.

"There was a lot of blood," Kala observed mildly, looking back at Della.

"I know." Della's sobs began softly under the black curtain of her hair. "I thought he was going to take my baby."

Kala waited until Della composed herself. "Only one last question for now, Mrs. Munroe, and then I think we should have someone check you over just to make sure your head is fine as you say. What did you do right after your husband was lying on the floor bleeding?"

"I called for an ambulance and the police from my bedroom as soon as I checked on Tommy. After I called, I went back to Tommy's room and picked him up to take him downstairs. We waited on the couch after I unlocked the front door. Tommy didn't wake up the whole time."

"You didn't try to stop Brian's bleeding?"

"No. I just wanted to be as far away from him as I could. I was sure he was going to wake up and come after me again."

"You didn't check to see if he was dead?"

"I didn't think I'd *killed* him. I thought he'd wake up and come after me." Della moaned and began rocking back and forth on the couch.

Kala turned off the tape recorder and looked over at Gundersund. He signalled to her that he was stepping outside to call for a doctor. They'd gotten what they needed but she still felt a twinge of disgust at herself for putting the woman through questioning when she'd just lost so much: a marriage that started out hopeful with love, and was now nothing but pain, loss, and that worm of guilt for no longer having to deal with an abusive husband. Kala reached over and touched Della's shoulder, the only gesture of comfort she could allow herself as the constable investigating his death.

—

"So what do you think?" Gundersund asked. He set a cup of coffee on the desk in front of Kala. She looked up from her computer screen. Gundersund was sipping from his cup, looking at her over the rim. His eyes had that curious look in them again that she found unnerving.

"Thanks." She picked up the mug and forced herself to focus on the case. "Della sounds credible. Combined with the alleged rape and bruises from this encounter after he broke in, I can't see enough for a prosecution. What do you think?"

"Same as you. It probably won't go to trial."

"Rouleau should give this to Chalmers and let me get back to the Sampson murder." She set down the coffee cup and resumed typing. Out of the corner of her eye, she watched Gundersund return to his desk. He sat down and began talking on his cellphone. He swivelled his chair around so that he had his back to her. Kala lifted her head and watched him for a moment. Whoever he was talking to was causing him grief. His shoulders had hunched forward and the fingers of his right hand tapped staccato against the side of his desk. His voice rose angrily and she heard him tell the person at the other end to just let it go.

Kala dropped her eyes back to the report on her screen. Most curious. Gundersund had somebody in his life who had the power to upset him.

15

DALAL SHAHAN WOKE up early, just as fingers of sunlight broke through the darkness of her room. She lay on her side with her eyes open, watching the sunbeams dance through the flimsy curtain onto the hardwood floor. *It would be nice to be a sunbeam,* she thought. Sunbeams made people happy.

Already, she could hear her mother moving around in the kitchen preparing breakfast. The spicy smell of beef haleem — wheat, lentils, and beef with coriander, cumin, and turmeric — drifted up the stairs and made her mouth water. There would be leftover samosas too, with green chutney from supper the evening before.

Dalal stepped out of bed and looked down at Meeza, still sleeping so peacefully with one arm flung over her head on the pillow. Meeza's other arm was wrapped around her stuffed teddy bear, Boo. Meeza had her own room but sometimes came to sleep with Dalal in the middle of the night when she got lonely. Meeza didn't like being alone much.

Dalal kept her eyes on Meeza's face as she skirted around her bed to the bookcase near the closet. She knelt and reached her hand behind the Quran her parents had given her on her tenth birthday. She let out a breath of relief to feel the thin diary still in its hiding place.

Ghazi hadn't found it on his last search of their room because she'd carried it to school in her knapsack two days before. Immediately upon arriving home after school, she'd told her mother she needed to use the bathroom upstairs. She'd tucked the book inside her underwear under her dress before getting off the bus. It had felt strange but comforting to have it next to her skin. She'd hurried upstairs and hidden the diary in the bookcase before scurrying across the hall into the bathroom. By the time Dalal entered the kitchen, her mother had already emptied her knapsack onto the kitchen table as she did every day when Dalal came home. Dalal felt a flush of guilt at this small rebellion but if she had to do it over, she would not change one thing.

Dalal pulled out the diary and straightened the books in an even row as they had been. She tucked the book under her arm as she crossed back to her bed and got under the covers. She rolled onto her side so that she faced away from the door and pulled the sheet over her head. When she was sure nobody was stirring across the hall, she opened the diary and squinted at the delicate swirls and loops in blue ink. The scrap of paper she used as a bookmark was still in place and she flipped to the spot she'd left off. She began reading.

> I got up this morning and heard them talking in the kitchen, like old women conspiring. Odd. They looked at me with guilty eyes when they saw me standing in the doorway. I pretended not to notice and ate my breakfast even though I wasn't hungry. I put on the black hijab and ugly long coat as expected and hurried for the bus. I prayed I wouldn't meet Susan and Josy and I was lucky today. If they

saw me in the head scarf and coat, they'd tell all the other girls. I hate, hate, hate their sly looks and superior way of looking at me. Brit met me in the park with my jeans and T-shirt. I changed behind the trees while she kept watch. She brought lip gloss and eye shadow and a little mirror. I'll have to remember to rub the makeup off before I leave school. Ghazi is hanging around more, spying on me and reporting back. If they knew, well, I won't think about that today. Chad Stephens smiled at me when I walked into history class. My heart is singing.

Oh joy of joys! Brit told me at our lockers this morning that Chad wants to take me out this Friday to the movies!!!! My heart is going to burst wide open, I am so, so happy. There has to be a way to be allowed out without them suspecting. I will go no matter what. I will find a way to have a night away from them if it's the last thing I do. I will have a life.

Dalal jumped as Ghazi's alarm clock began its wake up beeping in his room next to them. The wall muffled the annoying sound but Ghazi would let it go on a while before he woke enough to hit the snooze button. Dalal quickly closed the diary and decided she'd hide it in the bedclothes and take it to school again in her knapsack. She didn't trust her brother to stay out of their room today because he only had one class at the university this morning. He had all afternoon to search while she and Meeza were in school. He had all day to plot and scheme.

16

ROULEAU GATHERED THE team in the meeting room before lunch.

"Looks like we can wrap up the investigation into the Munroe death," Chalmers said, leaning back in his chair. "I spoke with the prosecutor this morning and they'll be pursuing involuntary manslaughter with provocation. She admits to killing her husband, but he'd broken into her house and was making off with the kid. She won't be doing any time, is my guess."

"Della Munroe told us that she was hanging up a mirror and left the hammer on the floor. Did that check out?" Kala asked.

"It did." Chalmers held up a photo. "The wrapping for the new mirror was in the recycle bin." He looked at her, a lazy smile spreading across his face. "Anything else?"

She met his eyes without smiling. "Yeah. Had the Munroes corresponded that day?"

"Nothing shows up in the phone or computer records." Woodhouse interrupted their staring contest. "We've had someone checking all morning. Della said she'd locked the door and he had a key, but she'd also put the chain lock on. When the chain stopped him from getting in, he broke the glass and reached in to undo it." He held up a photo of the broken window on the kitchen door before handing around the crime scene photos, adding, "Everything Della Munroe told us is checking out."

"On the other hand, she wasn't actually being physically threatened," said Gundersund. "The force she used was excessive. Anyone who takes a hammer to somebody's head has to be aware of the damage they can do."

"He'd ignored the restraining order and broken into their house. He was in the act of taking their son away. I'd say he was threatening her in other ways. Mental abuse can be more powerful than physical over time," Kala said. Her eyes had shifted to Gundersund's. He held her gaze.

Rouleau waited a few seconds before he broke the impasse. "It won't be up to us to argue her case, for or against. I want Chalmers and Woodhouse to finish up the investigation on this one. Stonechild, you can continue working with Gundersund on the Leah Sampson murder today. Still no solid leads or suspects, so you'll have to dig deeper into her life and the people she dealt with."

"Yes, sir," Kala said.

Gundersund looked at her. "Let's grab some lunch and go over the reports. We can plan our interview schedule."

"Perfect," Kala said. Her jaw jutted out dangerously. She looked at Rouleau. "Anything else?"

"I'm taking an hour to meet with a real estate agent to check out a house. I'll be on my cellphone if you need to reach me."

"Whereabouts?" asked Gundersund.

"Along the waterfront to the west of downtown."

"Nice area."

"It's not too far from Dad's, the only reason I'm giving it a look."

—

Rouleau leaned against the hood of his car and checked his watch. He'd give Laney Masterson five more minutes before driving downtown to pick up some lunch. He'd made initial contact with the real estate office by leaving a voice mail, but hadn't expected her to leap into action so soon. He wasn't even sure if it was the right time to leave his father alone. However, it would take a few months to finalize a sale and move in, so no harm getting the ball rolling.

He looked over at the house Laney had picked to show him. He'd specified a two-bedroom house, preferably a bungalow. This three-storey home wasn't even close to what he'd had in mind. The waste of his time irritated him. Her lateness made him doubly impatient, but he wanted to meet her if only to set her on the right track.

The sun beat down like a heat lamp and sweat trickled down his back, making his shirt cling uncomfortably. Grey clouds had gathered on the distant skyline but as of yet offered no relief. Rouleau worried that his shaved head would burn if he didn't soon get out of the sun and looked around for some shade. A few oak trees towered above the house in the backyard, but none in the front. He debated heading to the neighbour's yard where a couple of pine trees shaded the driveway. Before he roused himself to walk that far, a car engine sounded behind him. He turned to see a silver Nissan barrelling toward him at a speed that should have earned the driver a ticket and a few demerit points off their licence. They wheeled into an empty parking spot a few spaces down and the engine died. Rouleau squinted and made out a woman's ghostly face behind the sunlight reflecting off the front windshield.

The driver door was immediately flung open and a tall woman stepped out of the car. He was struck by how well put together she was, elegantly turned out in a white suit and red high heels with her auburn hair pulled into a bun at the nape of her neck. The bones in her face were sharp and angular and her eyes were hidden behind dark sunglasses. He could see enough to know that she was staring at him as she walked toward him. She held out a hand and he encircled her slender fingers with his own. Her grip was firm. In her forties, she had the body and movements of a much younger woman.

"Mr. Rouleau, so pleased to meet you," she said. Her voice was low and pleasing to his ear. "Have you had a chance to look around?" She waved a hand in a sweep. A diamond bracelet sparkled on her wrist.

"I decided to wait for you."

She flashed a quick smile as if acknowledging the implied rebuke, but didn't comment on her late arrival. She added brusque, business-like "Good. Then let's get started."

They walked up the sidewalk toward the front door. A white verandah wrapped around the front and side of the house.

"I know this is bigger than what you asked for in your voice mail, but the price is within your budget and the house is in excellent shape. The yard is well maintained and there are lovely trees in the backyard. I believe you'll enjoy living in this neighbourhood, that is, if you decide to buy."

She used a key to open the front door and they stepped inside. The front hall was narrow and cool, painted a creamy lilac. The only light came from an oval window near the ceiling.

She took her time showing him the downstairs — a large living room with a wood fireplace, small bedroom and bathroom, large kitchen with walk-in pantry, and formal dining room off the family room — and he let her talk about the updates and redone birch floors without interrupting. He wondered if the look of genuine appreciation on her face was feigned or real when she ran her fingers over the granite countertops and the oak mantle over the fireplace. She had all the jargon down.

Rouleau stopped her as she started up the winding stairs to the second floor. "No point going any farther," he said with unexpected regret. "It's a lovely home but isn't what I'm after. I've no desire to waste your time."

She turned, her feet resting on different steps, and frowned down at him. The confident glow in her lovely face had disappeared. She studied him for the first time as if she'd just realized he wasn't on board with her program. "Are you sure? This is the area of town you asked to see, but there isn't much available in your price range." She paused as if she wasn't used to such stupidity in her clients.

"It's too much house. I need something smaller. I'm sorry."

"No need to be sorry. I'm the one who brought you here." She retraced her steps and brushed past him, her high heels clicking on the hardwood as she crossed the hall and disappeared into the living room. Her floral scent lingered. A moment later, she emerged with her purse and folder. "I'll keep looking for you," she said, her eyes momentarily apologetic. She started toward the front door.

"No rush yet, but let me know if something comes up," Rouleau said, quickly stepping past her. His hand found the door knob before her and he held the door open.

They descended the front steps and walked toward his car. He looked up. The western clouds had scudded in quickly and he felt a dampness in the air that hadn't been there when they'd entered the house. Kingston weather could change on a dime.

"How do you know Heath?" he asked, stopping at the end of the walkway.

Laney turned and faced him. Her eyes clouded over. "He didn't tell you?"

"No."

"No, I suppose not." Her lips drooped in a scowl. She resumed walking toward her car, aiming her key fob at the passenger door. "Let's just say that we have a history together."

"I really didn't mean to pry," Rouleau said. He wished he'd never broached the subject. He felt like he'd stepped into something awkward and silently cursed Heath for not preparing him.

"It's okay. Had is the operative word." She turned and smiled for the first time, giving him a glimpse of what lay within. He noticed the crinkles around her blue-grey eyes. Under a coating of makeup, her face was tanned bronze from the sun. He pictured her stretched out in a lawn chair on a cruise ship with a drink in her manicured hand.

Rouleau nodded. "Well, let me know when you find something else. I should be able to meet you if given enough notice."

"I promise you something more suitable next time. Now that we've met, I have a better idea of what will please you." She smiled again, full wattage, before ducking her head to slide into her front seat.

Rouleau watched her car pull a u-turn and zip away from him down the street. She just barely stopped at the stop sign before whipping left and disappearing from view. He shook his head and got into his car to head back to the station. Laney Masterson looked to be a woman used to the privileged life where rules didn't apply to her. He turned the key in the ignition and wondered what had gone on between her and Heath. A wise man would turn and run the other way rather than get involved with either one of them. Rouleau glanced one more time at the house he'd never own, then cursed himself for being a fool because he was already looking forward to the next time Laney Masterson called. If that wasn't folly, he didn't know what was.

17

THE STOVE CLOCK buzzer gave its long, piercing signal. Gail Pankhurst jumped up from her chair, grabbed her rooster-shaped oven mitts, and pulled open the oven door. She slid out a pan and pushed on the nearest muffin with her index finger. Satisfied that they were ready, she grabbed the two tins and dumped the carrot muffins onto trivets she'd already arranged on the counter. While the muffins cooled, she changed into purple shorts, slightly tighter than she'd have liked, and an orange tank top that showed off her garden of tats. No use having them if nobody could see them.

She scrawled a note for her roommate Elaine on the back of an envelope, promising to clean up the mess upon her return. She added that she was on an errand of mercy that couldn't wait. Elaine would get herself into a snit over the mess anyhow, Gail knew, but she'd deal with it later.

She'd wearied of Elaine's cold shoulder and snide jabs. The animosity had all started when she'd announced to Elaine that she was gay and open to experimentation, probably not her best move in hindsight. Soon afterwards, they'd agreed that this would be the last year they roomed together. The main battle was yet to be fought, however. Gail would give up the Court Street apartment over her own dead body.

Elaine had tried to claim it, as if she'd forgotten who found the apartment in the first place. So much for high school friendship surviving university. Gail filed their relationship into her mental folder on human behaviour under the dysfunctional category. She'd go over their broken friendship later when it didn't sting quite so much. For now, it took all her energy to act like she was all for the split. She would not buckle and beg Elaine to stay. She would not.

Gail arranged the muffins in a tin that she placed into her knapsack. She searched under her bed for her sandals, then gathered the clothes that were scattered across the floor into one big heap. She tossed the lot onto her bed and kicked a stray bra into the corner. The clothes could damn well wait too.

She locked the apartment door and clumped down the stairs, taking the back exit into the yard where she retrieved her bike from the shed. Well, Elaine's bike really, but she never used it. Gail smiled and snapped her fingers, wiggling her hips before putting on her bike helmet. "You got it going on, sister," she said. A little self-mockery helped keep the blues away.

Exiting the driveway, she turned north on Barrie Street. The route would take her past Leah Sampson's apartment, but she felt ready to face the scene of the crime. She'd been more upset by the idea of a murder than Leah's death, although images of Leah kept coming back and disturbing her sleep. It was just the normal part of grieving, she told herself. Her job was to remain objective.

The gathering clouds were worrisome, but it was still a hot day with a cooker sun. Her hair would be plastered in sweat under her helmet by the time she reached her destination. As if she needed anything else to make her look less of a winner. She'd accepted that she'd never be a beauty and gone with the eccentric look, but she admitted to moments of model envy. "Ah screw it," she said out loud. She rubbed her Popeye tat, the greatest cartoon character of all time. "I y'am what I y'am." She hoisted her knapsack onto her back and swung a leg over the bike seat, giving herself a running start with her other foot.

She paused at the corner of Johnson and Barrie and looked a block to her right at the yellow tape surrounding the house where Leah had met her end. Her eyes misted over for a moment but she blinked away the tears. *Stupid cow.* She meant herself, but Leah deserved the moniker too. She must have done something totally asinine to get herself killed. A woman full of secrets and way too attracted to the male species. Her wandering eye had likely gotten her killed.

Gail had been keeping a file on Leah and Wolf for months. She put them under her "romance at work" category, detailing their relationship and then the breakup. She'd particularly liked that they grew up down the street from each other in the same town but didn't find love until they left Brockville. She'd sensed trouble several weeks before it happened. Not on Wolf's side; strictly on Leah's. Leah had always been evasive, disappearing for so called appointments. *Assignations* more like, and if Juicy was right, assignations with a married man.

As part of her research, Gail had begun charting Leah's comings and goings and snippets of conversations. How in the hell could she have missed that Leah was sleeping with someone else? Gail shook her head, disappointed with herself for overlooking such basic human behaviour. She'd always believed Leah and Wolf belonged together. Call her a romantic. Losing that dream was almost as bad as never seeing Leah again.

She put her bike back into gear and continued on her journey. The tires had to be soft because pedalling was more work than it should have been. Sweat was dripping off her forehead and her shirt was dark under her armpits. Another twenty torturous minutes winding in a northwesterly direction through neighbourhood streets and she found herself in front of Wolf's place. His little blue Volvo was in the driveway so she'd likely caught him at home. At last, something was going right.

She leaned her bike against a tree and climbed the steps to his front door. He didn't answer her ring right away, but she didn't give up. After the third time leaning on the buzzer, the door finally opened.

"I suppose telling you to go away won't work," Wolf said wearily, stepping aside so that she could enter.

"I brought muffins," she said with as much bounce in her voice as she could manage. She trailed after him into the kitchen. She took the baking out of her knapsack and put the muffins on the table before taking it upon herself to make coffee. She glanced at Wolf every so often. He'd sat in the chair near the window and slumped down with his chin on his chest, his long legs stretched out in front of him. His hair was uncombed and wild as if he'd spent the morning running his hands through it. His eyes were closed.

She leaned over the counter and pushed the window open. "Smells like a brewery in here. A brewery in a boys' locker room. Have you left the house at all this week?"

Wolf raised his head to watch her pour two cups of coffee and arrange muffins on a plate that she took out of the cupboard. "Why are you here?" he asked.

"Because you're in trouble and I can help." She'd decided that only the semblance of truthfulness would work with Wolf. "You're kidding yourself if you don't think the police have you squarely in their sights for Leah's murder. The scorned ex is always the prime suspect. You need to pull yourself together and figure out who killed Leah. I want to help."

"And why would you want to do that?"

"Let's say that I have a psychologist's interest in solving this atrocity. Leah was always kind to me. I know I'm not your traditional woman, but she never made me feel small. You never did either. In my world, that means a lot."

"And how can you be so certain I didn't kill her?"

"Because I'm a good judge of character." She paused to give him time to mull over her offer, her eyes never leaving his face. She'd have to rely on her memory to make notes in his file later.

"I told the police that I met a friend at the bar." His voice was flat, disinterested.

"And did you tell the truth?"

"I was supposed to, but by the time I arrived, he'd already been and gone."

"What time was that?"

"Near closing. I came back here first after I walked Leah home. I'd forgotten my wallet. Then I thought about some wording for my thesis and stopped to jot it down. Time got away."

Wolf had a reputation for being late, much like herself. Gail found his story plausible. "So after the police talk with your friend …"

"They'll be right back here I imagine." He bared his teeth in what could pass for a grin. "I'm fucked, as they say."

"Not if I say you came back to the centre after you dropped off Leah." Gail watched to see if he'd take the out she was offering him.

"You'd be lying."

"Just helping an innocent friend." She smiled. "We have to stick together."

"I don't know. On those police shows, lying never seems to work out very well."

"It might keep you out of jail long enough for us to figure out what happened."

He studied her. "It also gives you an alibi," he said. "If you're telling people I was with you, that means nobody saw what you were up to either."

"I was working the phone line."

"Only until eleven. Did anyone see you during the weekend?"

Gail stopped short of responding. Elaine had vacated their place Friday after class and returned Sunday evening. *Shit.* He was right. She didn't have an alibi either, but then, she didn't exactly need one.

"Do you have any idea who Leah was seeing before she died?" Gail asked. "I could do some digging."

Wolf looked at her, his mouth clamped shut. The silence lengthened. She tried not to back down from his gaze. Somehow, she'd lost control of the interview. When it became clear that he didn't intend to answer, she grabbed a muffin and took a bite. While she chewed, she stood and grabbed her knapsack and bike helmet. She paused in the doorway.

"You know where to find me," she said. "If you want me to say we were together part of the weekend, I'll back you up. You just have to let me know."

"I wouldn't hold my breath."

"Then be prepared for what's coming. The cops misinterpret evidence all the time to make it fit their theory. They can make square pegs fit into round holes if it suits them."

"Thanks, but I'll take my chances."

"Suit yourself."

She opened the door and saw that the clouds had closed in overhead like a grey blanket and the pavement was black and slick with rain. She'd be soaked through biking home, but at least it was a warm rain. It would feel better than sweat running down her body.

Her trip hadn't given her much that would inform her working files, but perhaps down the road there'd be something about Wolf's aversion to having her give him an alibi that she could work into a paper for one of the journals. His reaction had to be an anomaly. Most people she knew would do anything to avoid being charged with murder.

She'd begun a study of infidelity and would give anything to know what Wolf's reaction had been to Leah fooling around on him with a married man. Hopefully, he'd start thinking of her as an ally and would begin opening up. All she needed was to find proof that he couldn't be the killer. She'd present it to him and the police, and the rest would follow naturally. He had to spill his guts sometime and she was a good counsellor. Listening and observing were her specialties.

"See you later, Wolf," she said. "I'm always around if you need to talk."

She stepped outside and craned her neck way back to let the rain strike her face. If she was going to get wet, she may as well make the most of it. She looked back into the kitchen as she closed the door. Wolf was still sitting at the table, the full cup of coffee cooling in front of him, the carrot muffins untouched on the plate. He was one miserable sight and she hesitated. If he'd been at all receptive, she'd have gone back into the house and offered some comfort in a heartbeat, but he knew as much if not more about counselling as she did, and something told her he wouldn't appreciate her return.

Her hair and tank top were completely soaked by the time she reached the spot where she'd left her bike leaning against a tree. If she sped up her ride, she'd have just enough time to make it home and have a hot shower before heading to the help line for the evening shift. She'd be working alone for part of it and would use the opportunity to dig around the office files on Wolf's behalf. He'd owe her big time when she cleared his name, even if he didn't realize the trouble he was in yet. It might mean he'd help with her research and thesis down the road. She could live with having someone in her debt, especially someone brilliant like Wolf who was going places ... that is, if he managed to stay out of prison.

18

GUNDERSUND TUCKED HIS chin into his jacket collar and
ran the two blocks from where he'd safely parked his
Mustang on a side street to the Merchant Tap House,
dodging puddles and narrowly avoiding being drenched
by a speeding car. As he rounded the corner onto Princess
Street, he spotted Stonechild's black truck idling a few
blocks up, waiting for a blue van to pull out of a parking spot. *Good timing,* he thought. *Stonechild and I seem
to be getting onto the same wavelength more quickly than
normal for new partners.* He believed in that uncanny
sense of one another that partners developed over time.
Stonechild was prickly and liked working alone, but the
intelligence in her eyes was undeniable. It would take
time to find out more about her history. He bet it would
explain a lot.

He walked to the bar and ordered a beer for himself
and cranberry soda for Stonechild, taking both drinks into
the smaller room to the right of the entrance. It was becoming their debriefing spot. The lighting was low and the
room was empty of other patrons. It was the perfect place
to talk over their separate interviews without being overheard. Stonechild soon joined him, shaking the rain from
her hair. The dark strands glistened in the soft light from

the overhead lamps. Her eyes glittered like black onyx. Gundersund, realizing he was staring, lowered his eyes and looked into his beer.

"Thanks for the drink," she said, pulling up a chair kitty corner to him. "Kingston weather sure changes fast. The temperature must have dropped ten degrees." She slipped out of her rain jacket and turned to hang it over the back of her chair. "So what did you find out about Wolf's drinking partner Rick Carlson?"

Gundersund swallowed his mouthful of beer, then said, "Wolf never showed. Carlson waited an hour for him and then went home."

"Jucinda and Mark from the help line both told me that Wolf walked Leah home that night. Wolf had motive and now it looks like opportunity. He might have lost it and killed her if she rejected him again that night. It never fails to amaze me how people think they own each other."

"If I can't have you, nobody can." Gundersund was surprised to hear the bitterness in his own voice. Stonechild's bottomless dark eyes held his for a moment before flicking away. He took a breath and continued in a less strained tone. "I talked with the bartender on shift in the bar where Wolf said he met up with Carlson. Bartender says Wolf made it in just before closing. Looked around as if he was searching for someone and then left."

"That doesn't prove anything. He might have put in an appearance and then rushed back to Leah's apartment where he had her tied up."

Gundersund drank from his beer. "We don't have enough evidence yet to bring him in."

Stonechild nodded. "Besides, he's not the only one who could have done it."

"You got something more out of the housemates?"

"The girl upstairs, Becky, said that Leah used to come to her apartment to chat after her shifts a few times a week, but the last few months she'd stopped the visits."

"Any reason?"

"Becky thought Leah was evasive, as if she was hiding something that troubled her."

"That's about the same time that she and Wolf broke up."

Stonechild nodded. "I thought the same thing, but Becky said it was more than that. Leah was sad about Wolf but blamed herself. She said that Wolf believed she was having an affair and it was easier just to let him."

Gundersund took a drink of beer and thought over the possibilities. "Perhaps Wolf isn't the only one who felt like he owned her. A lover could be equally as possessive."

"Becky said the only reason she could think of that Leah wasn't more forthcoming was that she was having an affair and the man was married. She said it wasn't like Leah to be secretive."

"I think we need to get back to the help line tomorrow and ask more questions."

"I agree, but it'll be better if I go and work my way into their confidences. Two of us will just intimidate them."

Gundersund observed the defiant tilt to Stonechild's chin and the obstinate glint in her eyes that met his without flinching. Rouleau had warned him that working with her would take a careful hand.

"I still have to check out Leah's other housemate, Bobby Hamilton. I thought I'd visit his workplace and talk to his boss and co-workers. I'll get on that first thing while you continue ingratiating yourself at the help line."

Stonechild's features relaxed. She finished her drink and set the glass on the table. "Well, I'm going to push off. I have a hungry dog waiting for me at home. See you tomorrow, Gundersund."

"Until then." He tilted his beer glass in her direction and watched her walk away. She turned before she reached the door.

"If you don't have dinner plans this evening," she said, "I might just have an idea."

———

The rain slipped down the window pane and pooled on the open sill. Dalal put her index finger into the cool water and traced Joe's name and her own, encircling them in a heart. Today he'd pretended to avoid her because she'd warned him not to talk to her when anyone was around, but he had slipped her a note just before recess. He'd wanted to walk her home from school.

She'd met him in their usual spot near the fence at the back of the school property, out of sight of prying eyes. He'd held her hand for the briefest of moments before she had pulled hers away. His grasp had been warm and comforting, reminding her of the one time he'd dared to hug her. They'd been playing on the monkey bars and he'd grabbed her around the waist as she jumped onto the ground. Up close, with his breath warm on her cheek, his eyes had been as blue as her mother's good china. They'd made her heart pound hard and had taken her breath away. Today, she'd been firm.

"I can't walk home with you. It's not safe."

"Could you come for supper on Friday? My mother said it's okay and she'll make her famous pizza. You could say you're doing schoolwork at a friend's. You can even call me Josephine if it helps." He'd grinned.

"I can't promise anything." She'd started walking away from the fence, from him. "I wish I could."

There was a noise in the hall and Dalal turned to see Meeza jump across the floor toward her. Meeza was dressed in her best abaya, a deep sapphire blue. Her hair was tightly braided. She leaped onto the window seat and snuggled into Dalal.

Dalal laughed. "You seem happy," she said, looking down into her sister's glowing smile. She gently chided, "But why are you wearing your good clothes? Mother won't be happy if she sees you."

"It was Mother who told me to put them on. She's taking me to meet someone special. I'm to smile and only talk if he asks me questions."

Dalal's heart went as cold as frost on a January morning. Meeza reacted to the look on her face, her own eyes widening in fright. "What is it Dalal? Is something wrong?"

"No, no, I'm sorry if I scared you. Everything is just fine." Dalal paused, trying to still her racing fear. "Did you hear the name of this man you're going to meet?" she asked as casually as she could.

Meeza's face relaxed and she giggled. "I think she said his name is Mr. Khan. I have to go now. I wasn't supposed to tell you where I'm going, but I tell you everything." The happiness in her eyes disappeared, replaced by worry. "You won't tell Mother that I told you?"

"Of course not. You are my sister and I will always look out for you. This will be between you and me, Meeza. I'll see you when you come home."

Meeza leaned her lips close to Dalal's ear. "I love you, Dalal."

Dalal turned her lips toward Meeza's ear. "And I love you, little sister," she whispered.

She watched Meeza skip from her bedroom. Her mother's sharp voice scolded Meeza at the bottom of the stairs, telling her to put on her hijab and show some modesty. Just what was she thinking going out of the house in such a fashion? The sound of a sharp slap carried upstairs. Meeza's whimper was more than Dalal could bear. She jumped off the window seat and made it to the door before common sense made her stop. Defending Meeza would only make her mother angrier. The anger would make her hit Meeza harder while Dalal watched. It would not be the first time.

Dalal forced herself to stand motionless. She clenched her hands against her chest until she heard the front door slam and she knew they'd gone. She stepped forward and silently closed her bedroom door. She could hear Ghazi's music thumping through the wall, but she had to take this chance.

The diary was right where she'd hidden it in the bookcase. She listened for her brother's footsteps before carefully sliding the book out from its spot between two hardcover books. She crouched down and opened the cover. It took her several tries before she found the right page. The words swam before her eyes and she had to blink several times before she could see.

> Mr. Khan is pure evil. I'll run away before they force me to marry him. I hate him, hate him, hate him. I would rather die than sleep with such an ugly old toad.

Dalal slowly lowered the diary onto the floor. What was she going to do now?

19

ROULEAU SIGNED THE document Vera placed in front of him with a great sense of relief. It meant some human resources work and a party to plan, but Vera had assured him that she was way ahead of him. She'd already booked a venue and purchased the gift, a silver watch with Ed Chalmers's name engraved on the back.

"After this week, Ed is taking the next two weeks as holiday leave. Once that's done, one half of the dynamic duo will be officially in retirement." Vera smiled as he handed her the folder. "I've put the word out that we'll soon have an opening and there's already been a few nibbles."

"Any word from Heath?"

"He doesn't like to be in contact when he's on his wilderness retreat. How was your real estate appointment, by the way?"

"The house wasn't quite what I was after."

"I wouldn't worry. Laney will find what you want if it's out there. She's got her finger in most pies."

"How do you know Laney?"

"She's my cousin. We grew up on the same street. Chased the same boys."

Cousins? The downward turn in Vera's mouth when she spoke Laney's name spoke volumes. Rouleau refrained from probing deeper. Discretion appeared the wiser course. He'd save his questions for Gundersund. He checked his watch. Just past six o'clock and time to call it a day.

Vera left with the file but kept the door ajar. He heard her speaking with someone in the hall. Less than ten seconds later, she tapped lightly on the door before stepping back inside his office, an apologetic look on her face. "The defence lawyer Suzie Chen insists on seeing you now. I can tell her you're busy if you like, but she's adamant that she has to talk with you right away."

"Send her in." He was curious to hear what Brian Munroe's lawyer would have to say about his death at his wife's hand.

Vera moved aside as Suzie blew past her into Rouleau's office. Vera nodded at Rouleau and shut the door behind her as Suzie strode across the room to sit in the chair opposite him. Angry energy crackled from her like static electricity. Underneath her perfectly coiffed page boy haircut, her face was humourless, her black eyes shooting sparks. She slapped a file folder onto the desk and said, "Della Munroe murdered her husband. I believe that with every fibre of my being."

"There's nothing to back up your claim, unless you have evidence that we don't."

"You know I can't repeat what he told me even if he's dead. You need to keep looking at Della. She's as cold-hearted a bitch as they come and it kills me to think she's going to get away with this."

"Let me play Devil's advocate. The facts so far as we've been able to discern are that Della was raped. She says by her husband, even though he denied it. She had injuries that could not have been self-inflicted, from both the rape and last night. Brian broke into the home after she'd taken out a restraining order. He was on his way upstairs to take their son. According to Della, he said that she would never see their child alive again."

"The word according to Della." Sarcasm dripped from Suzie's glossy red lips. "Don't you find it just a wee bit convenient that there were no witnesses? Nobody to testify about this *supposed* abuse?"

"Munroe admitted to bruising her arm."

"On one occasion, I grant you, but she provoked him."

"Della's friend Celia Paules backs up her claims of physical abuse and his attempts to isolate her."

"Again, all the stories begin with Della. Look Rouleau, you appear to be a logical, dedicated sort of cop. I'm beseeching you to look at the events from Brian Munroe's side in this he said/she said. He's not here any longer to tell his version, but it doesn't mean there isn't one." She stood abruptly. "I won't even bother running this request past Heath since there's nothing political or sexy about a poor Black man being taken in by a psychopathic white chick, so his interest will be nil. I'm hoping you have the sense of decency that I think you have and give this a second look."

"And where would you have me start?" he asked.

"I've brought you Brian's notes to me that he wanted me to use in his defence." She pointed to the file she'd tossed onto his desk. "I feel safe letting you review them, but please, do not share with all and sundry. I'm putting myself out on a limb here, Rouleau. That lets you know how convinced I am about Munroe being set up for the rape and his own death."

Rouleau picked up the file. Chalmers and Woodhouse had plodded through the evidence, but they lacked intuition and initiative. Stonechild hadn't had time to do more than scratch the surface. "I'll give it another look. I can't promise any more than that."

Suzie Chen smiled for the first time. "Hiring you might just be the smartest thing that asshole Heath ever did. I wonder if he has any idea that he hasn't recruited another useless yes man." She bared her teeth in what passed as a smile. "Let me know what you find out. I'm counting on you to get to the truth, Rouleau. I'd really hate for Della Munroe to get away with what she did to that man."

—

The front door of the Sunshine Bakery was locked with a sign printed in black magic marker hanging in the window that read, "Closed until Further Notice." Rouleau peered through the glass and spotted a showcase of pastries and muffins with a half-filled coffee pot near the cash register. Baskets of breads and rolls filled the back wall behind the counter, each a forlorn reminder of Munroe's untimely death. The store had been left locked and deserted for nearly a week. Someone would need to clean out the food soon or it would get ugly. The room was small, the walls painted a canary yellow with large framed photos of lilacs and tulips filling the spaces. The cheeriness made Rouleau depressed. A woman called to him from the sidewalk and he turned.

"It's closed because of a death," she said. "You might want to try the Tim Hortons down the street." She looked like a student, early twenties, hair in two blond braids, T-shirt, red shorts, and sandals. A knapsack was slung over one shoulder. Her clear grey eyes regarded him sadly.

"Were you one of their customers?" he asked.

"I worked here part time. I was hoping someone would have opened up by now." She walked next to him and looked through the window. "Nothing's been moved so I'm guessing not."

Rouleau pulled his police ID out of his pocket. "I'm one of the detectives looking into Brian Munroe's death. I wonder if you have a few minutes to talk."

"I don't really know anything about how he died."

"I'm more interested in his life. Can I buy you a coffee at that Tim Hortons?"

"Sure. I never turn down a free cup of joe."

———

Erin MacDonald was a third-year business student at St. Lawrence College. She was holding down two part-time jobs: Tuesday to Thursday evenings at the bakery and Friday and Saturday lunch hours at a mall restaurant.

"My parents don't have much," she confided to Rouleau between bites of the jelly doughnut he'd bought her to go with the coffee. "I'm supporting myself, but that's okay. I'll just be a poor broke student one more year." She smiled, showing off deep dimples. She licked the powdered sugar from her lips. "So what do you want to know?"

"How long did you work at the Sunshine Bakery?"

"Brian hired me at Christmas last year. I just walked in with my resumé and he hired me on the spot. He was swamped with orders and understaffed."

"What did you think of him? Was he a good employer?"

"He worked hard and he always treated the staff fairly. I never saw him get angry or heard him raise his voice, except toward the end when he spoke to his wife on the phone. I think he was feeling the strain of whatever was going down between them. He really loved his little boy. Talked about him all the time. He had the photos of his son and wife on his desk in the little back office."

"Did you know he'd separated from his wife?"

"Yeah. He was sleeping on a couch in his office. Sad."

"Did you meet Della or see them interact?"

"She came by the bakery a few times." Erin fidgeted with her coffee cup, looking uncomfortable. "Very pretty."

"And?"

"It's just that while she seemed all friendly and nice on the surface, I just got this feeling she wasn't." Erin shrugged. "That's not evidence of anything."

"I'm wondering what gave you that feeling."

Erin tilted her head and watched a woman fit her baby into a high chair at the next table. She glanced his way. "Phoney. The way she spoke to Brian and their kid. It struck me that she was acting lovey-dovey. Everything she said was loud and sweet. Dripping saccharine. Brian looked uncomfortable every time she opened her mouth."

"Had she been by the bakery recently?"

"No, but two weeks ago she called just after I started my shift and asked to speak with Brian. At first he told me to tell her he was busy, but then he changed his mind and took the phone. I didn't hear what he said, but I could tell he was upset when he hung up."

Erin finished her coffee and looked apologetically at Rouleau. "I'm sorry, but I have a class and I'm already going to be late." He nodded and she stood, grabbing her knapsack from the back of her chair. She hesitated. "I liked Brian, Detective, and his death sucks, big time. Whatever was going on in his marriage, he didn't deserve to die that way. We're all really going to miss him." She tilted her head again as she thought about something else. Rouleau waited silently until she focused her eyes on him again. "The really odd thing is that the university girl who was murdered last week used to come into the bakery too, at least the last few months. I know it was her because of her photo in the paper. Leah, that's her name. We spoke a few times when I served her. Crazy that I know two people who died the same week."

Rouleau's pulse quickened. "What did you talk about?"

"Just school and the weather mainly. We weren't close or anything. She talked more to Brian, but only because he was around more often."

"Did she come into the bakery with anybody?"

"She was always alone. She'd take a table and I saw her get into conversations with people at other tables. I hadn't seen her for a while though."

"Here's my card with my phone number and email. Contact me if anything else comes to mind, no matter how insignificant it seems."

Erin took the card from him and tucked it into the pocket of her bag. "I will, but I really don't know anything else."

She left and Rouleau took his time finishing his coffee, thinking about what he'd learned from Erin and Suzie Chen. Neither had proof that Della was lying, yet each believed in Brian's worth. If Della had schemed to kill him, she'd done a good job setting up the scenario and covering her tracks. Rouleau wasn't entirely convinced she'd gone to such lengths. He remembered how traumatized she was after the rape and her devotion to her son. The physical evidence so far backed up her version of what happened the night she killed her husband. Brian might have been the devious one, spinning the image he wanted to project.

Rouleau drained the last of his coffee. Odd that Leah Sampson and Brian Munroe crossed paths and they both died within days of each other. Coincidence, or was something else in play? He was going to have to pull in Gundersund and Stonechild to see if they had any other connections between the two.

He looked toward the counter. His dad might like muffins for breakfast. He'd buy a half dozen, since the line at the cash register had disappeared for the moment. Rouleau checked his watch. Quarter after seven. His dad would be itching for company and waiting for his supper. Rouleau promised himself that he'd think more about the two cases later in the evening. For now, he had to put some energy into taking care of commitments on the home front. His father had been a worry at the back of Rouleau's thoughts all day. He'd been alone too long without someone to check in on him.

20

THIS TIME ROULEAU heard three voices when he stepped through the apartment door: his father, another man, and a woman. Oscar Peterson was spinning on his father's prized turntable, soothing jazz to calm the troubled day. Puzzled, Rouleau inhaled the smell of garlic, onions, wine, and tomatoes and heard the sounds of banging pots coming from the kitchen. His confusion was short-lived. Gundersund met him at the end of the hallway with two glasses of red wine and a big grin. Rouleau accepted one and looked over Gundersund's shoulder to see his father sitting on a chair in the kitchen and talking to Stonechild, who was stirring something on the stove. Her Lab Taiku lay at his father's feet. Rouleau felt the tightness in his chest loosen.

"You giving cooking lessons, Dad?" he asked.

His father stopped whatever he was saying to Kala and they both looked in his direction. Taiku lifted his head and thumped his tail against the floor.

"It's a dirty job," his dad smiled, the same gentle smile Rouleau had known since childhood. It was the smile of a man at peace with the world.

Rouleau felt some tension lift. *My father's back to himself.*

Kala waved a wooden spoon in the air and turned back to the stove. "You men take a seat," she said. "Except for you, Gundersund. I'll dish it up and you can deliver."

"That's about all I'm good for when it comes to the kitchen," Gundersund said.

"Unlike Stonechild, who is demonstrating hidden talents," Rouleau added. "Kala, you're now officially my most valuable detective."

"You won't get any argument from me." Gundersund set down his glass and took the tossed salad from the fridge. He grabbed a plate of rolls from the counter on his way past Rouleau to the dining room table.

Rouleau retrieved his father's crutches for him and they made their way into the dining room. The table was set, complete with table cloth, crystal goblets, and centerpiece of fresh cut daisies. Rouleau whistled.

Gundersund set down plates of spaghetti. "Not only can Stonechild cook, she classed up the joint." He picked up a pack of matches lying on the hutch and lit two yellow tapers in silver holders. "Can I give you a refill, Henri?" Gundersund asked.

"I wouldn't say no." Rouleau's father held out his glass.

Rouleau watched Kala smile at his dad as she took her seat next to him. He lifted his glass to her and she bowed her head. Gundersund's eyes were also on her, unreadable but clearly intrigued. Rouleau might have been worried if he thought Kala returned Gundersund's interest, but he knew her well enough to doubt in the likelihood. Her black eyes met his. He saw uncertainty. It echoed in her voice when she said, "I phoned to speak with you but Henri said that you'd called that you'd be late. We thought a real home-cooked meal might be in order. I hope you don't mind our intrusion."

"On the contrary. You've kept my father company and relieved my mind. I had no idea what I was going to cook tonight."

"This has been a marvellous surprise," his father added. "The three of you are working too hard with this murder investigation and deserve a few hours to unwind and think of something else."

Gundersund said, "To clarify, Stonechild was the brains behind this operation. I'm beginning to believe she can do anything she turns her hand to."

"Not everything." She picked up her fork.

Gundersund took a bite of the pasta and rich tomato sauce. "Is that ever good. Family recipe, Stonechild?"

Rouleau saw pain flash in her eyes before her face closed like a light shutting off. "No, not really," she said.

Rouleau exchanged glances with Gundersund. He'd caught her reaction and was aware of his blunder. Silence descended on the table.

Rouleau's father reached out a hand and touched Stonechild's wrist. She looked across at him. Something unspoken passed between them and the tension in her face softened. She returned his smile.

Henri picked up his wine glass and raised it in her direction, then in Gundersund's. "A toast to our guests and to a fine meal. An old man could not ask for better company."

"I second that," said Rouleau. "And for the duration of the meal, we'll take a break from our work and enjoy Stonechild's cooking."

"Good by me," Gundersund said, clearly relieved that the conversation had moved on.

—

Later, when Gundersund and Stonechild had gone, Rouleau sent his father to bed while he cleaned up the dishes. He filled the sink with soapy water to wash the good crystal, handed down through his father's family. The pots took a bit of scrubbing. The rest of the dishes and cutlery went into the dishwasher.

After he left the pots to air-dry in the rack, he poured two fingers of Scotch and took it outside onto the balcony. He leaned against the railing and looked out over the lake, a band of darkness with a cone of silvery light across its surface where the moonlight reflected off the water. The cloud cover had blown out as quickly as it had arrived.

He'd managed to fill in Gundersund and Stonechild about his talk with Erin MacDonald and the curious interaction between Leah Sampson and Brian Munroe. They'd accepted the information with the same guarded logic as his own. Kingston was a small enough city that people's paths crossed all the time. It might just be a coincidence that the two of them knew each other and died in violent ways within days of each other. On the other hand, their deaths could very well be related and needed to be checked out. The information gave the team renewed focus.

He sipped at the amber liquid. It burned the length of his throat, an old friend he rarely revisited. He'd let it worm its way into his nightly routine after his wife Frances left, but that had only lasted a short time. Whisky could drown a lot of pain, but it was not an answer in the long run.

His thoughts returned to Stonechild and Gundersund. She was a loner and a product of foster homes and frequent moves throughout her childhood. He could only guess at what lay behind the scars he'd glimpsed in her eyes in unguarded moments. Gundersund was separated, but Fiona was still in the picture from the stories he'd heard around the water cooler. Word was Gundersund would do anything to get her back.

"May I join you, son?"

Rouleau turned to see his father on his crutches beside the open sliding glass door. He jumped over to help him. "Of course, Dad. Can't sleep?"

"Just needed a drink of water." His father manoeuvred outside and leaned against the railing next to Rouleau. "Nice night."

They stood side by side without feeling the need to speak. After a few minutes of silence, Henri said, "I think it's time you found your own place, son. I'm managing well now and you don't need my daily upkeep to add to your responsibilities."

"I like being here for you."

"I know, and I appreciate all you've done, but it's time. I start back at the university on Monday. They're loaning me a research assistant for a few months. Grad student. He'll be able to do my heavy lifting. I intend to put in some late evenings."

"You're booting me out."

"In a manner of speaking."

Rouleau could picture his dad's smile in the darkness. He reached an arm around his father's shoulders. "Thanks, Dad," he said.

"No, son. Thank you. I know how much pressure you've been under to spend these last months looking after me while settling into a new life. I'm much better now and ready to get back on my feet, if you pardon the expression."

"Then I'll start seriously looking for real estate." He'd find a bungalow where his father could move in once he could no longer live on his own.

His heart lightened. It would be a chance to contact Laney Masterson again.

21

"TAKE NO NOTICE of me," Kala said to Jucinda Rivera. "I'm getting a feel of how this place operates, so please carry on as normal. If I have questions, I'll be sure to ask." She pointed to the couch. "I'll set up there."

"Great." Jucinda grimaced. She looked down at the textbook she'd been reading and used her feet to turn her chair so that her back was to her desk and the couch. Kala found the childish gesture non-productive but amusing. Probably a passive-aggressive personality, if she remembered her psych classes. She wouldn't have pegged this surly girl who dressed like a street walker in a low-cut top and black bra to be a counsellor. Someone answering a sex phone talk line maybe, but not talking university kids through their problems.

The phone on Jucinda's desk rang and she was forced to turn her chair back around. She reached out a manicured hand to pick up the receiver. Her eyes rolled toward the ceiling as she said, "Queen's Help Line. What can I do for you?" She leaned forward and cradled the phone receiver against her ear. Within seconds, her body language changed from disinterested to attentive listener as the caller spelled out their problem, which involved binge drinking as far as Kala could determine. Jucinda doled out information and choices in a cool but professional tone. Her eyes focused in on Kala as she hung up the phone. She shrugged.

"First year away from home, they're like babes in the woods." She opened a program on her computer and typed a notation into the log. Kala walked over to have a look.

"Do you log every call then?"

"We don't have call display and the caller remains anonymous, but we do enter time and length of call, problem, and advice given. We also get to know the repeat callers, although not by name. We give them a number, see? The last caller is new so I'm making a note of that."

Mark Withers, manager and wannabe beach boy, walked through the front door carrying two coffees. "Jucinda, sorry I'm late, but you wouldn't believe ..." He cut off whatever else he was going to say when he spotted Kala behind her. "You're back," he said. "I guess that means you haven't caught Leah's killer."

"Unfortunately not."

"We handed over Leah's computer and notes already."

"The lab is going through them. I'm just here to re-interview everyone and watch how this place functions."

"Don't you need permission from us to spend the day here?"

"This is a murder investigation. We don't need your permission, no."

Mark looked back at Jucinda. "New top?"

"Maybe."

"Nice." He put a coffee on her desk. "Nate will be in around ten and Gail and Wolf will be in at six for the night shift."

"I thought Wolf resigned from the help line," Kala said.

"He's doing a few shifts until we hire somebody to replace ... well, Leah." Mark and Jucinda exchanged glances.

"So, do you want to come into my office to ask me some questions?" Mark asked Kala.

"Not yet. I will in good time." Kala wanted them all off balance, outside their comfort zones. Waiting all day to be interviewed would heighten their anxiety.

"Well, suit yourself. I have paperwork to do."

He walked into his office, leaving his door open wide enough so that he could hear what was going on. Jucinda pointed toward his office and said under her breath, "Usually he shuts the door."

"Do you always sit at the same desk?" Kala asked.

"Yeah, unless I'm replacing someone and the other counsellor is staying on. Leah sat at that desk. Gail replaced her on late shift as a rule."

"Did you notice anything different about Leah the last month before she died? Anything or anyone bothering her?"

"Gail's the one you should be asking. She treats the rest of us like specimens for her research. I swear to God she takes notes."

"What did you think about Leah? Did you like her?"

"I didn't know her that well."

"You must have had an opinion. You worked on the same shift."

"She was okay. A little holier-than-thou, maybe."

"How so?"

The phone picked that moment to ring. Jucinda held a finger up in Kala's direction and took the call. Afterward, she typed notes into the computer. Kala waited until she was finished before repeating her question.

Jucinda sighed and rolled her eyes, something she did as regularly as breathing, Kala observed. "Leah acted nice, you know? Really concerned about people and generous. I bought it for a while."

"What did she do that made you change your mind about her?"

"I confided in her that I was interested in Wolf. He'd only started working here and it was before they started dating, so of course I felt like an idiot when I found out they'd become a couple. She gave me some explanation about how it just happened and she felt so bad, but bottom line, she could have had anybody and she picked Wolf even though she knew I was hot for him. Then I find out she's sleeping around on him. I was so mad ..." Jucinda pulled herself back and blinked at Kala. "I didn't kill her. I was angry, but not *that angry.*"

"Anyone would be upset. Do you know who she was seeing on the side?"

Jucinda glanced toward Mark Withers's office. "I couldn't say for certain."

"But you could guess."

"It wouldn't be right. I just saw them together from a distance."

"She might have been with Wolf then."

"Wolf was working the late shift when I saw Leah with the other guy. It was a month or so ago. I left Wolf talking to someone on the phone and started walking home. Leah was in a car a few streets over, sort of away from the street light in the shadows. I'm not even sure why I walked down that street. Fate, maybe. At first I thought I was hallucinating. I stood back in the shadows and watched for a while. It was definitely her but I never got a good look at the guy. She was on top of him. Kind of riding him, if you get my drift."

"What did you do with the information?"

"I told Wolf. He deserved to know the truth."

"And how did he react when you told him his girlfriend was cheating?"

"He didn't thank me, if that's what you're asking. He got real quiet and then acted like I hadn't said anything. They broke up the next day though. I did the guy a favour."

"Did Leah ever find out that you were the one who told Wolf?"

Jucinda shook her head. "She never acted like it."

Nate came for his shift soon after and Kala sat out of the way on the couch, taking in the rhythm of the day. If Mark was the beach boy and Jucinda the spiteful princess, then Nate struck her as the preppie academic. She approached his desk when Jucinda left to fill their sandwich order. She spotted the platinum wedding band on his finger. He looked up at her, his face impassive.

"My notes say that you work as a TA for Professor Dino Tadesco, is that correct?"

"I do. Dino's a good guy."

"He keeps this place afloat as well, I understand."

"Yeah. Without him we'd have closed our doors."

Kala rifled through her notebook to have Nate think she was refreshing her memory. It gave her time to study him. "Leah was in his class?"

"Yup."

"Did you work with her?"

"She was in the seminar class that I'm a TA for and I graded her papers."

Like pulling teeth. "What kind of a student was she?"

"Conscientious. Not brilliant, but she worked hard and did what she had to do to get decent marks."

"From the photos I've seen of her, she was very attractive."

Nate's eyes didn't waver from hers. "She was. Kind, too."

"I see you're married."

"I'm not the one Leah was sleeping with, Detective."

"Do you know who was?

"Not a clue."

"Surely you must have your suspicions."

"I only found out about it because Jucinda felt she had to share."

"What about Wolf? Was he still into Leah?"

"They were friends. Other than that, I don't know. Neither was much good at sharing their innermost feelings."

"Is your wife a student, Nate?"

"My wife?" For the first time, Kala heard his voice tremble with real emotion. He glared at her. "Trisha has nothing to do with this."

"I never said that she did."

"She works as a prison guard at the women's pen."

"Shift work?"

"Yeah. Trish was on nights when Leah went missing. I'm sure you have that in your notes already too."

"Actually, I don't, but thanks for clarifying."

His ears turned crimson at the tips and angry red patches stained his cheeks. Otherwise, his gaze remained level. *I'll bet you hate your body giving you away like that,* Kala thought. Hard to control the flush of blood to your face.

She returned to her spot on the couch and watched Nate for a while. If he knew she was studying him, he never let on. She bet he hid his emotions well for the most part. Like everyone who worked here, he knew the tricks of telling a believable lie and the tells when spinning a story. The psychology of the psychologists. Might make for an interesting study.

Kala's phone buzzed and she reached into her pocket. She checked the number before holding the phone to her ear. "Yes, Vera?"

"Sergeant Rouleau would like you to come to the station for one o'clock. Leah Sampson's parents will be here then and he wants you to speak with them. Gundersund will be here as well."

"Okay. I'm on my way."

22

GUNDERSUND CHECKED HIS rear-view and saw Stonechild make a left turn behind him into the lot. She followed him down the row of parked cars and slid into the empty space next to him. He waited for her to get out of her truck and join him where he stood checking his phone. When he looked up, she was as unreadable as ever, her body language distant. They fell into step and started for the main doors.

"Rouleau wants us to meet him in the lounge on the first floor. He and Fiona are with Leah's parents and will hand them off to us to carry on with the interview."

"They came in on their own?"

"Yeah. Mrs. Sampson's been sedated most of the week. They said they were finally feeling up to talking about their daughter."

"Okay." She tucked her hands into the pockets of her jeans. "Get anything new on Bobby Hamilton?"

"He was up on assault charges twice. The first time he received a suspended sentence."

"And the second?"

"Hamilton spent six months in the slammer. He got into an altercation with a guy who rear-ended his car. Hamilton chose to settle the matter with his fists even though the other guy was older and didn't put up any resistance. The judge ordered an anger management course, and Hamilton now tells everyone he's cured."

"Could have fooled me."

"His boss in city garbage said he shows up on time and does his job without complaint. Keeps to himself."

They kept walking. Stonechild had her head down, keeping pace with his long strides.

"Who did he assault the first time?" she asked.

They'd reached the main entrance and Gundersund leaned past Stonechild to grab the door. "The first time he beat on his mother. She tried to drop the charges, but the judge wouldn't let her. Bobby was high at the time of the assault and mad she'd turned down his music."

"Makes me glad I never had a kid."

"A teenage stoner kid anyhow."

They waited without talking outside the lounge. Gundersund checked his messages and kept a watch on Stonechild out of the corner of his eye. She leaned against the wall next to him with her arms folded across her chest. Her eyes were closed and she looked to be sleeping.

Ten minutes later, the door swung open across from him. Stonechild was instantly at attention. Rouleau and Fiona walked out together. Gundersund could see the Sampsons sitting together on the vinyl-covered couch against the far wall. They were a tiny couple, grey-haired with faces lined in grief.

Fiona had her game face on: lips a straight line, eyes evasive, no emotion to be seen. He knew from experience that she could play any role required of her. There was a reason she won at poker. She looked from Stonechild back to him. Her lips curled slightly upward as her eyes seemed to assess what he knew she'd consider a threat. It had taken him a while to understand the depths of her jealousy. She may not want to be married to him, but she didn't want anyone else to be either.

"Detectives," Fiona said looking at him. She nodded at Rouleau as he took his leave. She stepped closer to Stonechild and held out her hand. "You must be my husband's new partner. I'm Fiona Gundersund."

Stonechild reached out a hand and shook Fiona's. "Kala Stonechild," she said. Stonechild was as good a poker player as Gundersund's wife. She waited until Fiona had disappeared down the hall to glance his way. Gundersund's expression was apologetic and slightly amused.

"After you," he said, stepping back for her to enter the lounge.

Mrs. Sampson did all the talking while her husband sat next to her.

"Leah was the type of kid who brought home stray animals and people. She had such a big heart. We worried she'd get taken advantage of." Mrs. Sampson patted her husband's knee as she spoke. "We lived in Brockville, so Leah grew up in a small town with everyone knowing everyone. Kingston would have been a big city to Leah but she was determined to come here." Mrs. Sampson shook her head. "She wanted a career that helped people and there was no university in Brockville. We believed this was a safe town and were happy that she decided to stay close by."

"Did you know she was dating Wolf Edwards?"

"Of course. She adored Wolf but she wasn't sure if she was ready to settle down. Even as a child in Brockville, she wanted to see the world. We didn't have a great deal of money and our vacations weren't exotic. Camping in the province, mainly. Once we made it to Nova Scotia, remember dear?" She kept talking without waiting for a response. "We had to scrape to send her to university. We took out a loan and of course Leah worked and took out student loans. She had to work very hard at her schoolwork. It didn't come easily. We moved into an apartment in Montreal after Leah left. My brother owns the building and is giving us a discount in exchange for us looking after the property. Leah wasn't happy about it. Thought it was beneath us, but we have to live somehow. She has a lot of friends in Brockville though. She could always find somebody to stay with."

Stonechild leaned forward to capture her attention. "Do you know of anybody who might have wanted to hurt Leah? Did she say that anything was troubling her lately, or was there a change in her behaviour?"

"Oh my, no. Everybody loved our Leah. She had different boyfriends but they always parted friends. She didn't have a nasty bone in her body, did she dear?"

Mr. Sampson seemed to have waited for this cue to speak. "Leah called last month and said she wanted to come visit. Said she was going to finish her classes and take some time away to think. That was a change in pattern," Mr. Sampson said.

"Of course, she'd broken up with Wolf," Mrs. Sampson took the floor again. "I thought it was just the breakup that sparked her needing a change of scene." For the first time, her eyes clouded over and she reached to grab her husband's hand. "Maybe we missed something. Leah might have needed help and we should have seen it. I should have listened to you when you said you wanted to come see her last month. If only we had."

———

Gail had stopped for an extra large cappuccino on her way to work and the kid behind the counter took his sweet time frothing the milk. It didn't help that he was a trainee and his orders were already backed up. She'd been late leaving home so an extra twenty minutes wasn't the end of the world. She made it to the call centre at six thirty, half an hour late. Juicy had already left at five and Nate was antsy to leave.

"It might help if you could be on time for once. That way I wouldn't be late getting out of here every night." He scowled at her before gathering up the student papers he'd been reading. He stuffed them into his burlap bag.

She crossed to her desk and dropped into the chair. Nate was usually such a level, pudding personality. His file was a study in boredom. Something had to be up. "Who's my partner tonight?" she asked.

"Wolf, but he's going to be late. He called ten minutes ago."

"And where's Mark?"

"He left with Tadesco. They had a meeting with a possible funder."

"Are you sure the two of them weren't meeting up with Jack Daniels and Jim Beam? They seem to be spending a lot of time chumming it up in the pub lately."

Nate tightened the straps on his bag. He swung it over his shoulder and walked closer. "They wouldn't be pleased to hear you smearing them. Be careful what you say, Gail. Sometimes I think the walls have ears."

"I'm not scared. If they want to fire me from this low paying, thankless job, I wouldn't stand in their way."

"Tadesco's applying for department head and he's a little protective of his reputation right now. I've seen him angry a few times and he can be vindictive."

"Well, I'm not the one he needs to worry about."

"What do you mean by that?"

"You must have heard the rumours."

"What, that he's gay? That's just people talking."

"You know what they say about where there's smoke."

Nate held up a hand. "You go too far sometimes, Pankhurst. Stop spreading this shit or you're going to get into trouble. That female cop was here all morning, by the way."

"The Native?"

"She's observant and smart. Looks at you with those bottomless black eyes and gets you to say things you never meant to. I'd look out if I were you."

"Sounds like a threat."

"Hell, do whatever you want. Just don't say you weren't warned when it blows back. I'm late meeting Trish so I'm going to shove off."

"I consider myself warned."

He slammed the door behind him and Gail put her feet up on the desk, clasping her hands behind her head. It was satisfying to have one of her human experiments turn out as predicted. She'd made up the rumour about Tadesco a month ago, but only told Juicy, who predictably told Nate. Half the campus probably had heard by now that Tadesco was bent. One improbable little lie with no proof told to one person and it goes viral. Tadesco was even well liked, proving nobody was immune to malicious gossip. She felt a flush of guilt at the thought of what she'd started but pushed it away. She hadn't forced Juicy to tell anybody; in fact, she'd asked her not to. Tadesco wouldn't find out anyway and if he did, he'd laugh it off. He'd never know the rumour began with her.

She looked toward the front door. Nate was supposed to lock it on his way out, but she didn't remember hearing the click. He'd been in a big hurry and might have forgotten, or maybe he left it unlocked because Wolf was on his way. He should have known better though. The rule was not to leave a female counsellor alone in the unlocked office on evening shift. Gail put her coffee cup on the desk and swung her feet onto the floor, brushing away the feeling of unease. *I'm just jumpy because of Leah,* she thought. It's only normal to get paranoid when your co-worker's been murdered.

She was halfway to the door when the phone rang on her desk. She looked back and hesitated. Should she keep going and risk missing the caller or sprint back to her desk? By the time she made it to the door, the caller would probably have hung up and that could lead to trouble. A student thinking about suicide might be reaching out one last time. She'd talked one down just last week. There was really only one decision.

She managed to pick up the phone in time, sinking into her chair as a girl's tearful voice filled her ear. The door would have to wait, and Wolf should be here in a few minutes anyway. No point getting herself in a knot for the sake of ten or twenty minutes. What could it hurt to have the door unlocked until then, if it even was.

"Take a deep breath and start from the beginning," Gail said, putting her feet back up on the side of the desk. "We have nothing but time to sort this out.

23

"IS EVERYTHING OKAY, Dalal?" Miss Cummings's voice penetrated through her worries and Dalal saw her English teacher's concerned eyes staring at her from the front of the class. Dalal took a quick look around and saw her classmates watching her too. Joe met her eyes from two rows over and smiled encouragingly. She looked back at Miss Cummings.

"I didn't hear the question. Could you please repeat it?"

Miss Cummings watched her a moment more before picking Sally Jones to tell how Iago duped Othello into killing Desdemona.

Dalal looked down at her desk, even more miserable than before. She tried to concentrate the rest of the afternoon, but Miss Cummings didn't ask her any more questions. Finally, the three-forty bell rang and Dalal put away her books and pencils. She stood to file out with the rest of the class. Miss Cummings stopped her at the door.

"Dalal, could you please stay behind for a few minutes?"

"Yes, Miss Cummings."

She stood waiting for Miss Cummings near her desk until the last of the students had gone. Joe had lingered just outside the door and tried to signal her with his eyes, but she'd pretended not to see him. Finally Miss Cummings walked across the room and put her hand on Dalal's shoulder. She smelled of peppermint, pencil shavings, and the faintest trace of cigarette smoke. "Let's sit for a moment, Dalal."

"Okay."

They took the comfy reading chairs near the window. Dalal felt Miss Cummings studying her but she dared not lift her head. She knew that her teacher's eyes were the colour of warm toffee with darker flecks of green. Dalal wished her eyes could be the same colour. She often wondered what it would be like to have Miss Cummings as her mother. A few times she even dared to dream that it was true.

"You've been having trouble concentrating in class this week, Dalal. It is so unlike you that I wonder if something is on your mind. Perhaps it's something that I could help you with. I'm a good listener and I find that it always helps to share a problem."

It was tempting to give Miss Cummings what she wanted: the truth. *My family is going to marry my twelve-year-old sister to a man old enough to be her grandfather, but I'm not supposed to know. I cannot defy my parents or they will beat me and lock me in my room. Then they'll take Meeza away and I will never see her again. My family does not forgive if we are disrespectful or do not do their bidding. Meeza will probably disappear one day anyhow, no matter what I do or don't do. I thought it was me they would marry off first, not Meeza. We are as trapped as songbirds in a cage. Unless …*

"Look at me, Dalal, and tell me what you are thinking about." Miss Cummings's voice was more forceful this time, as if she was willing Dalal to give up her secrets.

Dalal met her probing eyes and tried not to show anything of herself. "Everything is fine, Miss Cummings. I've had a bit of the flu this week. It's been keeping me from sleeping and I'm tired all day. I'll rest more on the weekend and will be better on Monday."

Miss Cummings's eyes felt like lasers into her soul. Dalal knew that her teacher didn't believe her, but smiled as if she'd just told the truth.

"Can I go now? My mother needs me at home today."

Miss Cummings tried one last time. "Is everything going well at home?"

"Yes, Miss Cummings."

Those eyes searching her own and then the sigh and raised hand. "You can go then, Dalal. I'm here if you ever want to talk."

"Thank you, Miss." She left the classroom and started down the hall. Joe was waiting for her just around the corner near the water fountain.

"So what did she want?" he asked. "Was she mad you were daydreaming in class?"

Dalal shook her head. "She just wanted to know if everything was okay at home."

"Maybe you should tell her how strict your parents are. She could talk to them and get them to loosen up."

Dalal looked at Joe and back down at the ground. He really didn't get it. Nobody did.

Joe held the door open for her and they stepped outside into the bright sunshine. From the top of the steps, she checked the street and parking lot. No sign of Ghazi. Her shoulders relaxed.

"So have you asked about coming for supper tomorrow? We can play a little one-on-one basketball afterwards or just hang out if you want."

"I don't think so. I'd have to lie to get out of the house."

"Why don't you? My mom will back you up."

Dalal took a step down. "She'd go along with whatever story I come up with?"

"Yeah. I told her your family has you in this strangle-hold. My mom's cool. She thinks you should be able to so-cialize like other kids."

"What if my family comes to check up on me? They will, you know."

"You can say that you are doing a project with Meghan. She'll cover too. We've already discussed it."

His sister was in grade ten, a year ahead of her, but her parents wouldn't know that. It might just work. She almost gave in until reason and the fear returned. "It's too risky." She jumped down the last of the steps. She spotted Ghazi ahead of her getting out of his car. "My brother," she shout-ed without looking back. "Don't come near me."

She started running but Joe's voice followed her flight. "Meghan is going to call you tonight, so be ready to play along."

If Ghazi hadn't looked at her at just that moment, Dalal would have turned and told Joe not to let his sister do any-thing so foolish. Instead, she kept running toward her brother and didn't look back. She reached him out of breath.

"Your hijab isn't covering all your hair," Ghazi said.

"It slipped when I was running." Dalal tugged it back into place.

"You're late. I'll drive you home so you can get your homework done before you make supper." Ghazi looked back toward the school. He squinted into the sun. "Do you know that boy on the steps?"

She turned. "Not really. He's in one of my classes, that's all."

Ghazi shielded his eyes with one hand and stared at Joe a moment longer. Dalal looked at the ground and stopped breathing. At last Ghazi dropped his arm and pointed toward his black car across the street. "Let's go then. I have another errand to run after I drop you off."

24

AFTER A MEAL of scrambled eggs and toast, Kala called for Taiku and they set out for a walk up the road. The night was calm and the air cooler than it had been the past few evenings. She wasn't a fan of heat and welcomed the lower temperature. She felt the stress of the day slipping away as she walked past untamed stretches of trees and bush. Taiku stayed close for the first few minutes, but there was a rustling in the long grass and he raced ahead of her, tail and ears on alert until he was out of sight. She ran after him, calling his name, worried that he'd corner a skunk or porcupine. She had no energy to deal with either tonight.

She rounded the bend in the road and stopped midyell. Taiku was standing in the road growling at Gundersund and his border collie. She called for Taiku to stop and by the time she reached the dogs, Taiku was sniffing the collie, whose tail was wagging back and forth. Kala wasn't sorry that Taiku's first instinct was to be protective, but she was happy that he'd never attacked another dog or human. She had no doubt he would if she was truly threatened. Her eyes lifted to Gundersund standing a short distance behind the dogs. A grin spread across his face as he caught sight of her. He stepped forward and patted both dogs on their heads before walking over to meet her. "Looks like Minny and Taiku are hitting it off. Nice evening."

"Does your dog actually like being called Minny?" She was winded and felt at a disadvantage coming upon him so unexpectedly.

Gundersund laughed. "She's never complained. Fiona named her after a favourite aunt. Where did the name Taiku come from?"

"Not from a favourite aunt."

"You've neatly sidestepped my question." He smiled.

She smiled back at him. "I've made a religion of avoiding answering questions."

"I've noticed."

Kala inhaled the smell of sweet grass and rich earth and looked into the deepening shadows cast by the pine trees. The houses on Old Front Road were widely spaced with a tangle of woods between that gave the sense of being in the wilderness. The sun was sinking over the trees, and already stars were glittering through the darkening sky visible above the ribbon of road.

"The heat wave is over. It feels like fall's in the air." She looked back at him. "I think we should pay a visit to Professor Tadesco's office in the morning. Leah was in his class and he is often around the help line. He might be the other man in her life."

"Good idea. I can pick you up. It's on the way to the station."

"No, I'll meet you. I like to have my own vehicle."

"Suit yourself. Not everyone gets to ride in my Mustang though."

"I'm sure there'll be other opportunities."

They started walking side by side down the side of the road toward the dogs. The silence stretched between them.

She wanted to ask him about his wife, Fiona, but she'd made a pact with herself not to get involved. He hadn't struck her as married, though. It was odd that he'd never mentioned his wife.

"How old is your dog?" she asked instead.

"Minny's four. Taiku?"

"Eight."

The dogs had stood still for a moment, watching them getting closer before chasing each other down the road in the direction of Gundersund's house.

"We'd better corral them," Gundersund said. "It's a quiet night but traffic does travel this road." He whistled and Minny broke away from Taiku. Kala called Taiku to come. The dogs loped up next to them and Kala reached down to rub the fur behind Taiku's ears.

"Would you like to come in for a tea?" Gundersund asked. He'd crouched down next to Minny and looked up at her as he waited for her to respond.

Kala's instinct was to refuse. Nothing good could come of socializing with a partner. On the other hand, agreeing to a cup of tea might be a conciliatory gesture since it looked like they were going to be working together for the next while. "If you're sure it's okay."

"Why wouldn't it be?"

"No reason." *Except your wife might not appreciate me spending time alone with you after work hours since I heard the rumour that she's trying to get back with you.* She'd seen the way Fiona Gundersund had checked her out. Her look had been a challenging one when she'd introduced herself as Gundersund's wife. *Not ex-wife.* Kala had to admit that she wouldn't have placed the blond beauty Fiona with Gundersund. It would have made more sense for him to be the insecure one.

They walked another ten minutes up the road. His house was set back closer to the lake. Grey shingles. Cape Cod two-storey. They walked around the back to enter. The grass needed a mow and the garden was a mass of weeds with a few hardy perennials breaking through. A solitary lawn chair faced the water. The dogs raced around the yard and disappeared into the underbrush.

Gundersund watched her trying to decide whether to go after them. "They'll be fine," he said. "Minny never goes off the property. Coming?"

He started back toward the house, not waiting for her to follow. She took a last look in the direction of the lake and figured the dogs would be okay. There was another hour before complete darkness would descend.

Gundersund stood holding the door for her.

"I don't know why anybody would want to live in the city," she said as she reached him, "with all this beauty on our doorstep."

"Yeah, I'm really glad I moved out here."

Kala turned toward the side of the house. A few steps and she heard an engine getting closer. She stopped. "I think you have company," she said. "Isn't that a car pulling into your driveway?"

"I'm not expecting anyone." Gundersund shut the door and came back toward her.

Tires crunched on the gravel. They looked at each other and Gundersund shrugged. A car door slammed.

"Paul, I brought that wine. I thought we could …" Fiona strode around the corner and stopped. She looked at Kala and the smile slipped from her face, but only for a moment. "I see we have company."

Kala felt Gundersund move away from her. She looked at him but he was facing another direction, watching his wife walk toward them. Kala expected him to greet Fiona but he didn't say anything, even after Fiona reached them and stood in front of Gundersund waiting. Her eyes moved from Kala to Gundersund, where they remained. The silence stretched uncomfortably. Kala jumped into the empty space.

"I'm just on my way. I stopped by to confirm where we'll be meeting up in the morning."

Fiona's eyebrows arched in a puzzled line and she half turned, one hand raised toward the corner of the house. "I didn't see your car in the driveway."

"I'm staying at a friend's just down the road. My dog and I were out for a walk and I spotted Gund … your husband's car." Kala felt like she'd been caught doing something wrong. It was time to get out of here and let whatever was going on between the Gundersunds play out in private. She turned toward Gundersund. "I'll see you around eight tomorrow then."

He nodded. "I'll meet you outside his building at eight."

Kala called for Taiku and gave thanks when he bounded toward her. "Nice to see you," she said to Fiona, bending to grab Taiku's collar.

"Come by again," Fiona smiled, "when you have more time to visit."

Kala reached the corner of the house and looked back. Fiona had looped her arm through Gundersund's and was looking up into his face. He lifted his eyes to look over Fiona's head toward Kala. She had no idea what he was thinking, but doubted it was regret that she was leaving him to do whatever married couples did on a warm evening. She'd actually been looking forward to that cup of tea he'd promised, so all the regret was on her side.

She kept walking. When she made it home, she'd make herself a pot of Darjeeling and sit on the back deck with

Taiku to watch the sun set over the lake. She'd hold firm to her vow not to get involved with her co-workers in the future.

———

"Show's over, Fiona. You can let go of my arm." Gundersund shook her off and started back toward the house. He could hear her following close behind.

"She's a girl of few words," Fiona said. "Pretty, though, if you like that type."

Gundersund stopped and looked at her. "She's my partner, Fiona. Nothing more. Why are you here anyhow?"

"I wanted to put it right between us. I know I acted crazy last year but I've realized what's important." Her blue eyes were magnets drawing him in. He knew that she was aware of her effect on men, on him. Gundersund didn't want to go back there with her.

"I'm not up for doing this tonight. It's been a long day."

"I know something to take the stress away and help you relax."

He ignored the suggestion in her voice. "All I want is some sleep. Why don't I see you tomorrow?"

"I was hoping to have a tour of your new house."

"Another time."

He admitted to himself that it was tempting. Invite his wife inside and take up where they'd left off. Pretend the past year had never happened. There was a time not so long ago that he would have done anything to have her back. It hadn't even mattered that she'd left him for another man. He hadn't known how he was going to spend the rest of his life without her in it. She seemed to read his mind.

Her fingers traced along his forearm. The heat flickered like a pilot light in his belly. He looked down at her. Her blue eyes were wide-open, shining beacons.

She let her hand rest on his forearm. "Would it help if I told you I know I screwed up? I know you have every right to be angry with me, but I've changed. Being away from you made me realize how good we were together, what I'd thrown away by being so stupid. I was scared at the thought of a family, but now I'm ready to have a baby, Paul. I'd like to settle down and make a family. I'm done with all the rest."

He wanted to believe her. He'd been the one who'd wanted a child but she'd refused so many times, he'd given up on the idea. Now she was offering the only thing that could get him back into the marriage. Was this what he wanted? Could he trust her again?

"Let me sleep on it," he said finally. "I need some time, Fiona."

She reached up her hand and touched his cheek with the tips of her fingers. "I owe you that, I guess. When you're finished thinking it through, I'll be waiting with the wine chilled. This time I won't be going anywhere. It's time I came home."

—

Three calls later, Gail stood up from her desk and stretched her arms toward the ceiling. The last caller was a first-year biology major whose girlfriend left him on the weekend. He'd drunk himself into a depression and was thinking about dropping out of school. She'd convinced him to seek a counsellor, or at least he'd said he would call the number she gave him. She'd done all she could.

Pleasure spread through her veins like warm treacle. Damn, she was good at this job. There was something about the anonymity of the calls that kept her from feeling judged and let her say things she never would say face to face. The pain at the other end of the line was something she'd lived. She said the comforting things to them that she would have liked someone to have said to her on those days she'd thought about killing herself in high school.

She looked across at the clock on the wall and saw it was going on eight thirty. Where had the evening gone? Her eyes swung back to the empty desk across from her. And where the hell was Wolf? He'd become unreliable after he broke up with Leah, mooning around as if they were still a couple. Now he was all but lost in action.

Something cracked like a gunshot against the front door. Gail jumped at the noise, banging her knee against the desk. Her eyes swung toward the door and her mind started scrambling as she remembered that she hadn't checked the lock.

She took a step toward the door, then moved back to her desk and searched around in the drawer until her hand wrapped around a pair of scissors. She pulled them out and started back toward the door, walking as silently as she could across the floor. The detached, rational part of her thought about how ridiculous she was being, but the scared part of her was running the show.

She reached the door and held up her hand to test the handle. Slowly, slowly, she levered it down until it wouldn't move any farther. Relief made her weak. She let out her breath and slumped backwards against the wall. Nate had remembered after all. She was locked safely inside and whatever had hit the door was likely thrown by a passing student. She laughed at her fear of a moment before and pushed herself forward from the wall.

A sharp knock on the door behind her stopped Gail midstride. Her heart jumped like a frightened rabbit and she shrieked. She swung her fist up to her mouth and stifled a second scream. Once she got her emotions under control, she tiptoed back to the door and leaned her ear against the wood. The solid feel against her skin gave her strength.

"Is that you, Wolf?" she asked. No answer. "Wolf?" she yelled.

A man's voice penetrated the door. "Yes," he said and she let her breath out in one long sigh. Wolf had shown up after all. Damn the man for scaring her … and for being so late.

She grabbed the key from its hook on the wall and inserted it to unlock the deadbolt. Mark had set this system up against the wishes of the group. It took a key to lock the door from the outside and a key to open from the inside. Mark swore it was fail-safe, even after they raised concerns about fire. "The key will always be right here next to the door," he'd said. "You can put it into the lock at the ready if it makes you feel more secure."

Her hand hesitated for a moment as it crossed her mind that she hadn't exactly recognized Wolf's voice through the door. It might even have been a woman talking in a low voice if she was being honest. She could ask Wolf to identify himself again, but he'd think she was crazy. After all, who else could it possibly be? She pulled down on the handle.

"You're late, Wolf man," she said swinging the door open. She expected to see his hairy face and was momentarily startled that nobody was standing on the top step. "Where are you?" she called, getting royally pissed off at the infantile hide and seek game, as she took a step outside. She craned her neck to look down the street. It was eerily empty, dark shadows between the buildings. She hesitated. The hair on the back of her neck stood on end. She began to tremble in the cool evening air.

This didn't feel right.

Something clicked behind her and she began to turn. "Not funny, Wol—" her words were cut short by a *whoosh* of movement and lights as the raised brick smashed into the back of her skull. Her neck snapped forward and her teeth clamped together, cutting into her tongue. Blinding pain radiated from the back of her head the split second before her world went black. The force of the impact toppled her unconscious body onto the concrete steps like a sack of cement, where she lay with her head hanging over the edge, her arms and legs wantonly splayed. The scissors dropped into a hyacinth bush directly below. Mercifully, she didn't feel a thing when her face banged against the concrete as she was dragged back inside and rolled with a kick against the wall. Nor did she offer any resistance when her arms and legs were pulled back and she was hog-tied and left like a trussed-up chicken until the cleaner's arrival at six thirty the following morning.

25

IT FELT LIKE Kala had just closed her eyes when the alarm broke through her beautiful dream. The beautiful dream had been coming on the nights when she was overtired, like a returning old friend. In the land between sleep and awake, she was ten years old again and running in her deerskin moccasins down a dirt path through the woods near Birdtail Creek where Lily waited for her by the river. The running always took up a good part of the dream, and tonight was no exception. When she finally reached Lily, their conversation was always the same.

"You're late, but I told you I'd wait for you, Sun." In the dream, they used the childhood names they'd given each other. Lily crouched down and lit a cigarette, blowing smoke toward the river and squinting at something on the far bank. She wore her old buckskin jacket and her hair hung in two black braids halfway down her back.

Kala dropped down next to Lily and hugged her knees to her chest. "I had trouble finding you. I've been running and running."

"Well, now you've found me." Lily's mocking smile turned in her direction and it changed into her happy one — the smile she seldom used. Her eyes turned old. "I have a daughter now, Sun. I named her Dawn, after you. She's the best thing I ever did. I want you both to meet soon."

"I want to meet her too."

"Family, Sun. We're family, and no matter where me and Dawn go, that won't change."

"You'll come back for me, Lil?"

"You know I will. You can bet your life on it."

Kala leaned her head against Lily's shoulder and they sat silently in the falling autumn leaves until the darkness made Lily's face shadow over and recede into graininess, like a movie camera pulling back.

Kala reached over and slammed down on the clock's alarm button. She rolled onto her side and opened her eyes, watching the morning sunlight stream through the open window and letting the warm feeling from the dream settle into her for a few moments. This was as much of Lily as she would ever have, this fuzzy childhood memory from their lives on the rez some eighteen years ago mixed up with the present. Their reunion as adults half a year earlier had ended as quickly as it had materialized. Lily had disappeared with Dawn and left no forwarding address, but Kala would search no more. Their spirits would have to meet again in another world. The dream was nature's way of helping her to accept that.

Kala slipped out of the covers and padded naked to the bathroom, leaving Taiku spread sleeping across the foot of the bed. She turned on the faucets and let the water run hot before she stepped into the shower. She stood in its steaming stream as she washed her hair and soaped her body. Afterwards she dressed in clean jeans and a white blouse, leaving her shoulder-length hair loose to dry.

"Come, Taiku," she called. "Time to rise and shine."

Taiku raised his head from his paws and jumped from the bed, leading her out of the bedroom. They went downstairs into the kitchen. Kala started a pot of coffee and put on Marjory's sweater from the rack near the back door before stepping outside onto the deck. She and Taiku walked across the lawn down to the river's edge. Clouds had moved in overnight and the sun was hidden behind grey skies. A stiff wind crashed waves against the shoreline. Kala shivered and buttoned the sweater before following Taiku down to the narrow strip of beach, sidestepping the waves slurping up on the sand and rocks. They walked to the far point where Kala stopped to skip stones across the waves.

"Look at that, Taiku. Six skips. I'm becoming unbeatable."

Taiku sat down next to her, his tongue lolling out one side of his mouth, and looked out at the lake as if he was thinking over her words. She laughed and bent down to scratch his head. "Let's head home then and get you some breakfast."

The wind was against them walking back and she thought about the cup of hot coffee waiting for her. She even had enough time to toast a bagel to go with it. Still a half hour of peace before she had to meet Gundersund.

They were climbing up the short embankment onto the grass when she spotted him sitting on the stairs of the deck. Her heart gave a jump for which she mentally kicked herself. She would not let the man mean more to her than he should, even if there was something about him that made her happy to see him.

Gundersund stood at her approach and his eyes found hers. He started across the lawn to meet her halfway. She noticed that his hair was wet, slicked back from his forehead. He'd missed a dab of shaving cream on his cheek, all speaking to a rushed exit. He was dressed much like her in jeans and a light-blue denim shirt under a windbreaker. What she could see of the shirt looked wrinkled.

"I thought we agreed to meet at Tadesco's office?" Her voice came out gruff, but he didn't seem to notice.

"Trouble, Stonechild. We have to get to the help line centre instead. I tried to call, but when you didn't answer your phone, I thought I'd better come over to get you."

"I left my cell inside while we took our morning walk. Sorry. What happened?"

"The cleaner found a staff member unconscious when he opened up this morning. Somebody smashed her head in from behind and tied her up. She's in bad shape."

"Which one?"

"The girl with the tattoos. Gail Pankhurst."

"Damn." Kala wondered what she'd missed. Could she have prevented this? She had to put the guilty thoughts away. "I never had a chance to interview Gail yesterday. Looks like Leah Sampson's death is somehow linked to the help line."

"It's looking that way."

"Della Munroe also smashed in Brian's head from behind. I wonder if that means anything."

"I thought of that too. But Della didn't tie her husband up and tear apart his office."

"They were searching for something?"

"Apparently. Rouleau's going to meet us there."

Kala nodded and started past him. "Let me get Taiku some food and I'll be ready to go. Looks like we're about to have another long, messy day." She stopped and moved a step back toward him. "Two young women. What do they know that somebody is willing to kill them for?"

"It could be Leah's secret boyfriend. He might be desperate to keep the affair from being exposed."

"Someone said that Gail Pankhurst kept notes about her co-workers. You might be onto something. The fact both women work at the help line could be a red herring as far as the motive goes."

"We should also consider that the two attacks aren't connected."

"What do you think the odds of that are?"

"Low, but still needs considering."

Kala thought for a moment. "You haven't mentioned the other option."

"Which is?"

"Somebody phoned in information anonymously and Leah threatened to reveal what they told her. Maybe they'd done something so horrific that she was willing to break the code of silence."

She could see the skepticism in his face. "I don't know how she could have exposed anyone since they never identify themselves."

Kala accepted his doubt without protest and started up the steps after Taiku, but her mind was turning over possibilities. At the top, she stopped again and turned to face him. "What if she recognized their voice? What if she let on she knew who the caller was and they had to make sure she never told anybody what they'd done?"

Gundersund looked up at her. She could see him thinking about what she'd said. His voice came out harsh in the morning's silence. "Then whatever it is they're trying to hide must be pretty damn awful if they're willing to kill two women to make sure it never sees the light of day."

26

"I've sent Woodhouse and Chalmers to get a search warrant and then over to her apartment to go through her things." Rouleau led them across the office to the corner where Gail Pankhurst had been found trussed up and unconscious. He pointed to her dried blood. "She bled from her head but the cut was superficial. It was the force of the blow that did the damage."

Gundersund squatted down for a closer inspection. Kala looked at Rouleau. "Is she going to make it?"

"I don't know." His anger at what they'd done to the girl mirrored what he saw on Stonechild's face. "From the trail of blood, we can tell that after she was hit from behind on the steps she was dragged across the floor and left there by the wall. Somehow they got her to unlock the door. Mark Withers is outside. He said that Wolf was supposed to work last night but sent a text around nine that he'd been held up. Withers also said that Nate would have locked the door on his way out per their rules since Gail was on the night shift alone when he left her."

"Maybe he didn't lock it."

"There's blood on the top step so it appears she was lured outside or she was heading home and the attacker surprised her."

"Her bag is upside down by her chair. She would have had it with her at the door if she was on her way home." Stonechild stepped around papers strewn in fistfuls around the room and an overturned chair on the way to the desk where Gail had sat the day before. "She kept files on people. Could that be what they were looking for?"

"Maybe. The files would be on a computer, but I'd be surprised if she kept them on a common drive at work. Chalmers will pick up her home computer or laptop from her apartment. That said, she might have kept a notebook too. Mark Withers's office has also been ripped apart."

Gundersund moved next to Rouleau and said, "We should get him in here to see if anything is missing."

Rouleau agreed. "We'll let Forensics finish their work in his office first. Go find out if he knows anything else and I'll send word we're ready for him. Dino Tadesco was at home but said he'd be here within the half hour when Withers called him. He should have arrived by now."

Stonechild and Gundersund exchanged glances. "Fortuitous," Gundersund said. "Saves us a trip."

They walked outside and found Professor Tadesco and Mark Withers standing with a police officer at the bottom of the steps. Tadesco saw them first and broke away from the group. Gundersund hadn't met Tadesco before and studied the most likely candidate for Leah's lover as he approached. Tadesco could be Italian aristocracy, a tall man with slicked back black hair and a swarthy complexion. An open trench coat and loose silk scarf around his neck added to the European flair. He strode toward them like a man used to having people take him seriously. Gundersund thought the guy a serious fop.

"What the hell is going on?" Tadesco demanded. "How could this abomination happen again to one of our staff?"

He angrily ran a hand through his hair. "Have you any idea who could be behind this?"

"Nobody yet," said Stonechild. "We're hoping you might have some ideas."

Gundersund glanced at her. Had she also caught the false note in Tadesco's anger? He didn't know her well enough yet to tell the difference, but he'd swear there was irony behind her words. Tadesco plowed on, oblivious.

"This is insanity. Leah and Gail were both wonderful girls. Bright, dedicated to helping others. I can't imagine why anybody would want to hurt either one of them."

"So you knew them both well?" Gundersund turned his focus back on Tadesco and watched to see if he gave off any tells about his relationship with Leah Sampson.

"Of course." Tadesco waved him off and turned sideways to look at Mark, who'd stepped up next to him. "Mark, have you any idea about what is going on here?"

Mark shook his tangled blond hair. "Gail is quirky but harmless enough." He paled. "She wasn't beaten, was she?"

"We don't have that information yet," Gundersund said.

"Christ," Tadesco said. "Could this get any worse?"

"She could die," Gundersund said. He looked past Tadesco to the cop signalling to him on the top of the steps. "Come with me, Withers. Time to find out if anything is missing in your office."

Tadesco and Mark looked at each other. "We'll meet up later," Tadesco said. Mark nodded as if some message had passed between them. Gundersund exchanged a glance with Stonechild. She was watching both men intently.

After they'd gone, Kala said to Tadesco, "We *will* get to the bottom of this with some cooperation. Have you any information that could help us?"

"I wish I did. If this keeps going the way it is, the university will be pulling the plug on the help line. I can't tell you the politics of keeping the place going, but let's just say some will be more than happy to use the money elsewhere."

Kala looked across the street. Small groups of students were gathering on the sidewalk and along the roadway. A news truck had pulled up and a reporter was angling herself so that the cameraman had them in his shot. Tadesco followed the line of her eyes.

"Let's get out of here," he said. "I don't know about you, but I have no desire to be on the six o'clock news."

"Lead the way."

She followed him at a half run down the street to the next block. They ducked into another limestone building crawling with red ivy and walked side by side down the wide concrete stairs into the basement. Two couches and four chairs were arranged to their left. Lamps on coffee tables served as muted lighting, giving the space a private, cozy feel. Tadesco made for the chairs near the pillar. Kala was happy to see the room was empty of eavesdroppers.

"Coffee?" Tadesco asked, pointing to a vending machine in the corner of the lounge.

"Sure. Black is fine." She took a seat and waited while he fiddled with coins and buttons. He returned balancing two Styrofoam cups and handed one to her before sitting in the chair next to her. He sipped as he sat down. She smelled his musk scent, both expensive and inviting. It was the kind of scent that could make a woman want to bury her face in a man's neck.

"Terrible swill, but welcome this morning." He stretched out his long legs, elegantly draped in expensive black slacks. "I found this little spot quite by accident last year and use it as my refuge now and then. It's usually empty of students."

He smiled at her as if they were sharing a private moment. She could see the charm he used to make his way through life.

"I thought your office would be your refuge."

"God no. I can barely get any work done there. Students and faculty are stopping by *constantly*." His eyes were dark and his black lashes were long and thick. *Bedroom eyes.*

"Leah Sampson took your class last year and this semester. Was she one of the students stopping by to see you after class?"

"On occasion." He sipped his coffee and eyed her over the brim of the cup.

"Do you sleep with your students, Professor?" Kala asked.

He slowly lowered the cup. "I've never had relations with any of the women who work at the help line, if that's what you're asking. If Leah or Gail was having an affair — and I doubt very much if Gail has emerged from the closet — they were not having one with me."

Kala listened for the lie in his voice. She detected something off, but he sounded sincere about Leah and Gail. She thought over how he'd worded his response. "You didn't sleep with Leah or Gail. Have you slept with other students?"

His eyes widened before he looked down into his coffee cup. "I don't see the relevance or the need for me to answer."

She waited a bit to see if he'd fill the space with further explanation. He didn't and she figured best to let it go for now. "Have there been threats to the help line centre staff before this?"

She observed the lines in his face relax at the change in subject. "No. Nothing. We keep a low profile and don't broadcast our staff names or whereabouts."

"But somebody could find the location if they set their mind to it?"

"Sure. The location of the Queen's Help Line is in the school directory, although we only advertise the phone number in pamphlets and such. We don't hand out the address as a rule."

"Back to Leah Sampson. Do you know why she and Wolf Edwards broke up?"

"I heard through the grapevine that she'd met someone else."

Kala nodded. "We heard the same thing. Do you know the name of the new love interest?" She watched conflicted emotions dart across his face. It seemed he had loyalties to someone he was reluctant to implicate.

"Look, I thought it was Mark Withers at first to tell you the truth. He assured me, however, that he would not sleep with the staff. I believe him."

"Was Wolf angry with Leah when they broke up?"

"Initially they weren't speaking to each other. They were friends again a few weeks afterwards. Wolf isn't the type of man to hold a grudge."

"What kind of man is he?"

"Poetic, deep. He's a man whom people gravitate towards because he cares about them. I would no more believe him a killer than I would you, Inspector Stonechild."

"A strong vote of confidence."

"Well placed, I assure you."

Kala tried one more avenue through Tadesco's carefully constructed answers. "Did you know that Gail was keeping notes on her co-workers?"

Tadesco's laugh was loud and spontaneous. "Who would believe she's as good a counsellor as she is? I think it has something to do with all the pain in her own life. Being overweight, socially inept, and gay do not many friends make. Gail put up an eccentric front, but she was just getting by the best she could. If she was keeping notes, they were harmless observations."

Kala finished her coffee and stood. "I hope you're right, Professor, but somebody was desperate to find something in your help line offices. If you think of what it could be, here's my card. Call me anytime."

Tadesco stood as well and flicked the card against his wrist. He leaned in toward her and said, "I will most certainly be in touch if I remember anything that could help. You can count on it."

They walked up the stairs together and he shook her hand before he headed on foot toward his office. He pulled out his cell and held it to his ear as he strode away from her, his trench coat flapping around his long legs. Kala stood without moving and watched until he disappeared from view. She started back to the help line centre, his musky smell stubbornly filling her nostrils as she climbed the steps to find Gundersund and Rouleau.

27

ROULEAU LOOKED UP from his desk to find Stonechild hovering in the doorway, one hand lifted to knock. Her eyes were bright and excitement shone from her face.

"Have you got a moment, sir?"

He raised a hand and motioned for her to sit in the chair across from him. "You look like you've made a discovery," he said, leaning back in his chair, "or maybe I'm just being hopeful after Woodhouse called in that Gail's roommate reported that her laptop wasn't in their apartment."

Stonechild flashed a quick smile. "I believe I have. It might be nothing, but then again, you never know what will be important at this stage."

"What have you got?" He straightened and reached for the papers she passed across the desk.

"Professor Tadesco told me he hadn't slept with any women at the help line, but he was evasive when I asked if he'd slept with any other students. It got me wondering. I called the university and had them send me over his class lists for the past few years. Interestingly, Della Munroe was in Tadesco's class last year and again this semester. She might just like his teaching style or she could have something going on with him."

Rouleau studied the sheets, a tingling starting at the back of his neck, the sensation he got when facts started to realign. "It could be a coincidence."

"I know it's a bit of a long shot, but interesting nonetheless. The thing that I find odd is that Tadesco never mentioned her when we discussed Leah's murder and Gail's attack. If I had a student whose husband was also killed the same week, I'd probably mention it in passing."

"Yeah, that would seem like an obvious observation to make. If he's having a relationship with Della, do you think that he would admit to it if confronted?"

"I doubt it. He has too much to lose. I'm not even sure where an affair between the two of them would fit into our case." Stonechild looked less certain than when she'd entered his office. "Maybe it's just a coincidence that Della keeps taking his classes, like you said. An odd coincidence, but possible." She shrugged and took back the papers. "Any word yet on Gail Pankhurst's condition?"

"I checked ten minutes ago. She's still unconscious but stable. I have an officer on the door to her room."

"Gundersund and I are heading over to interview the people in the offices next to the help line centre."

"Good idea. Check in later."

"Will do." She hesitated at the door. "Do you think this person was after her laptop all along?"

"No idea, but it's the only thing that appears to be missing. It's not that valuable an item to fence."

"It's getting harder to separate what's important and what's collateral damage."

"We'll keep our minds open. You never know when something will pull all the pieces together."

———

Rouleau sat looking out the window and thinking about what Stonechild had told him. It was odd that the people in the Munroe and Sampson cases crossed paths, but perhaps not impossible with the university campus connections. The possibility that Della Munroe was having an affair with Tadesco would put a new spin on the story she'd given earlier. However, her involvement in a tryst really was nothing other than a hunch on Stonechild's part. It wasn't even strong enough to question her about. A hypothetical affair wouldn't hold much water in court. Yet, Stonechild had a sixth sense that he'd learned the hard way not to question.

He checked his watch. Going on three. He reached for the phone. His father picked up after two rings. He was just back from a few hours at his office on campus and settling in for a nap. This bought Rouleau some time. He offered to pick up some fish and chips on his way home if his father didn't mind waiting to eat for a few more hours. His dad said no problem.

Rouleau hung up and made an effort to reread the morning reports. The words blurred after ten minutes. He removed his reading glasses and rubbed his eyes. He could use a nap himself. He'd been on the move since he got the Pankhurst call at five fifteen.

Vera poked her head around the door. She was slightly winded, her blond hair in disarray. "I just came to warn you. I overheard that lawyer Suzie Chen talking on her cell outside the ladies washroom. She told somebody that she was on her way to rattle your cage about the Munroe case."

"I've got nothing new to tell her."

"I thought you might want to head home and miss another confrontation."

"Has anyone ever told you what a treasure you are?"

She smiled. "All the time. By the way, Heath is due back tomorrow."

"He's fished out the lake?"

"Oh, I don't think he ever catches anything." Her smile shifted sideways, turning up one side of her mouth. "But I'm sure you do." She was gone before he could formulate a reply. He shook his head and grabbed his jacket. Vera was turning into his Moneypenny. He was a far cry from James Bond, however.

He checked the hallway for Chen and hurried across to the fire escape. The best way to beat fatigue and to avoid an angry lawyer was to get out and do some investigating; leave his desk and get into the field. He felt his spirits rise before his foot hit the first step. The heaviness in his head had lifted by the time he reached the parking lot.

———

Della was moving around the living room, talking into her cellphone and pacing back and forth in front of the window. Once she stopped and looked out, her hand raised to the curtain. Her long black hair was tied up on top of her head but a piece had escaped and hung lankly across one eye. Her free hand pushed the hair away every so often but it always fell back. She wore a silky green dress that Rouleau imagined rustled when she moved. He could detect no grief in her face as she looked out onto the street, her mouth opening in laughter. She turned her back to the window and disappeared from sight.

Before opening the car door, Rouleau checked the side mirror. A car was racing up the street toward him and he hesitated. The red Explorer pulled into the driveway in front of Della Munroe's house and he slumped lower in the seat.

A short Mexican woman in a rainbow-coloured skirt got out of the driver's side and opened the back door. A small boy got out. He was a mixed-race child dressed in shorts and a Mickey Mouse T-shirt. He looked across the street toward Rouleau's car, and even from that distance, Rouleau could see that he had his mother's large blue eyes, although the black hair that surrounded his face was a mass of kinky curls inherited from his father. He was a startlingly handsome boy, a miniature model with a face that was going to break hearts. The woman took his hand and they walked to the front door. They waited nearly a minute for Della to answer, the boy hopping from one foot to the other while the woman kept hold of his hand. Finally, the door opened and the two stepped inside. Rouleau saw the flash of Della's green skirt before the door closed.

Rouleau debated watching the house a while longer or heading to the fish restaurant for takeout. It was going on five and if he left now his dad could eat his supper in front of the early news. He sat for a while longer, going over in his mind everything he knew about the Munroes and their marriage. While he reviewed the information, he kept an eye on the front door, but nobody came outside. The living room window remained empty. Twenty minutes later, he started up the car. He took one last look at the house. Something niggled in his memory but he couldn't pin it down.

He was turning onto Brock when it struck him. There hadn't been any mention of a nanny or domestic help in the reports. Had Della hired someone this week? He'd have thought the Munroes couldn't afford one from what he recalled of their finances. He made a note to himself to check the next morning when he got into work.

It was nearly five when he pulled into the fish restaurant downtown, a street over from Princess. The entire time he waited at the counter for his order, he pictured Della Munroe in her silky green dress standing in the window, laughing at whatever somebody had said over the phone. Head tossed back and red lips parted. The eyes that had looked out across the yard had been excited, happy even. Her recovery a week after killing her husband was nothing short of miraculous. It was enough to give a seasoned detective pause.

28

THE WHOLE FAMILY gathered around the dinner table to eat the meal Dalal had cooked after school. As instructed by her mother, she'd made a simple chicken korma simmered for an hour with ginger, garlic, and cashews, served over basmati rice. Her mother had shown a generosity of spirit by preparing a big bowl of phirni, Dalal's favourite dessert, a rice pudding made with cardamom and pistachios. Dalal worried that the delicious pudding was to soften whatever her mother was planning to do next. It wouldn't be the first time she'd prepared a treat and done something horrible soon afterward.

Her father was silent during supper. He only roused himself after dessert was served to ask Ghazi about his latest soccer game. Dalal tried to decipher the looks that passed between her mother and Ghazi during the meal, but she was at a loss. Meeza was quieter than usual, her eyes downcast and her head bowed, but she ate everything on her plate and asked for a second helping of phirni. For once, their mother placed another scoop into Meeza's bowl without chiding her for being a glutton.

Dalal became more and more agitated as the meal progressed. She practised a question in her mind but couldn't make the words come out of her mouth. Fear kept her from asking what she most wanted to know. Her father pushed his bowl away and placed his spoon on the table, and she knew it was now or never. She took a deep breath before speaking.

"Mother?" she began in a small, questioning voice.

"Yes, Dalal?" Her mother, father, and Ghazi fixed on her with their eyes. Even Meeza's spoonful of pudding stopped halfway to her mouth as she lifted her head. Her black eyes widened and she looked across at Dalal. Dalal wanted to crawl into a safe, dark hole, but the thought of Meghan's phone call kept her speaking.

"I've been working on a school project with a girl named Meghan in my class. She's invited me to her home after school tomorrow to finish it. She asked if I could stay for supper." Dalal folded her hands in her lap and lowered her head in the sign of submission that her parents liked to see.

"Where does this girl live?" her mother asked.

"A few blocks from the school. Her mother and father will be home tomorrow evening. She has assured me."

"What do you think, Burhan?" Her mother looked across the table at her father.

He didn't speak and Dalal stole a glance to gauge his reaction. He seemed deep in thought. She lowered her head again and waited.

"Dalal has been working hard and she is an obedient girl. I think we can let her finish this project with her schoolmate. Will it be too much of a burden for you to prepare the meal with Meeza?" he asked her mother. His voice brooked no dissension and Dalal dared to hope.

"I can prepare the meal," said her mother with a loud sigh. "If you think it is proper for Dalal to eat at this girl's house, I will gladly do the work at home."

"I do not see any harm," her father said.

Ghazi remained silent. Dalal couldn't believe her good fortune. She would get to spend an evening with Joe away from the suspicious eyes of her family.

———

She was nearly done her English homework when Ghazi walked into her room without knocking. He sat on the edge of her bed and waited for her to turn around. He tossed a foam football from one hand to the other. When he looked at her, Dalal felt a shiver travel up her spine but she kept her eyes steady on his.

"What do you want, Ghazi?"

"How come you never mentioned this girl Meghan before?"

"She's just a girl the teacher put me with to do a project. She seems okay."

"What is the project about?"

Dalal had expected this question and she was ready. "We had to pick an early American author and analyze their work."

"Really? And who are you analyzing?"

"Benjamin Franklin. He wrote the *Poor Richard's Almanack* from 1732 to 1758. It had a print run of ten thousand copies per year, which was very impressive for back then."

Ghazi shook his head and tossed the football into the air. He caught it with his left hand and leaned back against the pillows on her bed. "Fascinating," he mocked.

"I think so." She kept typing even though she'd already finished putting down all she had to say. What was he waiting for? The bed springs creaked and he shifted closer. She froze when she felt his fingers on the back of her neck. His breathing had gotten heavier, the opposite of hers, which had stopped altogether.

"Have any boys tried to touch you?" he asked harshly. "Like this?" His fingers moved around to the front of her neck and down the space between her breasts. She felt the heat of his fingers through her blouse. She shook her head hard from side to side.

"Have they ever tried to touch you here?" he whispered into her ear. His hand had moved to cover her right breast and his thumb rubbed against her nipple.

"Stop it, Ghazi." She batted at his hand, but he resisted and squeezed her nipple until she squealed.

"Stop it, Ghazi," he mimicked. His other hand had snaked under her shirt and was moving up her skin toward her other breast. He'd pinned her against his chest and his breath was hot and shallow in her ear.

"I'll scream," she said.

"You'll regret it," he said. "I'll make sure."

She stayed as still as she could while he massaged both breasts up and down in circular motions. Hot tears welled up behind her eyelids.

"Do you have the diary?" he asked. His breath was hot on the side of her face.

"I don't know what you're talking about. Leave me alone."

"You know where she …" he began, but a voice at the door to the room made him stop.

"Can I play?"

Dalal felt Ghazi's hands drop from her chest as she looked toward Meeza framed in the doorway, holding her teddy bear, Boo. She had a smile on her face, but her eyes were rimmed in red as if she'd been crying. Dalal stood and moved away from Ghazi.

"Come in Meeza," she said. "Ghazi is just leaving."

His eyes were angry bees staring into hers. Dalal glared back, trying to hold her ground, all the while fear beating like butterfly wings inside her.

"This isn't over," he said so quietly that Meeza could not possibly overhear. His hand pinched through the fabric covering Dalal's ribs and he gave a sharp twist before he pushed his way past Meeza and out of the room. Dalal waited until he'd slammed the door to his bedroom and the music from his stereo was once again beating through the wall before she crossed to her bed and lowered herself onto the edge, one hand clutching the place where he'd hurt her.

Meeza ran the short distance between them and flung herself into Dalal's arms. Dalal patted her head and wondered how much Meeza had seen. Her little sister was more intuitive than most, even with her limited mental capacities, and Dalal guessed this was the case now. Meeza sensed the danger lurking in their family even if she didn't understand it. It was up to Dalal to protect her … to protect them both.

29

GUNDERSUND WAITED FOR Stonechild in the hallway near the nurses' station. He checked his messages and saw one from Rouleau. He read it and speed dialed Rouleau's number. They finished talking just as Stonechild approached from the direction of Gail Pankhurst's room. Her face was grim.

"May as well go," she said. "Gail's been put into a medically induced coma. They're waiting for the brain swelling to go down and hope there isn't any lasting damage. We won't be able to talk to her today or maybe not all week. Maybe not ever if she doesn't pull through this."

Gundersund fell into step beside her. "Have her parents showed up?"

"Apparently not."

She'd expressed a lot in two clipped words. He had a good idea what she thought of parents who wouldn't make the trip to a severely injured child's hospital bedside. He pressed the elevator button. "Rouleau just told me that the same brand of rope used on Gail was used to tie up Leah Sampson. Forensics said it's an exact match. No prints."

"Had to be the same sick bastard."

"We just need to figure out what they were after."

They didn't speak in the elevator. Stonechild was wedged in between a patient in a wheelchair and the back wall.

Gundersund exited first and stood off to one side to wait for her while the others filed out. He and Stonechild began walking toward the front doors.

Gundersund resumed the conversation. "Rouleau said to carry on with the interviews. He's on his way to Toronto for the afternoon."

"Did he say why?"

"No. Just that he's checking something out."

"So who do we start with first today?"

"I think Wolf Edwards could do with another visit."

"I agree. Jucinda Rivera is working today and I'd like to speak with her after we're done with Wolf."

"Looks like a full morning."

"Looks like."

————

They found Wolf still in his pajamas, frying two eggs in a skillet. His black hair was curled in matted chaos around his head, his eyes bleary from too much alcohol and not enough sleep. He had them sit at the crowded kitchen table while he scraped the eggs onto a plate and turned off the burner. He poured three cups of coffee without asking and slid two in front of Gundersund and Stonechild. Then he sat down and pushed the runny egg yolks around his plate with a fork while he supported his chin with his free hand.

"You don't seem too concerned about Gail Pankhurst," commented Gundersund. Wolf had told them he'd already heard about her assault when he answered the door.

"Not much I can do," Wolf said. "Luckily, this blinding headache is keeping me from thinking too deeply about anything."

"Where were you two nights ago? Mark Withers told us that you were supposed to work with Gail but were a no-show."

Wolf put down his fork and closed his eyes. "Thanks for bringing up what I was trying not to think about. If I'd been at the help line like I was supposed to, I could have stopped Gail from being assaulted. After I got the call last night about the break in, I redoubled my Scotch intake."

"You were out drinking instead of going into work?" Stonechild asked.

"Yeah. I needed to stop thinking about the guilt I feel over Leah and alcohol seemed like the only way to shut off my mind. Now I have someone else to feel guilty about."

"And why do you feel guilty about Leah?" Gundersund asked.

"Because I walked her home that night and left her to some crazy killer. I keep thinking I could have saved her if only I'd walked her to her apartment door instead of stopping at the corner, or, I don't know, believed her when she told me to trust her."

"She told you that?"

"I thought she was covering up about an affair. Jucinda told me she'd seen Leah having sex in a car and with all the disappearing and secrecy on Leah's part, well, it all seemed to add up. I was sure she was having an affair and the guy was married."

"And now?"

"Now, I'm not sure." He groaned. "I'm supposed to be able to read people and figure out when they're bullshitting or telling the truth. With Leah, I let the green-eyed monster take over. I forgot to be objective."

"Jealousy can make you do things you regret," commented Stonechild.

Wolf looked at her, realization dawning in his eyes. "I didn't hurt her. I would *never* hurt her. My regret is that I didn't trust her."

"Can someone vouch for you in the bar the night of Gail's attack?" asked Gundersund.

"Maybe. I didn't stay too long in any one place. I came home at one point and drank some more before I passed out."

"Run it past me," Gundersund said, his notebook ready.

Stonechild waited while Wolf gave Gundersund a rough roadmap of his bar-hopping route. When they finished, she asked, "Now that you've had a few more days to think about it, Wolf, do you have any idea of either who Leah was involved with or what else she could have been mixed up in that got her killed?"

"I've thought about that a lot. I just have no idea who she could have been sleeping with. If it wasn't an affair, maybe it was a call she took over the help line that somebody regretted making. Like I said, Leah got secretive before we broke up. Once she disappeared overnight and wouldn't tell me who she'd been with or where. I imagined the worst. When she refused to tell me, I called off our relationship. If you can't trust the person you're with, what's the point of carrying on with them?"

Gundersund nodded. A hit close to home: Wolf could have been talking about him and Fiona. He'd also been consumed by the green-eyed monster, but in his case, Fiona had given him ample proof of her infidelity. He hadn't broken it off, however. Fiona had been the one to tell him they were over. What kind of a fool did that make him? An even bigger one now that he was considering taking her back.

Gundersund looked across at Stonechild. She had her head down, writing the last of the information that Wolf had doled out. He bet she never compromised her beliefs for anyone. She looked up, perhaps sensing his gaze. Her eyes went from questioning to unreadable in one split second.

"I think we've got all we need for now." She looked at Wolf, who was lifting a forkful of cold egg to his mouth. "We'll check out the bars you gave us. If you think of anything else we should know, give us a call right away."

"I know the drill," Wolf said. "I won't be leaving town."

—

"So what do you think?" Gundersund asked as they reached his car. "Is he lying?"

"I'm starting to believe him." Stonechild opened the passenger door. "Too bad if he's taken up drinking to ease the pain. It won't help in the long run." She tapped the car roof. "Time to track down Jucinda and grill her about this affair she witnessed. Maybe she can cough up a few more details like the make of the car wherein this illicit boinking took place."

"Is that the technical name for it?"

"According to Doctor Ruth."

"Are you up for some breakfast on the way?"

"Yeah. I could eat."

"They have a good breakfast at Morrison's on King. One of Kingston's landmark greasy spoons."

"As long as the coffee is hot."

—

Mark Withers was manning the phone when they entered the help line an hour later. He held up his pointer finger and directed them to the couch. They took seats and waited while he finished his call. The mess of the day before had been cleared away.

Mark hung up and walked over to them. He was wearing black shorts, a Planet Hollywood T-shirt, and sandals. His streaked blond hair was pulled back into a ponytail and a strap of black leather encircled his neck. Despite his youthful clothes, his boyish face was tired and he looked closer to his age, which Gundersund knew to be midthirties.

"Any word yet on Gail?" Mark asked.

"She's in an induced coma, but we're told she's stable. They'll be bringing her around when the brain swelling goes down, which could be anytime apparently," Gundersund said. "We expected Jucinda to be working today."

"She's coming in later. Nate should be here any minute. I'm running low on staff and nobody's lining up to replace them, oddly enough." He grimaced. "Word has gotten around that if you work here, you'd better have some life insurance."

"Nate and Jucinda aren't worried?"

"They are, actually. Good thing they both need the money, although I wouldn't be surprised if they're spending their free time looking for other jobs."

Nate picked that moment to enter. He slung his knapsack over the back of a chair and walked over. "Sorry I'm late, Mark. Any word on Gail?"

"She's hanging in," Mark said.

"Good."

"We've got a few questions for you, Nathan," Stonechild said. "Can we use your office, Mark?"

"Sure. I'll hold down the phones." Mark reached the desk in time to pick up on the second ring.

The cleanup in the outer office hadn't extended to Mark's lair. File folders and papers were tossed around the floor as if a gale-force wind had blown through. The garbage can lay on its side, fast food wrappers and coffee cups spread about, a half-eaten sandwich smushed into the carpet. Mark had cleared a place at his desk to work but hadn't bothered with anywhere else. Nathan righted a chair and sat down. Stonechild and Gundersund leaned against either side of the desk, looking down at him.

It was a cramped, sunless room and Gundersund felt like a clumsy giant in the enclosed space. He forced himself to ignore the nausea creeping up his throat. "You were home two nights ago I understand," he said.

Nathan nodded. "My wife and I celebrated our third wedding anniversary. I took her for dinner and a movie. We got home after eleven."

"Have you any insights into what happened here that night?" Gundersund decided an open question might elicit the most information at this point. Mark hadn't been able to identify anything missing and they were at a loss as to what was going on.

"Not a clue. We don't keep money or drugs on the premises. You can find us if you do a bit of research online, but who would want to target this place?"

"You keep records of the calls?"

"We do, but the entries are never linked to the callers because we never take names. We're an anonymous service and that's well advertised. We don't give out our names either and we sure wouldn't meet any of them. That would get us fired."

"We were told that Gail kept her own files on co-workers."

Nate laughed. "Gail looked at us as her petri dish. She'd say the most outrageous things to see how we'd react. I looked at what she was recording when she forgot her laptop last month. Most of it was silly stuff, although some of it could have been stretched into a study of some sort. She kept one on Leah and others on Wolf, Mark, and her flat-mate Elaine. From what I read, Elaine went ballistic when Gail came onto her."

"Did Gail record anything about an affair that Leah was having?"

"She never wrote anything about an affair. Believe me, if she'd known about it, she would have made notes. You'll be able to read through her files for yourself. She didn't even have a password on her laptop."

"The laptop is missing," Gundersund said. "And since you are the only one who read the files, we're going to bring you into the station and have you write down whatever you can remember." He pondered what it could mean if Gail hadn't recorded the name of Leah's lover. Would whoever did this think she had? Would just the thought of their name being recorded be enough for the person to break in and steal the laptop from her? Perhaps Gail had blackmailed him.

Nathan frowned. "Great. Serves me right for snooping, I guess. Can I do it after my shift?"

"Now would be better if you can arrange it."

"I'll see if Mark can hold down the fort for an hour."

Stonechild stopped Nathan at the door. "As Tadesco's TA, do you know a student named Della Munroe?"

Nathan's back stiffened, his hand on the door knob. He spoke without turning around. "Sure. Smart cookie. Why?"

"Had you heard there was an accident at her house last week?

"No. Is she okay?"

"She's fine. I wonder if you ever saw her with the professor outside of class?"

Nate took a step sideways. His eyes met hers and slid away. "Now that you mention it, yeah. She was in his office a couple of times when I went to drop off some papers. Lots of students went to talk to him after class, though. He had an open door policy."

"Good to know," Kala said. "Thanks."

Gundersund exchanged looks with Stonechild. He could see that she was as surprised as he was that news of Brian Munroe's death at Della's hand hadn't reached campus. He watched Nathan walk over to Mark.

"I'll bring Nathan back to the station and will meet you there once you finish up here," he said.

Kala stayed at the help line until Jucinda Rivera showed up for her shift. Mark left right after Jucinda arrived, although he would be returning later. This time Jucinda was dressed modestly in a loose sweater and jeans. Her motions were jerky as she pulled out a chair to sit down across from Kala in the outer office to be near the phones. She stretched her legs out, crossed at the ankles, and folded her arms across her chest, one hand gripping a Starbucks coffee. "The last damn place I want to be is here," she said. "I'm handing in my notice today."

"Do you believe somebody is targeting women at the help line?" Kala waited while Jucinda took a shaky sip from the cup.

"What do *you* think? Two of the three women who work here have been beaten to death or nearly. I don't plan to be the third."

"The theory has been floated that Leah Sampson was murdered because of an affair with a married man. You were the one who told Wolf that she was having sex in a car. Can you walk me through what you saw that evening?"

Kala was surprised to see the flash of guilt on Jucinda's face, the defiance in her eyes momentarily wavering. Jucinda blinked before fixating on a spot above Kala's head.

"I told him that I saw Leah a few streets over in a car I didn't recognize. I'd just got off shift at around nine o'clock."

"It was getting dark, I'm assuming."

"Yeah, but the car was under a streetlight."

Kala started to have a bad feeling. She watched until Jucinda began to squirm in the chair.

"Okay, I might not have actually *seen* her face, but for sure I recognized her shirt and hair."

"You didn't see her face, but by the illumination from a streetlight, you had definitive proof that the woman in the car was Leah Sampson. What was she wearing that was so distinctive?"

"A white blouse."

"And her hair?"

"Long and dark. She'd been wearing it the same way at work."

Kala couldn't keep the incredulity from her voice. "That's all you based it on? Were you aware that when Wolf confronted Leah, she never admitted to an affair? She asked him to trust her."

"Well, she would, wouldn't she? She was trying to save her bacon."

"I want you to think over what you saw again in that car very carefully. Could it have been someone other than Leah you saw having sex that evening?"

Kala stared at Jucinda while she waited for her response. Jucinda's eyes landed on hers then skidded away. One knee began to jiggle up and down.

"Maybe it wasn't her." The words came out barely audible.

"Can you say that louder?"

Jucinda sighed long and deep. "I *said* maybe it wasn't her, okay? I might have been wrong, but I really thought it was her at first." Her voice became pouty, "I still think it could have been."

Kala felt anger well up inside at this jealous backstabbing that likely lay behind the tragedy that followed. "You never believed it was her, did you? This was a way to get Leah out of the picture so you could make a move on her boyfriend Wolf Edwards. Am I correct?"

"You just had to look at her to know it was a matter of time before she fooled around on him. I did Wolf a favour." Jucinda mumbled the words from bowed head.

Kala fixed her eyes on Jucinda until she lifted her eyes, still defiant but not as confident. Kala let her anger harden her words. "And do you believe you did Leah a favour when you started this lie? Do you believe she's thanking you now?"

30

TRAFFIC WAS HEAVY on the 401 between Kingston and Toronto but moving at a good clip — twenty klicks over the speed limit. No accidents or bottlenecks until Rouleau spotted the CN Tower ahead in the distance when traffic abruptly narrowed to one lane and slowed to a snail's pace. He had time to study the map as he idled near an off-ramp. After ten minutes of stop and go, he passed a car flipped over and a long haul truck jackknifed sideways into the base of a concrete overpass. Police and a tow truck were clearing the scene. From what Rouleau could see, the ambulance had come and gone. As soon as he passed the last of the emergency vehicles, he carried on in the centre lane until he saw the Yonge Street exit.

He took Sheppard Avenue into North York and hung a right on Easton Road, and then a left on Florence. A lot more high rises spotted the neighbourhood than the last time he'd visited this area. He took Radine into the residential streets until he reached Stuart Avenue. The houses on the north side of Stuart were prime property, backing onto the ravine that cut north from the West Don River. It was an old working-class neighbourhood, but a goodly number of the small brick homes had been bought up by developers, torn down and spit into the landfill. Fancy oversized homes decked out in beige, cultured brick had taken their places, large price tags and small yards the new normal.

Rouleau checked the house number again on the paper lying on the passenger seat. Halfway down the block, he pulled over to the curb directly across from one of the original grand dwellings: two-storey gold brick with a turret and leaded windows. As he walked toward the front door he saw harbingers of decline in the tired paint around the door and fissures in the concrete foundation. The bushes under the bay window were overgrown and badly in need of a trim. It was as if the will to keep the place going was slipping away, although he still put the property at two million easy.

It took a few minutes before the front door was slowly opened by a Latina woman with grey hair and black eyes. She wore a pink nursing uniform and rubber-soled shoes. She looked at him quizzically before her eyes lit in recognition as she recovered the memory of his appointment.

"You are the detective from Kingston who called," she said, stepping aside to let him enter. "You've come at just the right time. Mr. Amato is having a good day. He's expecting you."

She led Rouleau into the back of the house to a sunny solarium. An emaciated man was stretched out on a couch, his head propped up by pillows and a red blanket covering his legs even though Rouleau found the room hot and suffocating. Tubes from a tank of oxygen were hooked into the man's nose. Classical music played softly from speakers hidden somewhere in the room. A medicinal smell cloyed Rouleau's senses.

"Do you need anything, Mr. Amato?" the nurse asked. When he shook his head no, she signalled for Rouleau to sit in the chair across from him and said, "I'll be back in ten minutes to see you out."

"I'm sorry to hear that you've been ill," Rouleau said, pulling the chair closer. His words sounded grossly inadequate to his own ears. The man before him with skin the colour of waxed paper and diminished size was obviously nearing the end. The nurse had told him that Amato had two months left to live on the outside when he called the evening before. "I just need to find out about your daughter, Della."

"Del-la." His papery voice rose just above a whisper.

"You were upset that she married Brian Munroe." Rouleau wanted to make the interview as easy as possible, to save the man from having to speak more than necessary.

"Began long before that." Mr. Amato paused, gathering his strength. "Della caused ... so much pain. Stole money. Lied all the time." Another pause. Another deep sucking of oxygen from the machine. "My wife and I gave up. Couldn't take it anymore. Had to think of Emily."

"Emily?"

"My other daughter. Lives nearby."

Rouleau nodded, surprised that her name hadn't been in any reports. "Is it okay if I speak with her?"

"Go ... easy." Mr. Amato smiled, his face softening at the thought of her. He coughed, a harsh rasp deep in his chest. His face contorted into a purplish knot and he pushed forward, trying to catch his breath. Rouleau rose to fetch the nurse. Mr. Amato waved him off and sucked in oxygen from the tank. "Am okay," he said. He took a few moments until his chest stopped its frantic in and out.

Rouleau lowered himself into the chair, anxiety making him lean forward to watch for any more signs of distress.

"Della's changed. Am hoping. My wife and I ... our fault." Deep regret settled over his face. His eyes fluttered closed as he sank into the pillows. "Need to make it right. It's just the two of them left now."

Rouleau lightly touched Mr. Amato's shoulder. The collarbone jutted sharply against his hand. Amato's wife had died a few years before. The two of them must be Emily and Della. Rouleau was suddenly too cognizant that this would be the one and only time he would meet this man, because his spirit was slipping away to a different plane. Rouleau wasn't sure if he believed in an afterlife. He hoped along with everybody else, but he didn't have the gift of blind faith. He spoke softly, not sure if Amato was still awake. "I'll let you rest now, Mr. Amato. Emily should be able to fill me in on the rest. I appreciate that you saw me today."

Mr. Amato's eyes fluttered open. The sound of his breathing was laboured as he pulled oxygen in sucking draws from the tubes. His eyes closed again but this time did not re-open. A harsh snoring sound started in his throat.

Rouleau watched for a moment more before standing. He stopped at the door and looked back. Mr. Amato had already drifted into a restless sleep. His mouth was open and pain lined his face.

The nurse met Rouleau in the hallway. "He's sinking fast," she said. "But something is making him hang on. When he gets it settled, I expect he'll be at peace enough to slip away."

She directed him down the street and around the corner to an older storey-and-a-half that had yet to be plowed under by developers. It was tucked in between two monoliths, three-car garages butting up against the property line on both sides. Rouleau studied the exterior: original red brick with wide concrete steps, a rose garden in vibrant bloom under the living room window. It was a well-kept house with a warm feel.

Emily Amato was a lesser version of her sister Della. Plump with black hair cut in a short bob. The dark almond-shaped eyes were the same, except for the kindness in these ones.

"I've made coffee," she said, leading him into her sun-filled kitchen that looked out over a garden of tomato plants and sunflowers. "Please have a biscotti. I made them yesterday."

Rouleau settled in and sipped the mocha brew topped with thick cream. The Italian biscuit was lemon-flavoured with vanilla-almond icing. He took a moment to savour the flavours while she watched him with troubled eyes. The room smelled of garlic, onions, and brown sugar.

"You have a sister. Della," he started awkwardly, aware that this woman had no reason to share her family secrets with him. "I'm trying to find out more about her."

"She's hurt somebody." Emily's eyes searched Rouleau's and found confirmation. "I knew one day … well, that one day, she would go too far."

"Can you tell me about her? I understand she was estranged from your family."

Emily's hands clenched into a single fist on the table. She bowed her head as if in prayer. "My sister was never right. In my earliest memories of her, she was manipulative, always the victim. My parents fell for her stories for a long time before they saw that she did nothing without calculation."

"Could you give an example?"

"I was born two years after Della. When I was five, she pushed me down the stairs. I was eleven when the stealing started. She took everything that mattered to me and either got rid of it or ruined it. She threatened to hurt me if I told. I got good at hiding when anyone or anything mattered to me. I learned that after she broke my cat's back legs."

"And your parents had no idea?"

"Not for a long time, or at least they weren't willing to admit it. They bent over backwards, trying to make her feel loved, hoping she'd outgrow this phase. Dad especially pandered to her demands. But it wasn't a phase. It's who she is. When Della was thirteen, she turned on our mother and made her life a living hell. It's a testament to my father and the strength of their marriage that they never divorced. When Della couldn't break them up, she faked having cancer. She was seventeen. She had us and everyone we knew believing she was on death's door. She even shaved her head so we'd think she was having chemo. People sent money that she never paid back. For my father, it was the final straw. When he found out how she'd used us, used all our friends, he kicked her out. He never saw her again until last month."

"She came to Toronto?"

"With her son. She'd somehow found out that Dad was ill and was trying to worm her way back in. You may have noticed that my father has money. He's also weak when it comes to Della. She told him that her husband Brian was abusive and she needed help to get her son away from him. Dad told her that he'd pray for her. He didn't promise her anything, thank God." Emily freed one hand and crossed herself.

"I imagine that didn't make her happy. You know that she killed Brian and claims it was self-defence after some escalating abuse."

The surprise in Emily's eyes sparked, then quickly disappeared. "Della phoned Dad that Brian had been killed, but she never said that she did it. She was distraught and begged him to send money so she could come home to Toronto. Dad told her she and Tommy could stay with him. I was livid when I heard. How did she kill him?"

"She hit him with a hammer in the back of the head. Twice. She said that he raped her a few days before and she took out a restraining order. She claims that he was trying to take Tommy away and she acted out of duress."

"Based on the fact you're here, you must have doubts about her innocence."

"I do."

Emily lifted her face to his. Rouleau saw anxiety in the creases and lines around her eyes. "Nothing that Della has ever done in her entire life has been without calculation, without concern for anyone but herself. I hope you can keep her away from my father these last weeks of his life. I dread how all this will end. She'll stop at nothing to get the inheritance. She'll sacrifice everything to get what she believes should be hers."

"You make her sound like a monster."

Emily looked Rouleau directly in the eyes. "If my sister is allowed free rein, I'm not sure any of us is safe. Me, least of all. If you don't find a way to convict Della of murdering her husband, Inspector Rouleau, I fear that you'll be investigating my murder next."

31

THE PIZZA SMOTHERED in gooey mozzarella cheese, pepperoni, and mushrooms was a rare treat for Dalal. Joe's mother insisted she have three pieces and then a large slice of chocolate cake with strawberry ice cream for an added bit of heaven. Dalal's mother scoffed at American food. She never gave Dalal or Meeza spending money in case they wasted it on foolish western food or clothes. She would have turned a shade of purple with steam coming out of her ears if she could see Dalal now. Dalal smiled thinking about this image of her mother while she sat quietly, enjoying the easy conversation and joking that went on between Joe and his sister and mom. Easy talking. No watching for words to set anybody off or waiting for a slap to reach across the table.

Joe's dad was away on a business trip in Vancouver, but Joe and Meghan had a video call with him after school. He'd even talked to Dalal through the marvel of technology in a way that her own father would never speak to her in person. He'd asked how her day went at school. She couldn't remember her father ever asking about her school work. Her parents had only spoken of Ghazi having a career. She dreamed of being a nurse, even if she just took the two-year college course and not the university degree as she would have wished. But she knew the time wasn't right to ask them. Her darkest fear was that it would never be the right time.

Dalal tried to store every moment of this visit inside to take out later when she was alone. This was how a real family lived; a family that loved each other and didn't put family honour above everything else. Her own mother was uncompromising about proper behaviour. She would not tolerate daughters who did not bend to her will. She believed in punishing the sinner.

There had been a time when Dalal had bought into it, believing her parents were always right. She'd been horrified when her older sister Nadirah had rebelled against them, staying out at night, taking off her hijab, wearing mascara and blue eye shadow and faded jeans. The fights between Nadirah and their mother had been brutal, until the Saturday night when Nadirah had been beaten with a broom handle. After that, she'd stopped arguing and had done whatever her mother asked of her at home. Yet Dalal knew it was all an act; secretly Nadirah was doing whatever she wanted once out of sight of her family.

Once Dalal had seen Nadirah with a white boy standing outside the 7-Eleven. Nadirah had been laughing and touching his face with her graceful fingertips. Dalal had stopped for a moment, caught between panic and the realization of how beautiful her sister was, her long black hair trailing down her back, her curves outlined in the tight jeans and silky blouse. Her black eyes had glowed with happiness like they never did at home. Dalal had run as fast as she could away from Nadirah and her rebellion, fear for her sister beating inside like a trapped bird. If Ghazi had happened by, Nadirah would have been locked in her room for the rest of the school term.

"I saw you," Dalal had said. "Ghazi will find out and tell. You'll be punished and it will be very bad."

"You worry too much." Nadirah had laughed off Dalal's whispered fears later when they lay on her bed after supper. "I just want to be like other girls. I just want them to stop telling me what to do. This is Canada, not India. Girls are free here. They aren't kept like butterflies in a jar. Someday, you will understand. You'll feel what I feel. I know you have the same questioning heart. Now go do your homework, little Dalal, while I write in my diary. When I tell the pages what I'm thinking, they never tell me that I should stop leading my own life like you and the rest of this family do." Nadirah had smiled to let Dalal know she was teasing her. She knew Dalal would never betray her.

Dalal had lain on her stomach on her own bed, working on her math homework, but she couldn't make the fear in her chest go away. Something terrible was going to happen. Nadirah's recklessness would be found out and *they* would make her pay.

"What are you thinking about?" Joe asked.

Dalal blinked. "Pardon?"

Joe laughed. "I asked you twice if you wanted to shoot some hoops but you didn't answer." He held up a basketball. "We have twenty minutes before my mother has to drive you home."

"I was just ... never mind. We could play twenty-one."

"Best out of three."

"You're on."

Joe hesitated. He looked down at her legs. "You could borrow some of Meghan's jeans if it would be easier. You're close to the same size."

She looked down too at the skirt that ended just above her running shoes. The head scarf was waiting just inside the front door for her to put back on. "I'll be fine," she said. "I'm used to running in this."

The net was screwed into the top of the garage and visible from the street. Dalal checked for Ghazi's car between throws, ready to run into the backyard if she spotted any sign of him. She kept her worry to herself, not wanting to ruin the last of their time together. Ghazi would have thought nothing about dragging her out of the driveway in front of everyone if he knew she was there with a boy.

She tried to shake off the sadness that suddenly filled her. This would be the one and only time she would be allowed to have supper with his family. Even now, a little bead of worry had worked its way into her mind. Why had her parents let her come tonight? Were they up to something and wanted her out of the way? She bent low and grabbed the ball from Joe as he bounced it past her on his way to the net. A quick turn and she threw the ball skyward. It bounced off the garage and dropped with a swoosh through the net.

"Gimme five!" Joe said, holding up his hand.

She slapped his palm.

"Next time you come, we'll get Meghan and Mom out here for a real game."

She turned her eyes away from his smiling ones. "Next time," she said as if she believed there would actually be one.

———

Taiku ran ahead of Kala and disappeared into the tall grass, his tail beating the stalks back and forth like a fan as he went. Kala walked along the side of the road, letting Taiku have free rein. He'd been shut up in the house all day and deserved an unhindered run. It was a cool evening after the stretch of late September heat. Even the shadows were getting longer for this time of day. Kala looked skyward. Soon the geese would be heading south. She would get the urge to leave too, restless for something she could never put her finger on. It was the same every year.

She half expected to meet Gundersund and his dog along the route and was surprised at how disappointed she felt when they didn't appear. The real surprise was that Gundersund was turning out to be good company: quiet for the most part but not because of a lack of intelligence. Like her, he didn't speak to fill in the silence. She was comfortable in his presence. The urge to keep moving and to be alone had ebbed for a little while. Rouleau and his dad were two others who might keep her from heading out as soon as they solved the Sampson murder and the Pankhurst assault, which hopefully wouldn't be upgraded to murder. The latest report had Gail stabilized but still in the coma. Maybe this year the birds heading south wouldn't get her gypsy blood flowing.

"Come, Taiku," Kala called. She held her fingers to her mouth and let out a shrill whistle. She stood stock still and waited. A moment later, he bounded out of a thicket and led the way toward home, stopping and looking at her every so often to make sure she was following.

She'd picked up a prepared curried chicken and rice dish on her way home that she put into the oven. It would have gone nicely with a glass of white wine and she closed her eyes, imagining the taste on her tongue. She wondered if she would be able to reintroduce alcohol into her life. Could she limit herself to one glass, or was she one of those people who couldn't stop once the drinking began? Her self-imposed sobriety surely was proof that she could practise restraint, or was she only deluding herself? The biggest part of her was scared to find out.

She'd just settled down at the kitchen table with a cup of tea when her cellphone rang. She looked at the number before answering.

"Shannon! What a nice surprise."

"I never know when to call you." Shannon's voice travelled across the miles from Northern Ontario. "Are you staying in Kingston?"

"For now. How's everything with you?"

"Good. I have some news though."

"Should I be sitting down?"

"Maybe. We received an alert across the wire about two armed robbers on the run. Nation-wide alert."

Kala felt her stomach drop. "Don't tell me," she said. "Lily."

"Yeah. Her and Gil Valiquette, a recent guest of Millhaven. I thought you should know. She might try to track you down."

"She told me that she'd stopped. Was anyone hurt?"

"They had a few people as hostages but let them go. They were holding up a liquor store. It doesn't look good for her, Kala. Valiquette must have dragged her back into the business."

"How could she be so stupid?" Kala rubbed her forehead. "Any word on Dawn, her daughter?"

"Nothing about a kid in the alert."

"Shit."

"So she hasn't made contact? You're like the only family she has, even if you're not blood relatives."

"She wanted nothing to do with me." Kala thought about Roger at the Birdtail Reserve in Northern Manitoba.

Lily might head there. "I'll keep an eye out but I don't expect to see her."

"Good. Sometimes working at a police station turns out to be worthwhile. I would never have known if I wasn't checking the alerts today."

"Well thanks for letting me know, but I don't think it'll matter to me one way or the other. As I said, we really aren't in each other's lives." Kala heard Shannon cover the receiver and call to someone.

"Gotta go," Shannon said. "I'm hosting book club and the first people just arrived. Talk soon?"

"Yeah, soon."

Kala closed the connection. She sat with her chin cupped in her hand, thinking about what to do. The problem was that if she tracked down Lily and her boyfriend, she might be forced to turn them in. Not only was she sworn to uphold the law, but there was also the girl to think about. Dawn was only twelve years old, still young enough to have a life if someone cared enough to give a damn. She could call Roger and warn him that Lily was likely on her way to him. It wouldn't be much but he might be able to stop her if forewarned.

The oven timer beeped and Kala jumped in her chair. Supper was ready. She looked at the phone and weighed the wisdom of contacting Roger, then stood and dumped her cold tea down the sink. *What was she thinking?* She'd promised herself not to get involved with Lily ever again. Lily didn't want saving, and she had nothing left to give. She felt the teapot with her fingers. It was hot still and there was enough tea for a fresh cup to go with her dinner. She would eat on the verandah and listen to the waves rolling onto the beach at the end of the property. The sky was clear and the stars would be out soon. There'd be enough light for her to take Taiku down to the water for a last run before bed. She'd jog alongside him and wear herself out and hopefully sleep would come quickly so that she could shut out the day.

32

THE DOOR WAS unlocked and the house was silent when Dalal stepped through the back door. Joe's mom had dropped her off in front of the house but no eyes had been watching from behind the living room curtains. Dalal breathed a sigh of relief but the worry was still with her. Just what was her family up to?

Ghazi's car was gone from the driveway but her father's was in its usual spot. Dalal walked to the kitchen but her parents weren't there. Dirty dishes and cooking pots filled the sink and spread across the counter. Her mother had made shrimp biryani by the smell of ginger, garlic, and chilies and the leftover basmati rice, cashews, and raisins in the serving bowl. Trust her to make Dalal's favourite meal the one time she was away for supper. Dalal looked through the kitchen window. They were both sitting in the swing, her father reading the paper and her mother knitting. To anybody else, they would look like a normal family, spending quiet time together and enjoying each other's company.

Dalal opened the door and called to them that she was home. The yell startled her mother. Her surprised look flashed guilt and anger in quick succession, and Dalal felt the worry in her belly growing. Her mother called her to come over. Her father looked up, saw her, and looked back at the paper. Dalal crossed the lawn to stand in front of them.

"Your project is finished?" her mother asked. Her mouth settled back into its familiar scowl.

"Yes. Thank you for letting me go to Meghan's. We'll get a good mark. I am sure of it."

Her father grunted.

"Where are Ghazi and Meeza?" Dalal asked.

"Ghazi is out with his friends." That flash of something odd crossed her mother's face again. "Meeza is in her room. She has the flu and went to bed early. Do not disturb her, whatever you do."

Dalal found both curious. Ghazi didn't have any friends that she knew of. Meeza had been fine that morning when they left for school together.

"I'll go finish my other homework," Dalal said, shifting her knapsack from one shoulder to the other. "If you don't need anything, Mother."

"Clean up the kitchen first," her mother said.

"Yes, Mother."

She didn't make it upstairs until eight o'clock. Meeza's door was shut and Dalal paused before knocking. She put her ear against the wood and heard what sounded like a wounded animal crying inside: a keening wail that made the hairs on her neck stand on end. Dalal walked back to the head of the stairs. Her parents had come inside while she worked in the kitchen. They were watching a show on television and the volume was up high. Her father was going deaf but refused to go to a doctor. Dalal tiptoed back to Meeza's door and turned the handle. *Locked.* It must be locked from the outside. She knocked as loudly as she dared.

"Meeza? Meeza? Are you okay?"

The wailing quieted, but Meeza didn't answer. Dalal waited as long as she safely could before crossing the hall to her own room. She shut the door and felt in her knapsack for Nadirah's diary. It was time to do something. She prayed that she hadn't left it too late.

33

THE TEAM MET in Rouleau's office at eight a.m. the following morning. Vera had let him know on his way in that Heath was expecting a briefing at nine. Chalmers took the seat closest to the door, which Rouleau thought was a symbolic move in light of his pending retirement. Woodhouse and Gundersund sat next to each other and Stonechild picked a spot on the other side of room. They looked tired, or maybe he was projecting his own weariness.

"We need to make another stab at finding something on Della Munroe," Rouleau began, and explained what he'd uncovered with her family in Toronto.

"She's done a good job covering her tracks," Chalmers said. "It's her word against a dead man's. We've got no definitive forensics proof either way, but what we do have points to her innocence."

"Will her sister testify?" Stonechild asked.

"Yes, but it won't be enough." Rouleau looked at her. She'd been eager to tell him something when she first came in, but he'd wanted to get this case out of the way first.

"We could bring Della in and grill her again," Woodhouse said. "Get her to contradict what she told us. She must have tricked Brian into coming by the house and set the whole thing up."

"She sounds like one sick fuck," Chalmers said. He looked across at Stonechild. "Excuse my French," he added.

Rouleau decided to ignore him. "Right, so what have you got on the Sampson murder? Stonechild?" He nodded at her.

"We might be on the wrong track with her too. Turns out she wasn't having an affair, at least not in the front seat of a car. Jucinda Rivera told Wolf that Leah was getting it on in the car without actually seeing her. Jucinda based her story on black hair and a white blouse, but after pressing her she admitted that she didn't believe it was Leah when she told Wolf. Jucinda appears to have wanted Wolf for herself."

"Same outcome though," Chalmers said. "Wolf and everyone believed she was having it on with a married man. The motive's still there."

"Except," Kala said, "that it rules out the lover as a suspect since there wasn't one, and it makes me wonder why Leah let everyone believe she was cheating. From all accounts, she was still in love with Wolf. Doesn't add up."

Chalmers's voice got more forceful. "It adds up. She was cheating with somebody else and thought she'd been caught. She broke it off with the other guy and he got even."

"There's no proof she was," insisted Stonechild. "Plus, why would this phantom lover torture her? What would be the point?" They locked eyes.

Chalmers smiled out of the side of his mouth. "Women are natural-born cheaters. Just ask Gundersund."

The room went quiet. All eyes turned as one toward Gundersund. He looked at Chalmers. "Speaking of sick fucks."

Rouleau stood. "That's enough. Chalmers and Woodhouse, go back and re-interview everyone who knew the Munroes. Gundersund and Stonechild, carry on with your lines of enquiry. I have to fill in Heath."

Rouleau watched them file out and shook his head. Chalmers had offered to stay on a few extra days rather than use up all his vacation. It would have been better if he'd taken the full two weeks before his official retirement kicked in. Maybe with his partner gone, Woodhouse would fall into line. Hopefully a new partner would spark something in Woodhouse. The problem was that now Rouleau had to find Chalmers's replacement. Good recruits weren't exactly lining up at the door. Vera had vetoed all the applicants so far. She was going to have to work some magic.

Rouleau made his nine a.m. meeting with Heath, who looked rested and wind-burned after his fishing trip. He listened to Rouleau's debrief of the two cases without comment. After a suitable pause, he steepled his fingers under his chin and said, "Sounds like you have it all in hand. Would be good to make an arrest for the Sampson murder soon since whoever killed her and beat up Pankhurst appears to be ramping up. The Munroe killing is more contained within the family. I understand you haven't found a house to your liking?"

"Not yet."

"Laney is good. She'll find you something soon, I imagine. Chalmers's party is set for next Friday night. Vera has made all the arrangements. You'll put your cases on hold for a few hours of team-building."

"If nothing else breaks open."

"Granted. Is Stonechild planning to stay on the team?"

"She's considering it. We haven't any potential replacements for Chalmers yet."

"Vera's on the case. She has some new resumés for you." The phone on Heath's desk rang. "Anything else before I take this?"

"Not a thing."

"Good. Be sure to keep me in the loop."

———

"So what was that Chalmers dig about?" Kala asked Woodhouse when she met him in the hallway.

"You don't know?"

"Would I ask if I did?"

"Touché. Gundersund's wife left him to live with another guy. A doctor rolling in dough."

"I saw her at Gundersund's house the other night. They both seemed okay."

"Word is the doctor wised up and dumped her. I'm not surprised she's worming her way back in with Gundersund. He's got this blind spot when it comes to Fiona. She's good looking and all that but none of us can figure it out. The woman's a barracuda in a lab coat. Well, see you later."

"Yeah. Later."

Kala waited in the hall for Gundersund to finish in the washroom. They fell into step on their way outside. She felt uncomfortable walking next to him across the parking lot, knowing that she'd betrayed his privacy. He didn't appear to notice her discomfort since he barely acknowledged her presence. His jaw was set and he wasn't talking. They reached her truck.

"I'll spend the morning at the help line and we can meet at the Merchant for lunch if you like. My turn to buy." She knew it was guilt behind her offer. Maybe a bit of pity thrown in too.

Gundersund looked at her and saw something in her eyes that made him flinch. "Let's leave it open. I'll call when we get done talking to Della's classmates." He'd been given a uniformed sidekick for the morning who'd already started the car.

"Great. Let me know if you find out anything interesting."

———

The only one answering the phones when Kala arrived at the centre twenty minutes later was Mark Withers. She took a seat at the empty desk next to him and waited for him to finish a call. She couldn't help but tune in to his end of the conversation. He was talking a student into going to the hospital to get his depression meds adjusted. After a great deal of coaxing on Mark's part, he hung up the phone and turned to face her. His surfer boy good looks were fraying. She threw him a smile. He looked like he could use it.

"Hard morning?"

"My staff have all been killed, assaulted, or harassed by police. I'm forced to man the line until Nate, the only one left, I might add, shows up at noon. The university is threatening to cut our funding … and, oh yeah, my wife is getting pissed because I'm never home anymore. It's been a bloody hard morning, and month for that matter." He managed a bleak smile. "So what do you need from me today?"

"You seem close to Dino Tadesco."

Mark shifted away from her, a subtle body movement but one that Kala read as resistance to her probing. He wouldn't be telling her the entire truth.

"We hang now and then."

"Did he also *hang* with others on staff? Wolf or Leah?" She hated the word hang. It was so imprecise, it could have meant anything.

"Not so much. He wasn't sleeping with either of them if that's what you're asking." Mark laughed.

"Was he sleeping around on his wife with someone else? A student?"

"I have no idea."

"But you must have insight into his fidelity, or lack thereof, since you spend a lot of time together in bars after work."

Anger flashed across his boyish face, but only for a second. "You people really do check under every rock, don't you? All I know is that we didn't fool around on our wives when we were together and we never discussed doing it. Not every man screws around, Detective."

"So you say."

The phone rang, interrupting what he was about to reply. "Hello?" He turned away from her, but immediately turned back around, his expression puzzled. "Leah Sampson? May I ask how you got her name?"

Kala moved her chair closer. "Man or woman?" she whispered.

Mark covered the receiver with his hand. "Girl, young," he mouthed. He uncovered the receiver. "So, this was how long ago?"

Kala put out her hand. "I'll take it."

Mark covered the receiver again with his hand. "Goes against our rules …"

Kala wriggled her fingers. "I'm overruling your rules. Give it here. Tell her you're handing her over to Leah as requested."

Mark tried to outstare her. He lost. After a few beats he said into the phone, "I'll just pass you over. One moment." He gave Kala the receiver without another word but his angry face spoke volumes.

"How can I help you?" Kala asked, Mark quickly forgotten. As hoped, the girl assumed she was speaking with Leah Sampson. Kala listened closely to the timbre of the speaker's voice. She placed her at about twelve but she could have been older.

"I was told to call you if I needed to reach my sister."

"Can you tell me your name?"

Kala listened to the in and out of the girl's breathing. Finally, a deep inhale of air and, "My sister's name is Nadirah. I need to speak with her."

Nadirah. The name sounded Middle Eastern or Indian. Kala spoke carefully. She couldn't let on that she had no idea who Nadirah was or what her connection had been with Leah Sampson. "I wonder if you and I should meet ... so that I can fill in Nadirah about why you need to reach her. It will help when I arrange for her to contact you."

Another pause.

"Can you tell me your name?" Kala asked softly. "I'd like to help."

"I can't ... not now."

"Are you in school? I could come to you."

"No, not here. Maybe I can meet you someplace. I'll call you back after I check."

"When will you call back?" Kala didn't want to let her go. She felt in her gut that this child was the link to what had happened to Leah.

"I'll know tomorrow. I'll call around this time."

"I'll be waiting for your call tomorrow at this same time," Kala repeated.

Mark jotted something down and turned the paper toward her. She read the words: *Is she in danger?* Kala nodded in his direction.

"Are you safe?" she asked.

The breathing quickened on the other end of the line. "No," the girl's voice was just above a whisper. "We are not safe."

Before Kala could respond, the dial tone hummed in her ear. She hung up the phone and tried to put together what had just happened.

"So?" Mark asked. "Did you get her name?"

Kala pulled herself back from the minefields and focused on his face. She felt the urgency to act, but felt completely helpless. Could she have done something to keep the girl talking? Had she let the opportunity slip away?

"No, she didn't give her name, but Leah must have gotten involved in a situation that got out of control. You said that your staff don't give out their names or make personal contact with callers, correct?"

"You got that right. If they did, they'd be fired. Anonymity on both ends is the foundation of the help line."

"I think Leah might have broken your number one rule. This girl mentioned that her sister's name is Nadirah. Does that ring any bells?"

"Never heard that name before. It's unusual enough that I would have remembered if Leah had mentioned it."

"Leah must have kept whatever she was doing to help this person a secret."

They were both silent. Kala didn't have to spell it out. Whatever Leah had done in secret had probably led to her death.

"Let's hope the kid calls back tomorrow," Mark said. "Hopefully she won't find out in the meantime that Leah Sampson doesn't exist anymore."

34

"NADIRAH IS A Muslim name," Kala said to Gundersund. She scrolled through the list of girls' names on the site. "From India," she added.

Gundersund looked up from his computer. "There can be serious family issues in their communities. Girls aren't regarded the same as boys in some immigrant families from that neck of the world. We had some cultural sensitivity training last year. Bit of an eye opener."

"Do we have any database that would help us to find this family if we did a search of the name Nadirah?"

"Depends on whether Nadirah had a driver's licence or police record. It's still tough without a surname. She might have been a prostitute. That might explain why the little sister doesn't know where she is. I'll run a check."

"Thanks."

"Sure," Gundersund said. "The family could be abusive and the little sister's in trouble now that her sister has taken to the streets."

Kala rubbed her forehead. She smiled as a thought broke through her fatigue. "Nadirah must have been a student at Queen's if she called the help line. I could call records to check."

"I'll get someone on that too," Gundersund said. "You look like you need some lunch." He checked his watch. "It's going on three."

"Maybe that's why I'm feeling light-headed." Kala stood. "Can I get you anything?"

"I ate at one so I'm good, thanks."

"I'll be back in twenty minutes."

She took the stairs to the cafeteria and ordered a roast beef sandwich and a coffee. On second thought, she asked the girl to add a salad. It had been a while since she'd eaten anything green and leafy.

She found a spot out of the way of traffic and sat down to eat. She wanted to take a break from work but the kid's voice on the help line phone that morning was still playing in her brain. It raised disturbing images of Dawn on the run with Lily and her con boyfriend. Two innocent young girls in trouble and all Kala could do was search through databases and spin her wheels. The inaction was driving her crazy. She was chomping to do something to somebody. The feeling that time was slipping away while trouble brewed like a gathering storm was getting tough to shake.

———

Gundersund found Stonechild staring out the window, sipping on the last of her coffee. He stood for a moment just inside the doorway to the cafeteria and watched her unseen. She was deep in thought in the middle of a room filled with chatting officers and clinking dishes, the only one sitting alone. She didn't appear bothered by her solitary lunch. The stillness of her features was Zen-like.

He heard his name and glanced to his left. Fiona was waving to him from the far corner of the room where she sat with some of the forensics team. She wore a blue dress that he'd bought for her the summer before she moved out. It was silky, the top tight and flattering while the skirt fell away from her waist just enough to hint at her curves as she moved. He hadn't seen her wear it all year. Her hair was loose and her lips painted a creamy red. She motioned for him to join them, but he pointed to Stonechild and mouthed the word "working." Fiona's gaze shifted toward Stonechild and her smile evaporated.

He crossed the floor and squeezed past two tables to where Stonechild sat oblivious to his approach. He waited for her to focus in on him.

She blinked. "What are you doing here?" she asked.

"Sorry to interrupt your lunch but we've got to move. Call from the hospital just came in. They've brought Gail Pankhurst back to the land of the living and the doctor says we can speak with her for a few minutes." The relief on Stonechild's face made him smile.

She jumped up. "Let's go. I'll drive."

He glanced over his shoulder at Fiona as he followed Stonechild toward the door. The unguarded look on her face could have turned water into ice. One part of him didn't like to think where her jealousy, no matter how misplaced, could lead. The other part was secretly pleased that she even cared.

—

Dr. Blais warned them that they'd only have a few minutes, if that. "Gail started waking up in the night but we waited until now to call you."

"Has she suffered any brain damage?" Stonechild asked.

"Not that we can tell. The swelling has gone down and she's stable. Barring any setbacks, I expect her to fully recover. She could have headaches and dizziness for some time, but we'll have to wait and see. The recuperative powers of the young are amazing."

"Has she said anything about the attack?" Gundersund asked.

Dr. Blais shifted her tired eyes to his. "No. She might not remember any of the trauma."

He nodded. "That's my fear. I've had other people who survived horrific events blank out chunks of time."

They took places around the bed. Gail was a large mound under the white sheet. Her arm was hooked to an intravenous drip and a machine monitored her vitals. Gundersund thought her Mickey Mouse and Betty Boop tattoos made her look young and vulnerable. Colourful cartoons with her as canvas. She was a girl crying out for attention if he'd ever seen one. "Have any family members been to visit her?" he asked Dr. Blais.

"No. Her mother calls twice a day."

Stonechild shook her head and met his eyes. He could see that they were on the same wavelength.

They'd agreed that Stonechild should ask the questions since Gail had already met her. Gundersund had suggested that his size and gender might frighten the girl after what she'd been through. Dr. Blais picked up one of Gail's hands and rubbed it gently between both of her own. "Gail, you have visitors. Officer Stonechild would like to ask you a few questions if you're up for it." She waited until Gail started coming around before stepping back.

Gail's eyes blinked open. They were faded blue but vivid against the paleness of her skin. She turned her cheek into the pillow where Stonechild stood squarely in her line of vision. "'Kay," she said.

"Gail, do you remember what happened to you?"

"Someone at the door. Wolf. I opened it and then ... I can't remember." Her face contorted as if she was about to cry.

Stonechild touched her shoulder. "It's okay. Nobody can hurt you anymore. We're here to keep you safe. Was it Wolf who was at the door?"

"Waiting for him. Don't know."

"The person who knocked you on the head took your laptop. I understand that you were keeping notes on people. Did you keep any notes on Leah Sampson?"

"My laptop? Experiments. For my thesis."

"And Leah?"

"Yes, Leah."

"Did Leah mention a caller named Nadirah? Think hard, Gail. This is important."

Gundersund watched memories flit across Gail's face as she strained to place the name.

"No. But Leah took long breaks. Left early. Once, gone overnight ... never knew where."

"You recorded all this in your files?"

"Yes."

Dr. Blais held up a finger. They had one more minute.

Stonechild looked at Gundersund. Her eyes asked if he had a question. He nodded to let her know that she was doing fine.

"Did you keep notes on everyone at the help line?"

"Uh huh."

"Did you notice anybody else leaving early?"

It took longer this time for Gail to respond. Gundersund thought they'd lost her to sleep when she said, "Nate. Gone sometimes."

"Thank you, Gail. We'll let you sleep now. You've done great." Stonechild lifted a hand and lay it against Gail's cheek with great tenderness.

Gundersund's breath caught in his throat.

Dr. Blais straightened the sheet around Gail's waist and checked the IV. She motioned toward the hallway and they followed her out.

"I don't expect she'll be awake much the rest of the day," she said. "It could take her a long time to remember what happened."

"An officer will stay with her to make sure she's not targeted again," Gundersund said. "No visitors except family for now."

"If any family come," said Dr. Blais with a sideways smile, "I'll be more than happy to let them see her."

35

DALAL EXPECTED TO see Meeza sitting on the couch watching television when she came home from school, but the living room was silent and empty. Nobody was in the kitchen or the backyard either, not even her mother. She knew that Ghazi was off somewhere doing whatever it was he did after school. She wasn't altogether sure what, but she was relieved to have him out of the house. She climbed the stairs and listened for sounds of her mother. Her parents' bedroom door at the end of the hall was closed, so her mother was likely having an afternoon nap. Meeza's door was also closed.

Dalal silently crossed the carpet and knocked lightly. When Meeza didn't answer, she tried the door knob. The handle turned easily and the door swung open. Dalal stepped inside and closed the door shut behind her. Meeza's bed was made and the window was wide open, a breeze billowing the curtains into the room. Boo and Meeza's two favourite dolls sat on her pillow, their glassy eyes seeing all and seeing nothing. The dolls were well-loved, their hair frizzy and sparse from too many brushings. There was no sign of her little sister.

Dalal left Meeza's room and was near the head of the stairs when she heard the front door open and then slam shut. She froze in place and craned her neck to look over the banister. The top of Meeza's favourite violet-coloured head scarf was directly below. Her mother's shrill voice travelled up the stairwell.

"You go up to your room and don't come out. I don't want you talking to your sister. I've left a suitcase next to the closet. Pack up all your clean clothes. Mr. Khan will be coming for you on the weekend. Now get moving."

"I don't want to go with Mr. Khan," Meeza's voice, a childish whine.

"You stupid, ungrateful girl. He's being very generous taking you off my hands. If we wait much longer, you won't be worth anything."

"But he's mean. He hits me."

"He only hit you because you didn't do as he asked. You will do what he says from now on, do you hear me, Meeza? I will not have you do anything to damage the family's reputation. Mr. Khan will be your husband soon. You will obey him as you obey me."

Dalal stepped away from the stairs and tiptoed to her room. She shut her door before Meeza's heavy footsteps made their way up the stairs to her own room. Her heart beat as if a small bird was trapped inside her chest. *What to do? What to do?* Her eyes searched the bedroom. Tears filled and threatened to overflow. The room turned blurry.

"Dalal!" Her mother screamed up the stairs.

She must have spotted Dalal's shoes by the front door. Dalal dove for her bed, grabbing a book and pencil from her desk on the way by. She had her eyes closed pretending to be asleep with the open book on her stomach when her mother flung open the door.

"Sleeping at this hour of the day. You lazy girl," her mother said, but her eyes darted around the room, more assessing than angry.

Dalal sat up and yawned. "Sorry, Mother. I was studying and must have fallen asleep. Do you need me to make supper?"

"No. You study. I'll make supper tonight." She started to pull the door closed but stopped and said, "Meeza has the flu so we'll let her sleep tonight. Stay away so you don't catch it."

Dalal's heart turned. *How many other lies?* "Okay, Mother. I hope she feels better soon."

Her mother's eyes searched hers and Dalal kept her expression innocent of bad thoughts.

"I'm sure she'll be better soon. With any luck, the rest of us won't catch what she's got." Her mother's lips curved upward in a smile. She backed out of the room, pulling the door closed behind her, but not before Dalal saw the hardness in her black eyes.

After she'd gone, Dalal hugged her legs to her chest and lay one hot cheek against her knee. At the same time, she yanked the elastics from her hair with her right hand and flung them onto the floor. Her hair, freed from its braid, fell around her to her waist. Rage and despair flooded through her. Her mother had talked about Meeza as if she were a bug under her foot.

Dalal sobbed into her pant leg. She'd tried to be the good daughter after Nadirah had abandoned them. She'd swallowed all of the insults and cried away the slaps alone in her room. She'd done everything asked of her, but not anymore. Her mother's smile as she made fun of Meeza had let Dalal finally see the truth. Whatever she did would never make her mother love her or Meeza.

Dalal wiped her tears and breathed in deep gulps of air until she felt calm enough to think. Now was not the time to break. Meeza needed her.

She stood and walked on silent feet to the closet. She wouldn't be able to take many clothes, but that didn't matter. When they found Nadirah, they'd buy new clothes. She caught sight of herself in the mirror above the dresser. She almost didn't recognize the face that looked back at her. Her eyes were huge and blazing, not those of a child any longer. They sparkled with unshed tears. She tightened her lips together in a tight line. The time for crying was over. She would stop letting her family do things to her and Meeza, even if it meant never seeing them again. If Nadirah could find the strength to do it, then so could she.

———

Kala waited until Gail's eyes opened before standing to look down at her. "How're you feeling?"

Gail grimaced before smiling. "Okay. More questions?"

"No. I'm just a visitor this evening. I wanted to make sure you were doing okay, and I brought these." Kala lifted up a vase of daisies and mums.

Gail's eyes brightened. "Nice," she said. Her voice was weak, the words slurring. "Any news …?"

"On who hurt you? No, not yet. We're working on it though, rest assured. Are you thirsty?" Kala picked up the glass of water and directed the straw to Gail's lips. She managed a swallow before her eyes closed again and she drifted back into sleep. The nurse had warned Kala that Gail would fall in and out of consciousness for a while yet.

Kala sat back down and pulled a slim book of poetry from her bag. Dylan Thomas. She didn't understand half of what he was saying, but she loved the beauty of his words. She began reading aloud to the sleeping girl, hoping the sound of her voice would bring comfort. She'd once read that even patients in comas were aware of people talking to them or music playing. At least it gave loved ones the sense that they weren't helpless.

It was peaceful in the room, only one lamp turned on to give her enough light to read by. Kala read several more pages aloud. She lifted her eyes periodically to look at Gail's face turned toward her on the pillow. The girl looked so pale, like a lost child. Kala found the cartoon characters adorning her arms touching in a way that surprised her.

A tap at the door and Kala turned. The uniformed officer Cal was standing just inside.

"I'm back from dinner. Thanks again for spelling me off."

"My pleasure."

He ducked back outside and Kala stood and stretched. She gently squeezed Gail's hand before following him out of the room. Cal had already settled in his chair, drinking coffee and reading the newspaper. He looked up.

"Thanks, Stonechild. It was good to have the chance to eat. You've been her only visitor, by the way, aside from us."

"Yeah, I heard."

"If it was my kid in there, I'd move heaven and earth to be here."

"It can be a sad world."

She carried on down the hall to the elevator and pressed the down button. The bell dinged and the door slid open. Nate stepped out, holding a bouquet of pink roses from the grocery store. His eyes met hers and shifted toward the floor. His personal details flipped through her mind. The good-looking, quiet one, married three years, and Tadesco's Ph.D teaching assistant with a master's in psychology. She watched a bright red work its way up his neck and into his face. Kala let the elevator descend without her. She started walking alongside him toward Gail's room.

"You won't be able to visit, I'm afraid," Kala said.

"I'll just leave the flowers then." His voice was low, defensive.

Nate's discomfort intrigued her. She stood behind him while he gave the bouquet to the nurse on the desk. He straightened his shoulders as if about to face the firing squad before he turned. This time, his eyes held hers without wavering. "I guess we need to talk."

"Let's get a coffee in the cafeteria." She nodded to Cal, who'd stood and was watching them with interest from his post.

She paid for their coffees and they found a table away from the hospital staff lingering over their meals. Nate took his time pouring packets of sugar and plastic containers of cream into his coffee.

Kala waited without comment. She'd had time to guess at what was triggering his guilty conscience. If true, she owed Professor Tadesco an apology.

"This isn't something I'm proud of," he began at last, as if reading her mind. "I wasn't going to say anything until I'd told my wife." He stirred his coffee so hard that it slopped onto the table.

"My job isn't to judge you."

"Yeah, well, you couldn't think any worse of me than I already think of myself. She came into my office a few months ago to discuss a mark I'd given her on her paper. She thought it was too low." He took a slurp of coffee. The red was back, creeping up from his shirt collar. Kala drank from her own cup but stayed silent.

"She shut the door. I remember thinking I should go over and open it. Maybe I had a premonition. Anyhow, I didn't and the next thing I knew, she was on my side of the desk, pulling her shirt over her head. I was looking up at her and she bent over so that her bare breasts were inches from my face. She had my zipper down before I'd recovered from the shock."

"Just to confirm, this is Della Munroe you're talking about?"

"Yeah. *Her.* We got it on a few times in my office, but I kept thinking somebody was going to walk in and I told her it had to stop. We met once in a washroom. I realized the insanity of what we were doing and ended it after that. Plus, I could hardly live with the guilt afterwards."

"Did you try it in a car?"

"No. That wasn't me."

"You're sure?"

"I would have remembered."

Kala had been willing to bet that Della was the mystery woman in the car now that Leah was vindicated. Had she guessed wrong? "I understand how you might have been blindsided the first time, but why the other times?"

The corner of Nate's mouth rose in a half smile. "I'd like to bedazzle you with psychological insight, but it was just my dick overriding my brain." He groaned. "She knew how to work it."

With effort, Kala kept her eyes on his face and no lower. She cleared her throat. "Did Della ever mention her husband Brian?"

"Not really. I got the impression she was getting ready to leave him though."

"What makes you say that?"

"Just that when I told her it wasn't going to work, she said no problem. She wasn't going to be around much longer."

"She said that?"

"She was mad. I don't think she meant to say it."

"So, when you heard that she killed her husband, what did you think?"

Nate rubbed his forehead. "I didn't know what to think. My first thought was that he was a first-rate asshole and that's why she was fooling around with me."

"You don't sound convinced."

"Della Munroe seduced me to get a better mark on her paper. I have no doubt about that now. I accept that I screwed up big time and could lose my job if this comes out. Right now, all I care about is fixing my marriage."

"This might not have to come out."

"I don't want my wife embarrassed. She just told me she's pregnant." Nate's face crumpled and he covered his eyes. "Christ, I've been an idiot."

Kala knew exactly what he was speaking about. She'd been the other woman not so long ago. The difference was that she'd really loved the man. She'd left town to give him a chance to fix his marriage.

"You can make it work," she said, "if you both want to."

"Maybe. I've done a lot of damage."

"I have another question about Gail's files on her co-workers. You read them and gave Gundersund what you remembered. I read your notes back at the station and found the details a bit skimpy."

"That's because I skimmed her files. They weren't exactly scintillating."

"Can you remember any more details about her file on Leah Sampson?"

He pondered for a moment. "Gail recorded every tidbit of information she knew, right down to favourite foods and what we did in our time off. Boring stuff. She also liked to lance grenades and see how people reacted."

"Grenades?"

"She'd toss out something outrageous and hurtful, then wait to see how we reacted. We all knew she was doing it. For instance, Gail might say to Leah that she saw Wolf in the bar talking to another woman. Then she'd record Leah's reaction. Childish."

"She made up lies?"

"More like fibs. The others used to have a laugh about it when she wasn't around."

"Did she write anything about Leah and Wolf's relationship?"

"I skipped over most of what Gail wrote about them because it felt, I don't know, sick having them under Gail's microscope. I remember she wrote about them coming from Brockville. There was nothing about Leah cheating on him though. And nothing about me with Della. I had to be sure."

Kala thought for a moment. "Did Gail record anything unusual about Leah and any of the callers in the last month before she died?"

"Like a stalker?"

"Maybe, or anybody giving her trouble over the phone, no matter how minor."

"Not that she ever said. A caller wouldn't have known anything to identify Leah by anyway because she wouldn't have shared any personal information. We're not allowed to give them our name or to ask them theirs. If we think we know the caller on the other end, we're supposed to give their call to our partner and erase it from our memory bank."

"That's what I've heard."

And I'd buy it if it weren't for the fact that one scared little girl who's desperate to find her sister knows Leah Sampson by name.

36

"DAD, BREAKFAST IS ready." Rouleau finished scraping the scrambled eggs onto two plates and grabbed the bread from the toaster. While he waited for his father to exit his bedroom, Rouleau poured two cups of coffee and took the lot over to the table. He looked down the hallway toward his father's closed door. "Dad?"

"Coming, son. Get started without me." His dad's voice came out muffled through the door.

"Okay, but your eggs are getting cold."

Rouleau took a seat and began eating. As he sipped Colombian coffee, he watched the rain beating against the patio door. The wind was rattling the glass in gusty bursts. It would have been a good day to stay in and watch a couple of movies, if only he had the luxury. Instead he'd be spending the morning in meetings with a hurried house viewing scheduled during lunch. Laney Masterson had set up a showing at a place off Montreal Road in a newer subdivision. He was looking forward to seeing her as much as the possibility of finally finding his own place.

He finished his coffee and got up to get a second. He was at the counter pouring one more for the road when he heard his father's bedroom door open. Rouleau glanced at the clock above the stove. He could spare a few more minutes. His dad's crutches were slowly clumping their way down the hall.

"Pretty ugly out there today," Rouleau said. "You planning to go into the office?" He lowered his cup onto the counter at the sight of his father. "Is something wrong, Dad?

His father had manoeuvred himself into the chair by the time Rouleau reached him. His face under uncombed hair was as pale as linen. He'd put on a sweatshirt but left on his pajama bottoms, an uncharacteristic attire. Rouleau didn't know what was more alarming: his father's skin colour or his dishevelled appearance.

"I'm fine. I thought you had to get to work early this morning."

"Work can wait. What's going on, Dad?"

His father reached for the fork Rouleau had set beside his plate. His fingers were trembling so much that he left it and dropped his hand into his lap. "The nurse is coming later. I'll be fine."

Rouleau knew his dad's gruff voice was meant to close down the discussion. It heightened his alarm.

"You're white as a ghost, Dad. Are you in pain?"

"Nothing I can't handle."

"You should go to the clinic. I'll postpone my morning meeting and take you in."

"You'll do no such thing. I'm not going back to that place."

"I'm not giving you a choice." Rouleau pulled out his cellphone. "Should I call an ambulance or are you going to let me take you to get checked out?"

"You don't have time for this. I can take a cab."

"I'm taking you, Dad, *point finale*. See if you can manage a few bites of toast while I get your raincoat."

Rouleau hit Vera's number on speed dial. He'd be working by phone for the morning at least. If he wasn't already fully aware, this was his new reality of being the only child of an aging parent.

———

Gundersund hung up the phone. "That was Vera. Rouleau won't be in this morning. He's taking his father to a doctor. We're to carry on and call him if something breaks."

He looked across at Stonechild, leaning against a filing cabinet and drinking a cup of Tim Hortons coffee that she'd picked up on the way into the station. Her hair hung in damp strands around her face. Her skin looked drawn and tired. She'd come in later than usual and said she'd slept in.

"Rough night?" he asked.

"Just trouble sleeping, that is until it was time to get up. Then I could have slept for hours."

"So what have you got on the burner today?"

"I'm planning to read through the files on the Munroe case again. Nate from the help line dropped by the hospital last night and we had a heart to heart. Turns out he was having sex with the one and only Della Munroe."

It took Gundersund a second to absorb what she'd said. "He admitted to that?"

"He did. I was hoping to run it by Rouleau this morning. He's closer to this case than I am and might be able to put some of the pieces together."

Gundersund started thinking out loud. "So Leah Sampson wasn't killed by the 'other man' because there wasn't one. However, Wolf didn't know that so he isn't in the clear yet. On the Munroe case, we now find out that

Della isn't the innocent she let on. These two cases are starting to intersect all over the place."

"I know. I'm not sure what the connections mean yet, but Della has uncomfortably entered the world of the help line through an affair with Nate and classes with Tadesco."

"Means absolutely nothing," said Woodhouse. He was sitting at his desk and leaned back in his chair. He crossed his hands over the paunch straining his shirt buttons. "I still say that Sampson's boyfriend killed her. Della Munroe is just a red herring."

Gundersund looked across at Stonechild. She was watching Woodhouse as if he was from another planet. Gundersund smiled. "What makes you think that?" he asked Woodhouse.

"Wolf was the last one to see Leah alive. They had a volatile relationship and he was jealous she was moving on. Whether she was banging somebody else or not, doesn't matter because he *believed* she was. Could be this Nate guy was banging Sampson too. Wolf found out, went into a rage, and killed her."

Gundersund looked from Woodhouse to Stonechild. Her eyes were an unfathomable black that he could have sworn glittered with disbelief.

"You've just put on a stunning display of mental gymnastics," she said to Woodhouse, "connecting all those dots." Her voice was deadpan.

The smile dropped from his face. "And I suppose you have a better idea?"

"It just so happens I do."

The phone rang on Woodhouse's desk, and he broke his stare. He picked it up and turned his back on them in one fluid movement.

Gundersund crossed over to Stonechild. "And what is your new line of thinking?" Unlike Woodhouse, he'd already learned that she never offered an idle opinion.

She glanced at him and then back down at her coffee cup. "I think this has something to do with the little girl who called in. I'm heading back to the help line in the hopes that she calls back like she promised."

"There you are! Together as always."

They both turned. Fiona was walking toward them, carrying a brown paper bag and a tray with two coffees. Her smile took in both of them before she focused her eyes on Gundersund. She was wearing a tight black dress with her hair tumbling around her shoulders in layered waves. Gundersund's eyes widened at the sight of her. She looked stunning, the new dress a not-so-subtle seduction ploy. Perhaps a few months ago he would have jumped at what she was offering, but something in him hesitated. She knew him so well that she believed he could be lured back by sex. The sad thing was, she was probably right if their past history bore out.

She walked her fingers down his arm. "Sorry to interrupt, but I know you never eat breakfast and I couldn't resist treating you. I thought you could come downstairs and go over the tox report on Brian Munroe in my office. It just came in."

"Do you have time to hear the results?" he asked Stonechild. If he thought she would save him from a private viewing with his wife, he was mistaken.

"You go ahead," Stonechild said. "I'll be heading over to the university."

He nodded at Fiona. "Let's go then." He turned to Stonechild. "Call me if something happens and I'll be on standby."

Stonechild nodded but he could tell she had no intention of following through.

Woodhouse hung up the phone and groaned. "That was Rouleau. I'm to take up surveillance on Della Munroe. Just how I want to spend my day."

"Where's Chalmers?" Gundersund asked.

"Using up some of his holidays. This won't take two of us anyhow. A monkey could sit in a car all day, watching a house."

Stonechild met Gundersund's eyes and smiled. "Too easy," she mouthed.

He smiled back, all the time wondering why he felt more in sync with his new partner than his wife. "Check in later," he said.

"Will do."

This time he thought she might actually mean it. He followed Fiona's trail of expensive perfume out of the office, feeling like a bass with a lure caught in its mouth.

37

THE AFTERNOON SPED by without a break. Kala checked in with Gundersund at five o'clock.

"The girl didn't call back," she said. The disappointment she heard in her own voice was nothing compared to what she was feeling. The young girl knew something that could lead to Leah Sampson's murderer, Kala was sure of it. "I'll see you tomorrow." She hung up and grabbed her jacket from the back of the chair.

Mark Withers looked up from the other desk. "If the girl calls when you're not here, whoever's on the line will give her your cell number."

"Thanks. There's always an outside chance. I'll keep my cell close by."

She covered her head with a newspaper and dodged puddles on her run into the restaurant to pick up a roast chicken sandwich, maple doughnut, and coffee on the way back to the station. She hadn't bothered to tell Gundersund that she'd be returning to finish going over the Munroe file on her own time. Something niggled at the back of her memory bank and she wanted to be certain that she'd absorbed everything so that she could put her mind at ease.

By the time she pulled into the station parking lot, the rain was picking up, slanting into the windshield by the force of the wind. She rooted around in the passenger seat for a sweater that she tucked under her shirt as she dashed for the entrance.

The office was empty and cool without any warm bodies to counter the air conditioning. Cold rain had chilled her and she slipped out of her shirt and put on the pullover. She'd have to suffer through with wet jeans. The suddenness of the change from the heat of a week before was startling. Autumn was just around the corner and the heat in the building would need to be turned on soon. It was a depressing thought. Still, they should have a few more weeks of warmer temperatures in October.

She settled in at her desk and hungrily polished off her supper before accessing the database where the reports were housed. She licked the last of the maple sugar sweetness from her fingers while the latest forensics report loaded onto the screen. She scanned the results before leaning in to give it a thorough read. Brian Munroe hadn't been on any drugs or consumed alcohol before he broke into the marital home. No earth-shattering findings that would warrant Fiona waylaying Gundersund for a morning meeting. She had to admit that he hadn't seemed to mind though.

Kala sipped on the coffee, which was now lukewarm, but the caffeine would keep her alert enough to wade through the documents. Reading files on a computer screen was tiring at the best of times. She much preferred reading from paper with her feet up.

She downloaded the photos from the crime scene. Brian had been struck from behind when he reached the top of the stairs. He was face down, his feet closer to the first bedroom doorway than the stairs. It was the bedroom where their son slept. Blood darkened his hair and stained the beige carpet. The force of the hammer striking his head had sent blood spraying onto the walls. She scrolled to the close up. The wound was devastating, caving in part of his skull like a smashed watermelon. Della must have heard the crack as his skull fractured and felt his warm blood strike her face and hands. She'd stepped around him to get their son from his bed. Even under duress, how had she seriously believed he was still alive and able to come after her?

Only Della's handprints were found on the hammer, which she claimed to have been using to hang a mirror at the bottom of the stairs. Photos of the mirror and packaging bore this out. Della had claimed that she'd reacted spontaneously with no intent to kill him. Brian had broken in to take their son. Kala studied the photos of the broken window in the back door. Shards of glass had fallen inside the kitchen, also confirming that the glass had been broken from the outside.

She searched for photos of Della but none were on file. A note said that her clothing was taken away for processing but it was still in the queue. Kala read through the statements and interviews. Nothing popped out.

She leaned back in the chair and stretched, then ran her fingers through her tangled hair. It was almost dry. Flipping over her wrist, she saw by her watch that it was nearly nine o'clock. She'd do one last check of her emails before heading home to take Taiku for a quick walk if the rain had let up at all.

A new email message dinged in her mailbox. Kala clicked it open. Vera was burning the late-night oil too. She wanted the entire team to know that Rouleau would be off the next day as well. He was available by phone if anything urgent came up. Kala cursed at emails that gave no explanations. She idly scrolled down and clicked on the message from the university registrar that confirmed Della Munroe was enrolled in Tadesco's class. Kala had been rushed when it arrived and hadn't opened the attachment. She did so now.

The entire class list filled the screen. Kala skimmed it. Thirty-two students: twenty-seven women and five men. She half hoped to find the name Nadirah but there was only one Muslim name and it looked to be a male — Ghazi Shahan. Finding Nadirah this way would have been too easy, she supposed. The world didn't work that way.

She gave one last look to the list before shutting down the computer for the night. It had been another disappointing day, spinning her wheels. Hopefully something would break tomorrow. Hopefully the girl would call.

38

GHAZI CAME INTO my room again last night. I was nearly asleep when he climbed into bed and covered my mouth with his hand. I could feel his erection through my nightgown. He rubbed up against me like he was a dog in heat while he called me filthy names like "cunt" and "whore." I jerked him off without a fight this time. It was just easier and way less painful than getting pinched and punched. I threatened to tell Mother last Saturday when he forced me to go down on him, but Ghazi said I'd regret it big time. I'm not even certain that she doesn't know. Her golden boy blinds her to all else. I hate him!!! At least he's careful not to "damage" me for my future husband. Big joke.

Ghazi said that he's going to pick me up tomorrow to go to his class and take notes for him like I did last week. He called me his slave and said from now on I have to do whatever he wants. He's met someone and they're planning to screw like dogs somewhere

private — his words, not mine. It would be
nice if he gives it all to her and leaves me
alone. I can't let on that I like going to his
class. This is as close to a university education
as I'll ever get. I wish I was a bird and could
just fly away from here. My only regret would
be leaving Dalal and Meeza.

A noise in the hallway. Dalal tucked the diary under her
mattress and listened. Her parents were downstairs watching television and Ghazi was still out, as far as she knew. He
never came home early anymore. She'd heard her mother
scolding him for missing supper so often. Tonight she'd
eaten a silent meal with her mother and father, Meeza still
"sick" in her room and Ghazi out, doing whatever it was
he did after class. Maybe he was with this woman Nadirah
talked about in her diary.

Dalal pulled the book out from its hiding place and
turned to the page she'd meant to read all along.

I finally called the number on the bulletin
board that I saw at the entrance to the building. "Queen's Help Line: Anonymous help
a phone call away," or that's what the poster
said. I hung up the first time someone answered. It took me two more tries before I
spoke to a woman. I didn't have to give my
name and she said she couldn't read my phone
number. It wouldn't have mattered anyhow. I
used a payphone. Thankfully Ghazi was late
picking me up because it all came spilling out
like this anonymous woman had turned on
a tap inside me. It felt good to tell somebody

what is going on in our family. Probably stupid. She gasped when I spoke about Ghazi like
she had a hard time believing me at first. Then
she told me that I should speak with someone
about it who could help me, like the police.
Another big joke. Ghazi just wrote the exam
to become a cop. He passed and is scheduled
for a physical. If they take my brother, what
other animals do they take? I said I'd think
about it and hung up just before Ghazi sa-
shayed through the front door like king shit.
I hate the sight of him.

Dalal rolled onto her back and dropped the diary onto
her chest, folding her hands across the cover. She could
almost recite the last section by heart. Every time she
read the part where Nadirah recognized the voice of the
woman on the help line ask a question in the psychology
class, Dalal rejoiced along with her. *Leah*. Such a pretty
name. Nadirah had followed her from class and worked
up the nerve to talk to her. This girl Leah had said she
couldn't help at first. But Nadirah called her again at the
help line and Leah had finally changed her mind. They'd
met secretly a few times at the Sunshine Bakery, not far
from campus but far enough to be away from prying eyes.
They'd been careful though. They sat at different tables
and pretended not to know each other when customers
came into the shop.

They'd come up with a plan. And now Leah Sampson
would bring them to Nadirah.

Dalal heard her mother's footsteps heavy on the stairs
and stuffed the book under her pillow before the door
opened. She didn't question her mother's sixth sense

when it came to sniffing out lying. Her mother was always suspicious. If only she knew that this time it was with reason.

"I'm going to have my bath now and then am going to bed," her mother said, her eyes darting around the room and back to Dalal's face. "It's been a long day and I'm tired." Under her arm, she held her silk pajamas and faded flower robe with the big pockets.

"Can I see Meeza?" Dalal asked. She knew her mother would wonder if she didn't ask. "I'm worried. She hasn't even left her room to go to the bathroom."

"Your sister's fine. I have a pot in her room for that."

"Yuck."

"She's too weak to make it to the toilet. A few more days and she won't be infectious."

"Maybe she should see a doctor."

"Meeza has a virus, nothing more. Her temperature has come down and the fever has broken. I'm checking on her now. You can see her when she's better."

Her mother pulled the door closed. Dalal jumped from the bed and listened with her ear against the door. She heard the key scrape in the lock to Meeza's room and then the rise and fall of her sister's voice, pleading to be let out. Her mother's voice rose in an angry hiss before the door to Meeza's room slammed shut.

—

Dalal had racked her brain for two days, trying to figure out how to get Meeza out of her room without anyone knowing. Without fail, her mother had locked Meeza in after every visit and kept the key with her at all times. She never left the house. Meeza would be turned over to Mr.

Khan on the weekend and escape was getting more and more hopeless.

Just before eleven o'clock Dalal heard her father climb the stairs and enter her parents' bedroom. She crept across the floor to her bedroom door and opened it a crack. The bedsprings creaked when he lay down next to her mother. She listened to him toss and turn for a full five minutes before he got comfortable and silence spread down the hallway to Dalal's sentry post.

She looked toward Ghazi's room. A light was on under his door. He'd come home around ten and talked to her father before going into his room. The music was beating through the wall so the chance of him hearing her walk across the carpet was slim. For practice, Dalal walked as silently as she could in bare feet to the bathroom to brush her teeth while she worked up the nerve to slip into her parents' room to find the key. The thought of what her mother would do to her if she caught her sent a long shiver down the length of her back.

The bathroom smelled of rosewater from her mother's recent soak in the tub. Dalal brushed her teeth and placed her toothbrush back in the holder. She swung the door shut with her foot to sit on the toilet while she bought herself some time. Lifting her skirt, she sat on the toilet seat and rested her elbows on her thighs with her chin resting on her bent fingers. She finished peeing and looked up. Her eyes widened. She froze at the possibility hanging before her on the back of the door.

Her mother's flowered housecoat.

She took a moment to still her heart and suck in her breath. *Please, please, please.* She lowered her skirt and washed her hands. Gently, gently, she crossed to the door. Her right hand reached into the first pocket and her fingertips searched. *Nothing.* She held her breath and regrouped. Her hand snaked into the remaining pocket. This time her hand brushed against a hard object and victoriously wrapped around the key to Meeza's room.

Dalal scooted back to her room and shut the door. Her knapsack was packed in the closet and she grabbed it and retrieved Nadirah's diary from under her pillow. She ran across the room and searched her desk for anything she'd missed that might come in handy. She stashed away her comb and some loose change from the top drawer and raced over to the door to her room.

Slow down, she ordered herself with her hand on the doorknob. *Don't blow this chance.* She leaned an ear against the door and listened. Ghazi had turned off his music and was either going to sleep or waiting for her to make a move. The question was, which? She crouched on the floor and opened her door a crack. The light was off under his door. Was he watching and listening in the dark like her? Well, she would outwait him.

Dalal rested against the wall in the shadows and checked her watch. Ten minutes, twenty minutes, half an hour, crept by. She dozed. The night's silence drew her in like ether and she fell into a deep, dark slumber. The minutes, then hours ticked by.

When her eyes snapped open, the room had lightened slightly and a tidal wave of terror rushed through her. She grabbed the knapsack from the floor and scrambled to her feet. The time for caution was long past. She stepped into the hall and made it across the landing to Meeza's door. As silently as she could, she jiggled the key in the lock until the tumbler clicked. She didn't even chance a look down the hallway. She closed the door after her and found her way to Meeza's bedside. Her sister was curled into herself under the covers, her face troubled even in sleep. Dalal clasped one hand over Meeza's mouth and shook her shoulder until her eyes opened as wide as silver dollars.

"It's me, Meeza. I've come to take you out of here. Will you come with me? You'll have to be quiet as a mouse."

At Meeza's nodding head, Dalal released her hand from her mouth. The emptiness in Meeza's eyes frightened her and she rubbed Meeza's cheek gently with the back of her knuckles. "Where's your bag?" Dalal stared with dismay at the luggage near the closet. "Put on your skirt and a T-shirt. We'll buy you some clothes when we find Nadirah. You can bring Boo."

Meeza nodded again and got out of bed. She crossed to the suitcase and took out the clothes on top. Dalal helped her change before handing Meeza her teddy bear. Meeza clasped him close under one arm with her hand near her face. She put her thumb into her mouth and took Dalal's hand with her other. She hadn't said a word the entire time.

They made it down the stairs and outside just as the grandfather clock in the living room struck five o'clock. They had a few hours to make their escape before their mother would notice them gone. Dalal knew a place where they could hide until she felt safe enough to call for help.

39

WOLF GOT TO the help line just after Mark. He'd decided that he might as well give Mark a few hours while he waited for the okay from the police to leave town. Answering calls might take his mind off the drunken black hole he'd wallowed in since Leah died. It was past time he pulled himself together.

"Thanks for coming in, man," Mark said. His hair was pulled back in a ponytail and he wore tan khakis and a white shirt. "I'm interviewing people today and wasn't sure how I was going to swing it."

"Yeah, no problem."

Wolf steered away from Leah's chair and sat at Jucinda's desk.

"Java?" Mark lifted the coffeepot skyward and Wolf nodded. Another cup might chase away the beer fog.

"Been to see Gail?" Wolf asked, taking the mug from Mark.

Mark leaned against the desk and sipped on his coffee before answering. "Nate went over with some flowers but didn't get in. They have a cop on the door. Family only, or at least it was when he went. You?"

"Thinking about it. I was kind of waiting until they don't think I was the one who beat her up."

"I hear you, man, but none of us seriously thinks you did it. The cops'll come around. That Stonechild's been hanging here a lot. I expect she'll be back soon."

"Great."

Wolf took a few calls but the line was quieter than usual. He thought word had gotten around that the place was jinxed.

Mark exited his office at ten. "I'm just heading to the deli for a sandwich. Want anything?"

Wolf looked up from the *Psychology Today* magazine he was flipping through. "No thanks. I'll grab something when Nate shows up at two."

"Good enough."

After Mark had been gone twenty minutes, Wolf took a chance and went to the washroom. The phone was ringing when he got back and he dashed across the room. He picked it up and was relieved not to hear a dial tone.

"Help line," he said, catching his breath. "What can I do for you?"

"I have to speak to Leah Sampson."

The voice was a girl's, older than twelve, but not by much. Wolf lowered himself onto the chair, gripping tightly onto the receiver. "Did Leah give you her name?"

"Nadirah."

"Excuse me?"

"My sister, Nadirah, gave me her name. Can I speak to Leah, please?"

"Are Nadirah and Leah friends?"

There was silence on the other end of the line and Wolf feared he'd lost her. He had to keep talking. "I'm Leah's boyfriend. She's not here today, but she asked me to look after her callers. Can I help you with anything?" He leaned onto his knees and strained to understand what this caller asking for Leah could mean. How could this girl know her name? Was this part of the puzzle that had led to Leah's murder?

"We need to find Nadirah. Leah knows where she is. Nadirah said if we were in trouble to call Leah at this number."

"Leah knows where she is." He echoed her words, giving non-judgmental, positive reinforcement as trained. He had no idea what he was wading into.

"Can you come get us?" Her voice wavered. The fear was stark.

"Of course I can. Where are you?" He spoke gently, keeping the urgency from his voice.

She'd covered the mouthpiece and he heard her talking to someone. She released her hand. "We're at the Frontenac Mall. Near the Harvey's." More talking to someone and then her voice, stronger. "What's your name?"

"Wolf. They call me Wolf. I'm tall with dark brown hair and a beard. I'm wearing blue jeans and a white shirt with red flowers embroidered under the collar." Silence again. He needed to convince her. "Leah would want me to help you. She'd want to make sure you're safe."

The long silence again before the girl said at last, "Please come."

"I don't know your name. How will I know who you are?"

"You don't need to know. We'll find you."

The phone went dead in his hand. He leaped up and started toward the door before remembering he was alone. "Damn!" He returned to the desk while hitting Mark's number on his cellphone. The phone went directly to voice mail. "Have to leave, Mark. An emergency. Get back right away."

He snapped the phone shut and found a pen and paper to leave Mark a note as added insurance. The guy was due back any minute and the place would be safe until then. The phones had been quiet and hopefully nobody needing help would call in the next ten minutes. If Mark made a stink later, Wolf would deal with it.

———

Kala waited at the top of the crest of land for Taiku. He'd run the length of the beach and swum in the lake but disappeared into the underbrush when he realized they were heading back to the cottage. It was his old trick to gain time outside. Kala couldn't blame him. She'd been putting in long days and he'd been shut up alone in a stranger's house. She checked her watch. Twenty more minutes wouldn't hurt anything.

She found a lichen-encrusted slab of rock and sat down to wait. A white mist hung over the water. Gulls circled overhead, their shrill call breaking the morning silence. The breeze had died down and the lake was still. She couldn't see much past the shoreline and felt alone and cocooned in a foggy netherworld. Her navy pullover was enough to keep the chill out once she tightened the hood over her head and tucked her hands into the pockets. She closed her eyes and cleared her mind, letting the morning peace seep into her being.

Taiku finally darted out of the bush just as she thought it was time to go in search. He stood in front of her with tongue hanging to one side of his mouth and tail down. A leaf and twig had entangled themselves in his fur.

"Got that out of your system, then?" she asked. She called him to come and knelt down to remove the debris.

She slung an arm around his neck. "When these cases are over, I promise we'll go on a canoe trip. We've both earned one."

Back in the house, she fed him and went upstairs to change for work. Her cellphone rang as she finished braiding her hair. She checked the number before answering.

"Roger?"

"Hey, Kala. Good to hear your voice. I guess you know why I'm calling."

"Lily?"

"Yup. She showed up here at Birdtail with that con Gil Valiquette she's hooked up with and her daughter Dawn, oh 'bout twenty-four hours ago. I tried to talk her into going to the cops, but she wasn't having any of it. She always was more bull-headed than was good for her."

"It's not really any of my business, Roger. Lily made that clear when she took off without leaving a forwarding address." Kala didn't quite succeed in keeping the bitterness from her voice.

Roger was silent for a moment before saying, "I could talk your ear off about why that girl runs away from people who care about her. You of all people oughta know. She's in trouble and she's dragging that girl Dawn down with her."

Kala considered what he said. His concern overrode her resolve not to get involved. "What do you want me to do? Are they still there with you?"

"Nah, they headed west to Calgary before light. They were gone when I woke up. I was scared to call you with Valiquette watching me the entire time they were here. I was hoping you had some contacts who might intervene, you know, unofficially. The guy she's with is a first-class loser and I'd like to see him locked up. She's scared of him."

"She said that?"

"No, but I could tell from the way he spoke to her that there's a problem. She kept trying to keep Dawn away from him. The man is trouble through and through."

"They robbed a liquor store with a gun, Roger. They took hostages, which raises this crime into another category altogether. I got a call a few days ago."

"Shit. I knew it had to be something like that. He's behind it, Kala. Lily wouldn't do anything like that. Not with Dawn to look after. I know Lily's been trying to turn her life around, but this guy is pulling her back down. Can you help?"

"I'm not promising anything, but I can try. She'll still be charged once the police catch up with them, but the court will have to look at her entire history. That should count in her favour, having such a lousy childhood and all." *And they'd never find out the half.*

"Well, that's all I can ask. If she calls, I'll let her know you're working things from your end. Maybe if she sees a way out ..."

"You can give her my cell number. I'll do what I can."

"Thanks, kid. And how about you? Doing okay down there in Kingston?"

"Yeah. I'm doing okay. Not sure if I'm going to stay here into the winter, but I'm working on a few cases for Rouleau and will see them through. Speaking of which, I'd better get a move on."

"Well, talk to you soon, then. Let me know if you hear anything from Lily."

"Take care, Roger."

Kala leaned against the doorframe and looked out the kitchen window without seeing anything. She felt an urgency to drop everything here and go rescue Lily and Dawn from this man who had Lily under his thumb. If only she hadn't gotten so deeply involved in the Leah Sampson murder case. The best she could do now was to call Shannon in the Dryden OPP office and get her to use her contacts in Calgary to help out. Shannon had cop friends in every city and most towns across the country. The important next step would be to get Lily and Dawn away from this guy.

Kala slammed the palm of her hand against the wall. "Damn. Damn. Damn, Lily. Why do you keep messing up?"

She pulled her cell out of her pocket and opened the address book to find Shannon's number. She tried to ignore the flicker of hope that she'd be reunited with Lily and Dawn when this was over. That was a road that would likely lead to more heartache. Still, knowing that Lily might have had little choice but to leave Ottawa without saying goodbye meant she could have misread the situation.

That could count for something.

—

Kala found a parking spot across the street from the University Help Line. It was later than she'd meant, but she comforted herself with the knowledge that Mark Withers was going to have the girl call her cellphone if she decided to make contact. Kala had to concede that the odds of a call were diminishing with every day that passed.

She got out of the truck and locked the door. Two cars passed by before she was able to dash across the road. She reached the sidewalk when the help line front door burst open. Wolf was halfway down the stairs before he saw her.

"I'm glad you're here," he said. "I got a call from some kid who was asking for Leah and I'm on my way to meet her."

"I've been waiting for her to call again. Didn't Mark tell you?"

"No. He must have forgotten. I'm off to meet her now at the food court in the Frontenac Mall, although it sounds like she's got somebody else with her."

Kala waved him off. "Thanks for the information, but you can stand down. I'll be going alone." She turned and took a step away from him.

"You need me," Wolf yelled above the rumble of a passing truck.

"Excuse me?" Kala half turned and squinted up at him. The angle of the sun hurt her eyes as she tried to make out his features through beams of light.

"She's expecting to see a man of my description. She sounded jumpy and I doubt she'll show herself except to me."

Kala hesitated. This kid was scared and could run. Wolf moved down two steps closer.

"You need me," he said again. "Admit it. You can't make contact alone."

It was crazy to bring along a civilian, who was still considered a murder suspect. Things could turn ugly real fast. Still, her options weren't all that plentiful and time was ticking. There was only one choice really.

"We'll take my truck," she said, scowling up at him. She turned her back and began walking. "Get a move on," she tossed over her shoulder. "I don't want them bolting before we get there."

40

FOR THE SECOND straight day, Zach Woodhouse parked his car a few doors down from the Munroe driveway just after seven a.m. He had a clear view of the house but wasn't in direct view if Della looked out the window. The day before, a couple of times, he'd seen her standing in the living room, arms crossed and looking out. A mom and little girl came midmorning and drove away with the Munroe kid but had him back before lunchtime. Della hadn't left the house.

Woodhouse organized his Thermos of coffee, large bottle of coke, three peanut butter sandwiches, two Coffee Crisps, and two packs of chips on the seat and hunkered down. It was going to be a sunny, warm day once the morning chill burned off. Thank Christ for small mercies. The windshield and windows were tinted so he was barely visible from the outside. He'd brought binoculars and took a few seconds to scan the Munroe yard and windows. All quiet on the western front. Not a creature was stirring.

Damn that old dog Chalmers for bailing again today, although Woodhouse had to admit he'd have done the same that close to retirement. If Chalmers was here with him now, he'd have the seat back and would be sawing logs. They'd go for a long liquid lunch around noon and claim overtime.

The report would be fabricated accordingly. Woodhouse hated to think about the changes that were sure to happen with Chalmers gone.

He shifted the seat back to give himself more room to stretch out his legs. He ate one of the sandwiches and polished off the coffee. Some of her neighbours left for work or school. It wasn't the best end of town, but safe enough during the day. A few blocks over on Princess Street you could get yourself tattooed and pierced before going for a drink in a scum line bar. Could probably get a mini-skirted escort out on the street, no problem. Could even join a biker gang if you were so inclined.

The morning passed slowly. He had a bladder like a camel's hump but even it had limits. The pressure was getting uncomfortable. Nobody would be the wiser if he headed over to the community centre down the street to relieve himself. After all, if Rouleau had cared that much, he would have sent someone to spell him off now and then. They wouldn't have left him alone all day like an outcast on a deserted island.

A side mirror check and he caught the glint of sunlight bouncing off a car as it slowly pulled into a space three houses down. Woodhouse kept his eyes on the mirror, hoping some hot chick in short shorts and a skin-tight top would slide out of the open door. He was disappointed to see a young East Indian kid in his midtwenties finally step onto the street. Disappointment turned to suspicion as it normally did whenever he saw a member of the jihad nation. As Chalmers liked to say, nothing wrong with keeping a watchful eye on the movements of citizens from the terrorist countries.

The kid took his time locking his car, a new black Nissan Sentra, before he checked up and down the street.

"Now just what are you up to, my lovely?" Woodhouse said out loud.

He picked up his binoculars and angled the side mirror to read the licence plate. He repeated the number to himself a couple of times as he searched for a pen in the front dash. He jotted down the plate number at the top of the newspaper he'd picked up along with the bag of salt and vinegar chips. Task completed, he looked up and surveyed the street. Where had the kid gone? It was like he'd disappeared into thin air. Woodhouse sighed. They were a race that had learned to make themselves invisible when need be. Stonechild's people had the same gene. Mostly because they were always up to no good. He picked up the paper again. He may as well check out the sports page and find out if the Jays had gotten another win against the Red Sox. He could wait twenty more minutes before he'd have to answer nature's call.

———

Della Munroe turned on *The Little Mermaid* and settled Tommy in front of the television with a bowl of Cheerios while she considered how to get rid of Ghazi, waiting for her in the other room. She also needed a few minutes to collect herself so that he wouldn't sense her rage. Of all the stupid things for him to do, showing up at her doorstep had to be the stupidest.

"You stay here, Tommy, and Mommy will be back in a few minutes."

He lifted his chin and looked at her, with his father's curly hair flopping in his face. It would be a life-long reminder of her sins.

She took a moment to rake her hands through her hair and to smooth down her purple silk blouse. A glance in the mirror and three deep breaths. *Just get rid of him,* she told herself. *Whatever it takes.*

Ghazi was sitting at the table when she entered the kitchen. His eyes were black and angry, the expression on his face was dangerous. She felt a momentary sense of foreboding combined with a rush of heat between her legs. For a split second, she was back to the first time she saw him standing in the hall outside the psychology classroom. He was so perfectly delicious: twenty-two years of raging testosterone. All dark smouldering eyes with the body of a male athlete. He'd been a worthy partner in the sack once he learned to follow her lead. He liked it as rough as she did. After a few months, she'd lost track of who was the teacher and who was the student. The plan came later when she realized he could help her get rid of Brian. It hadn't taken much convincing to have Ghazi take the roughness up a notch and fake the rape. He'd framed it as a favour to help her get away from her domineering husband. Ghazi had started confiding in her after that. She'd found him seriously depraved, dangerous … and exciting. It was too bad he'd become a major liability. His appearance here today confirmed it.

She forced a dazzling smile.

"I wasn't expecting to see you. I thought we'd agreed to cool it until my … predicament concluded."

"I thought you might want to come with me on another adventure. I know how much you enjoyed hearing about my last one."

"Who?"

"My whoring sister Nadirah. I want to get to her before she influences my other sisters any further. I think they're on their way to find her. Luckily, I've figured out where she is."

"How did you do that? Leah never told you anything as I recall, even with your ample … persuasion." Della shivered as she remembered his lurid description of what he'd done to her. She still didn't understand the lengths he'd gone to over his so-called family honour. It was as twisted an obsession as she'd ever seen.

"I got her co-worker's laptop, which surprised me with intimate details of Leah's life. For instance, Leah grew up in Brockville near to where her family still owns a cottage on the St. Lawrence River. I've got a map of the area and found the location on Google Earth, or close enough that I can get there. It's secluded and the perfect place for Nadirah to hole up."

"Your sister could be anywhere. She might have left the country even."

"Not without her sisters. I know Nadirah. She'll want to stay close by until she thinks it's safe to make contact. Then she'll try to get my other sisters to join her. Dalal anyway. Now the two of them have gone missing."

"Why haven't you gone to get Nadirah already?"

"My father wanted me to hold back and overrode my mother, but now she's decided that Nadirah's behaviour must be punished. We can't wait any longer."

"What do you intend to do when you find her?"

Ghazi straightened and puffed out his chest as if he was a warrior on a holy crusade. "Save my family's honour. She's better off dead than carrying on like a common slut."

"Surely your parents wouldn't be pleased if you kill her."

"Who do you think sent me to avenge our honour and bring back Dalal and Meeza before they also bring shame on the family name?"

He stood and paced from one end of the room to the other, stopping a foot from where she stood. He reached up and grabbed the back of her neck, pulling her to him. His mouth was on hers like a sledgehammer and his tongue forced its way between her lips. She gave in to his deep kiss but broke away as his hand reached up under her blouse and fumbled with the clasp on the front of her bra.

"Not here," she gasped. "Tommy's in the other room and could come to find me any minute." She pushed him back and stepped away.

"Fine time for you to act like the good mother." His eyes blazed but he didn't move toward her. "I just wanted to see you one more time, Della, before ... I wanted you to come with me."

She kept her eyes on him, acutely aware of how unstable he was. The look in his eyes was crazy with the fervent passion of the demented. Why hadn't she seen it before? She needed time to figure out how to neutralize him without being linked to him. They'd been very careful not to be seen together; if she could just get rid of him now, she'd buy some time to come up with a plan.

She traced her hand down his chest. "Baby, I can't just leave Tommy here alone. You go take care of your sisters and we'll meet up to celebrate, I promise. I'll post a message on the board at the entrance of the University Centre next week like I did before. It'll give a time and place to meet up in that code we set up. I'll want a full account of how it goes down today. The wait will be just so sooo exciting." She slowly circled her tongue around her lips before leaning in to kiss him one more time. She bit his bottom lip before lifting her mouth to whisper into his ear, "Now be my good boy. You go do what you need to do and don't let anyone see you leave. We have to be careful."

The tension left his body as her hands moved their way down his back. He stepped away from her and smiled a cheeky, little-boy smile. "Okay. One more week. But don't keep me waiting any longer. I can't live without you. You and me belong together, even if we have to keep our love a secret."

He didn't say from his mother, but she knew that was the fear still barely keeping him in line. She cringed at the veiled threat implicit in his words and their pact that would keep her under his thumb. Letting him pretend to rape her might have been a mistake. The thought of spending her life as the object of his latest obsession was chilling. She ran her fingers across his cheek.

"I want you bad too, Ghazi. Just be a wee bit patient and I'll make the wait well worth your while. We're going to party like there's no tomorrow, and nobody is going to get in our way. I promise you that."

———

Woodhouse might have missed seeing the East Indian kid come out of Della Munroe's driveway if he hadn't looked up from the sports section at just that moment. His blood quickened when he realized the boy had come from the back of her house as cool as you please, dark sunglasses hiding his eyes. He turned his head to look up and down the street again before sidling across the road and passing just in front of Woodhouse's car. Woodhouse was worried the kid had spotted him, but relaxed when he hustled on by without anything more than a glance at his car.

Woodhouse tried to ingrain a description of the kid in his memory. He was good-looking enough if you liked that sort: brown-skinned, stylish short haircut, masculine features, and physically fit. He wasn't carrying any merchandise so probably hadn't been on a robbery mission. He'd only been in the Munroe yard for all of fifteen minutes so likely hadn't gotten into too much mischief. The question was, had he been inside the house visiting? If so, why had he come out the back way and why did he keep looking around as if trying to see if anyone had followed him?

Woodhouse heard the Nissan start up, and a few seconds later the kid sped by, one hand holding a cellphone to his ear. He would have liked to stop the kid on principle, but figured he'd better not blow his cover. He looked down at the licence plate number scrawled on the newspaper lying next to him on the passenger seat. Might not hurt to phone the number in and get someone to check on the owner. At the very least, he'd look like he was being thorough, and that wouldn't be a bad thing with Rouleau in charge and a new partner soon. Odds were that he wasn't going to be lucky enough to get another Chalmers in this lifetime.

Woodhouse turned the key in the ignition and eased his car away from the curb. First things first. He'd make the call as soon as he got back from the community centre, otherwise his bladder would be exploding all over the front seat. He winced at the image and at the never-ending hazing that would follow as sure as the sun was going to rise tomorrow. He tried to think of anything but the pressure in his bladder as he sped up the street to a community toilet and some blessed relief.

41

"I'LL HANG BACK until the girls make contact. When you've explained that I'm also here to help, give me a thumbs up. I'll come over and will take it from there." Kala checked to make sure Wolf understood she was in charge. They were climbing the stairs to the second floor where the food court was located. He nodded but remained silent. She sensed uncoiled energy and hoped he wouldn't blow this chance to get close to the girls. Even more, she hoped this encounter was going to lead somewhere.

At the head of the stairs, she held back and let Wolf walk ahead toward the Harvey's. He bought a coffee, took a seat at one of the tables, and put his elbows on the armrests, leaning slightly forward, his eyes scanning the other tables without staring at anyone for long. The usual senior citizens sat in groups of two and four, cups of coffee on the tables in front of them. A table of six teenage girls was raising the noise level as everyone spoke that much louder to be heard over their laughter and shrieks. Canned music filled what there were of the empty spaces.

Kala skirted around to a spot closer to an exit where Wolf could see her when he turned around. She'd surveyed the people sitting at the tables and walking by but hadn't seen anyone who fit the description of East Indian pre-teens.

The greasy smell of French fries and burgers made her mouth water. Breakfast had been a blueberry yoghurt cup gobbled down on her way out the door.

After ten minutes, Wolf was getting restless. Kala noticed him changing position, crossing and uncrossing his arms, angling his body toward different parts of the room. He'd spotted her early on but managed to avoid glancing her way more than a few times. She thought about buying some fries and taking a seat at the other end of the room at one of the tables. She felt conspicuous lurking around the fringes.

She'd taken two steps toward the Harvey's cashier when she spotted them at the far end of the food court: two girls wearing headscarves, black T-shirts, and long skirts, one blue and the other a green zigzag pattern. The taller one looked about fifteen. Very pretty face with high cheekbones and almond-shaped eyes. The other was a few years younger with a plumper face and mouth drooping slightly open as if she didn't understand what was going on around her.

They held hands as they approached and passed a few feet from her. They'd spotted Wolf and changed course to walk toward him. He stood and smiled as they reached his table. He motioned with his hand for them to sit across from him. They appeared tentative, but sat in the seats after the older girl took a careful look around.

Kala waited for Wolf's signal. He finally lifted his hand in her direction and she walked over after she also took a look around to see if anyone was watching. Satisfied that the girls hadn't been followed, Kala took the empty seat next to Wolf.

"I'm glad you've agreed to meet us," she said to the taller girl, smiling to ease her fear.

"Wolf told me that Leah couldn't come but you're her friend." The girl's eyes darted between Kala and Wolf. She was still holding her sister's hand, which rested on the table.

Kala nodded. "That's right. We both want to help you. I work for the police but I'm here as Leah's friend. Can you tell me your names?"

"I'm Dalal Shahan and this is my sister Meeza. We need to find my sister Nadirah. Did Leah tell you where she is?"

"No, but maybe we can sort it out. Did Nadirah run away?"

Meeza's head lifted and she focused her eyes on Kala. "She's as good as dead to us," she said, her voice robotic and shrill.

Dalal shushed her before explaining. "She's just repeating ... My mother wasn't happy that Nadirah ran away. She's not going to be happy with us either. We can't go back."

"How did Nadirah know Leah?" Wolf interjected. "Where does Leah fit into this?"

"They talked through the help line but Nadirah was too scared to do anything like call the police. She got lucky though. Ghazi was taking the same class as Leah at the university, but he skipped it a few times and had Nadirah go in his place. Nadirah recognized Leah's voice from the help line and approached her. Leah agreed to help her leave home because Nadirah was so desperate. My sister wrote everything in her diary."

Ghazi. Kala remembered the name from Tadesco's class list. She placed her hand on Wolf's forearm to stop him from talking. "Why did Nadirah have to leave home?" she asked.

"My family believed that she was becoming wild and needed to be controlled. They arranged for her to marry a man, Mr. Khan. Nadirah refused and my parents locked her in her room for a month. When Nadirah got out, she pretended to go along with the idea of marrying Mr. Khan, but she was making plans with Leah to disappear. My parents and my brother Ghazi were very angry when Nadirah left. They've been trying to find her."

All eyes turned to Meeza, who'd let out a sob. She'd begun shaking uncontrollably. Dalal wrapped an arm around her shoulder, pulling her closer. "It's okay, Meeza. I won't let anything happen. You will not have to see Mr. Khan ever again."

Kala met Wolf's eyes while Dalal continued to murmur into her sister's ear.

"Has something happened to make Meeza afraid?" Kala asked.

Dalal scowled. "They decided that Meeza would take Nadirah's place so they locked Meeza in her room all week. She's ... not handling it very well. Mr. Khan was coming for her today but we ran away. We won't go back." Her jaw jutted out in defiance. "You can't make us go back."

What kind of family would give their daughters away? It was beyond comprehension. Kala felt a rage inside that she would have liked to let out. "You're very brave girls, Dalal. We won't make you go back. We're going to help you," she said. "Where are your parents and Ghazi now?"

Dalal's eyes widened and she looked around the food court as if she suddenly remembered where they were. Panic crossed her face. "They're probably looking for us. We need to find Nadirah. We're going to live with her. She promised."

A memory of Lily and her ten-year-old self caught in Kala's throat. Lily had made the same promise to her so many years before. A promise that never came true. She coughed to clear the image and to return to the frightened young girls in front of her. "You have no idea where she might have gone?"

Both girls shook their heads.

"I think I might," Wolf said, his face animated. "Leah would have brought your sister somewhere safe where your family would never find her." He smiled at Dalal. "Leah would want me to reunite you. I know that for certain. There's only one place she would have brought your sister and I can take us there in an hour or less if we get on the road now."

"The three of you will have to wait here in Kingston. Tell me where she is and I'll go get her," Kala said.

"You won't find it on your own," Wolf said stubbornly. "You'll waste time trying to find the side road and the laneway to Leah's family cottage. You still need me."

"I have a map. It can't be that hard."

"It's not marked on maps."

"We have to come with you," Dalal said. "We have to find Nadirah."

"I want Nadirah," Meeza wailed. "I want Nadirah now!"

Kala looked at Dalal's and Wolf's determined faces and Meeza's mouth widening into a howl. She wasn't going to be able to leave them without a scene. If this place was so hard to find, Ghazi and his parents would have the same difficulty, even if they'd figured out where Leah could have hidden Nadirah. It might be safer to keep these girls with her rather than let their family track them down.

"Well, let's get going then," she said. "I'll put a call in to my boss so he knows what we're up to."

She didn't add that she'd wait until they were on their way out of Kingston before calling. Rouleau likely would veto the plan if she called any earlier.

Rouleau woke up to find his father's doctor leaning over him, shaking his shoulder. The fog lifted quickly. "Is my father okay?" he asked, pushing himself upright. "Has something happened?"

"He's awake," she said, "and asking for you. All of his vitals are stable so he's come through the surgery with flying colours."

"Good. He had me worried."

Rouleau followed her through to the semi-private room where they'd moved his dad. He was hooked up to beeping machines and an intravenous drip. Rouleau sat near the head of the bed and covered his father's hand with his own.

"How are you feeling, Dad?"

"Been better." His dad said the words slowly, but managed a shaky smile afterward.

"Doc says you'll be home soon. They'll keep you overnight to keep an eye. It was a blocked artery, but all clear now. No lasting damage."

His father's eyes closed and his breathing deepened. The doctor finished checking the heart monitor and smiled at Rouleau.

"He'll be sleeping the day away if you want to go home and get some sleep. We'll call you if there's any change."

"I'd like to stay a few more minutes if that's okay."

"Certainly."

She left after writing on his father's chart and giving a word to the nurse.

Rouleau held his father's hand and watched the shallow in and out of his father's chest. He tried not to think of what could have been. A few more hours and he wouldn't have made it. The enormity of what Rouleau nearly lost made

him want to gather his father into his arms and flee to somewhere safe, where time stood still and they both had their
youth and health. A time when his father was the strong one
and he was still a child. That time was long past and was
now but a bittersweet memory. It was a sad truth that the
passage of time left no prisoners. Yet, they had been blessed
with a reprieve.

Rouleau kissed his father on the cheek and brushed a
lock of white hair back from his forehead. He stood and
watched him sleep a while longer, until the fear constricting
his own breathing loosened enough for him to walk away
and leave his father in the capable hands of Hotel Dieu's
medical staff.

Vera reached him as he was driving north on Division
toward the station. He put the phone on speaker.

"How's your father?"

"Doing well. I'm on my way in."

"Stonechild's been trying to reach you."

"I had to turn my phone off in the cardiac unit. Is everything alright?"

"She has a lead that she's following up on and wanted to
let you know. She's on her way to Brockville."

"Brockville?" Rouleau racked his tired mind. "Leah
Sampson grew up there."

"A girl called the university help line looking for her sister, Nadirah. Stonechild believes that Leah has her holed up
near Brockville."

"Why?"

"Nadirah's family is after her. They aren't happy that she
ran away."

"An honour killing?"

"That's Stonechild's fear. She asked us to pick up
Nadirah's brother Ghazi and the parents. She's convinced

they had a hand in Leah's murder. Heath agreed there was enough evidence to question them. I sent a unit over about five minutes ago."

"Good. Where's Gundersund?"

"He called in sick. Should I try to reach him?"

"I don't see the need at this point. I'll be in the office in ten minutes. I'll interview Nadirah's family when they arrive."

Vera disconnected and Rouleau increased pressure on the gas pedal, the overwhelming fatigue replaced by a surge of adrenaline.

———

The noise of the shower woke Gundersund for the second time that morning. He moaned and rolled onto his side to check the clock. Five after eleven. Damn.

He rolled out of bed and tried to ignore the pounding in his head as he stood up. His clothes were scattered across the floor. He searched around for his jeans and found them under the bed. Grabbing a clean sweatshirt from the pile on the dresser, he dressed quickly. The effort cost him and he sat back on the bed, pressing his temples between his hands while he concentrated on not puking.

The shower stopped and a moment later Fiona strolled out of the ensuite vigorously drying her hair with a towel. She wore a smile on her face and not much else.

"How are you feeling, lover?" she asked.

"Fiona, I'm not sure how …"

She lifted a hand to stop him talking while her mouth settled into a straight line. "You don't have to say anything, Paul. I know that tone of voice."

She walked over to the chair where her clothes were neatly folded and began dressing with her back to him. "Last night was fun but you're questioning it this morning." She hooked her bra in the back before turning. "You didn't have any questions last night." She attempted a cheeky smile but her bottom lip trembled and the words came out more desperate than teasing.

He looked at his beautiful wife and felt so empty he could have cried. He couldn't forget what she'd done to their marriage; he knew that now. He'd known it even as he'd drunkenly lowered himself onto her the night before in the darkness of his bedroom while she called out his name. He'd made love to her, but the feeling of being close to her never came. Just a hollow sadness. His last thought had been of Stonechild as he drifted off to sleep.

Fiona met his eyes and her face paled. The towel dropped to the floor. She crossed the short distance to him and knelt at his feet, her cheek resting against his leg. He rested his hand lightly on her damp hair.

"It's not going to work, Fiona," he said. "You must know it too. I thought maybe, but I can't get past you leaving me last year. I can't go back there, to what we were. I wish I could."

She looked up at him. Her eyes shimmered with tears. "I wish I could take back what I did. It doesn't feel over for me. Can't you just give us some more time? I'll prove to you that I've changed."

"It's not that easy. I honestly wish it was."

After she left, he put on a pot of coffee and retrieved his cellphone from his jacket hanging on the back of a kitchen chair. He scrolled through the missed calls and recognized Stonechild's cell number. She'd tried to reach him twice but hadn't left a message. Her last call had been half an hour ago.

He hit her number and poured himself a cup of coffee while he waited for her to pick up. His headache was becoming manageable after two pain killers but he still felt rough. Now add guilt to the mix. He had let Fiona convince him to call in sick and in doing so had left his partner in the lurch.

No answer.

Worried, he dialed Vera's number. She picked up after one ring.

"Gundersund."

"I've tried to reach Stonechild. Is something going on?"

"She's on her way to Brockville, chasing down a lead. Rouleau's on his way in."

"She's not picking up. What happened?"

"The girl called back to the help line. Stonechild thinks Leah Sampson was killed because she hid the girl's sister Nadirah at the family cottage near Brockville. We've got some officers picking up the brother and parents now."

"The girl's family killed Leah?"

"That's Stonechild's premise. Can you hang on a minute?"

"Sure."

He heard muffled talking and then Vera was back. "They brought in the father but the mother and brother are missing."

"Do you have the location of the cottage?"

"No. Wolf is with Stonechild and he's taking her there."

"Listen. I'm going to start heading to Brockville in my car. If she calls in, get her exact location and phone me on my cell. Do you have any info on the brother's vehicle?"

"Not yet. I'll call as soon as we know anything."

"And I'll be on my way to find Stonechild."

42

NADIRAH SHAHAN SAT on the dock and dangled her feet into the lake. She'd made friends with a flock of ducks who paddled nearby but just out of reach. Ducks she'd been bribing with crumbs so that they'd stick around and not leave her all alone.

"No more bread for you," she said aloud. They looked in her direction but didn't come any closer. It was almost startling to hear her own voice. She'd been here for nearly a month and hadn't spoken to anyone. That would change soon. Leah was overdue for a visit and had promised to bring a bus ticket and money for a fresh start in Halifax. Nadirah frowned and tried not to worry about Leah's long silence. They'd agreed to make as little contact as possible through September, but she'd been expecting Leah's arrival for over a week. Leah had promised to check up on Dalal and Meeza and would try to get word to Dalal about her sister's whereabouts. Nadirah worried about them too. Still, the best thing would be for her to relocate and send for them once she was settled and had a job.

It was a lovely morning: sunny and warm, although not with the heat of a few weeks before. "You ducks should be thinking about trekking south," she said. "You don't want to get trapped here for the winter." A twinge of guilt struck her at the thought that she was responsible for their lingering so long as the weather began to turn the corner into autumn.

She stood and looked at the sparkles of sunshine shimmering across the water. The water reminded her of Kingston and homesickness welled up. No matter how awful her family could be, she still loved her sisters and father, even her mother if it came down to it. She'd tried to be a good daughter but her mother wouldn't bend an iota. She'd tried to understand the old ways that her mother clung to so desperately from her own childhood in India, but could not. Perhaps it was her own failings keeping her from doing as her mother asked. She'd been told often enough that she was the bad seed, bringing dishonour on a respectable family. Her mother thought Mr. Khan was the answer to mending her oldest daughter's rebellious ways and had refused to see Ghazi for what he was. Nadirah trembled at the thought of what her life had become at home and what it would be if she hadn't found Leah.

She walked back down the dock toward shore and started up the path that wound upward through bushes and pine trees to the cottage. She was out of milk and fresh fruit and had taken the last loaf of bread from the small freezer. She'd have peanut butter toast and tea with powdered milk for lunch. Leah had to come soon. She'd know how little food was left and wouldn't let it go on too long. She must be having trouble getting away.

The sound of tires on gravel greeted Nadirah as she reached the deck jutting out over the cliff at the top of the hill. Her heart jumped happily at the thought of Leah's arrival, and she ran lightly across the deck and through the sliding glass door into the cottage to meet her at the front door. The front door looked out toward the parking area and the rutted track that passed by the property. She pictured the purple coneflower, Queen Anne's lace, and buttercups that grew in profusion amidst the raspberry bushes and cedar just outside the door. Leah had been right about the cottage being secluded and free from passersby. It was a safe haven, but Nadirah had never quite gotten used to being so alone. She could now admit that she'd been worried about Leah leaving her there much longer.

She flung open the door and raised a hand in greeting. Horror filled her like a douse of ice water. She barely had time to realize her mistake before Ghazi had shut off the engine and stepped outside the car. Her mother's face turned to glare at her through the front passenger window.

"Hello, Nadirah," he said. "We've come to put you out of your misery."

———

Kala kept her speed just above the limit, the two girls wedged between her and Wolf. The sisters barely spoke the entire time. Wolf sat stone-faced, watching out the passenger window.

Kala looked across at him. "You been to this cottage?"

"Leah had parties at her cottage in high school and I went to a couple. Her parents moved to Montreal after she left home for university and only kept the cottage because Leah planned to use it more when school was finished. She loved the place." He pointed to a sign. "Take that exit. The road to the cottage is five minutes from here."

She'd ignored her ringing phone, concentrating on her driving. When she got the chance, she'd check in with work before the last leg of the trip. Very likely it was Vera or Rouleau trying to reach her. She took the exit and spotted a gas station and country diner.

She looked at the girls. "Anyone need to use the washroom?" she asked.

"Yes," Dalal said.

"I'll take them in and will get them a drink," Wolf said.

"Great. I'll get some gas and will check in at work," Kala said. "See you back here in ten minutes."

She watched the three of them cross the parking lot and enter the restaurant while she filled the tank. When she finished, she pulled into a parking spot next to the main entrance.

Gundersund had called a couple of times. Rouleau's number popped up last. She returned his call first. "Hello, sir. How's your dad?"

"Out of surgery and doing well. Where are you?"

"At the truck stop at the 659 exit west of Brockville and about to take the back roads to the Sampson cottage on Charleston Lake. Wolf is with me and knows the way. I should also tell you that I have Nadirah Shahan's two younger sisters with me. They ran away from home and it seemed safer to keep them with me."

She was relieved when Rouleau didn't get upset with her. She knew bringing them along wasn't the best move. After a brief silence, he asked, "How old?"

"Dalal looks to be about fifteen and Meeza's around eleven. The parents were giving Meeza away to some man this weekend. That's why they ran away as far as I can tell."

"We've had a slight hiccup at our end. Mr. Shahan is at the station but his wife and son Ghazi are nowhere to be found."

"Is there any way they could have found Nadirah? I'm making the assumption that Wolf is right about Leah bringing her to this cottage. It makes sense though. Leah was secretive and leaving the office for meetings, which Nadirah's sister now says were with Nadirah at the Sunshine Bakery. Leah disappeared for a day and everybody thought she was having it off with a married man. It could have been the day she brought Nadirah to the cottage. I still haven't figured out how Ghazi made the connection between Leah and Nadirah though."

"He might have followed his sister to the bakery. He would have recognized Leah from the psychology class. Dalal tells me that he was forever following them around and spying on them."

"Makes sense."

"We have no way of knowing what else Ghazi has figured out. Gail Pankhurst kept details about everyone on her laptop. She might have known about Leah's hometown and cottage. You have to be extremely cautious since he could be headed the same place you are. I'd prefer you wait for Gundersund. He's on his way."

"How far back?"

"About half an hour."

"If Ghazi has figured out that Nadirah is at this cottage, she could be in real danger. I'm convinced that he killed Leah and put Gail into a coma trying to find out where she was hiding out. I can't wait around here for Gundersund."

"Do you have your firearm?"

"No. There wasn't time."

"I don't want you taking the civilians to the cottage. Can you get there without Wolf?"

"It would be quicker with him, but I'll get Wolf to draw a map. He says we're about fifteen minutes away."

"Good. I'll have Gundersund stop at the gas station to get directions from Wolf as well. I'll also put a call in to the local police, but I doubt they'll get there in time even if they take this seriously. We don't even know if she's at this cottage. Be careful, Kala. You have no idea what you're walking in on."

"I will be, sir."

"I'd like to see you back here in one piece."

"That's my plan."

———

Wolf wasn't kidding about the cottage being hard to find. Kala passed the track twice before she spotted a carved board with the word "Sampsons" nailed to a tree stump set in an overgrown thicket of raspberry bushes. She wondered if Ghazi could really have found this location on his own. She doubted it and for the moment felt optimistic that Nadirah was safe if she was holed up here.

She would have enjoyed this drive into the woods if she hadn't been so worried about Nadirah. Oak and cedar trees were interspersed with pine and balsam trees. Sunlight streamed through openings in the green canopy with glimpses of a satin blue sky. The smell of vegetation and rich earth assailed her through the open window. This would be a lovely spot as the leaves changed colour over the next few weeks. Maybe she'd make a return trip to the lake when life calmed down.

The truck jostled along the track and Kala bounced up and down like a bed spring for about a kilometre before a grassy opening appeared on her right. The opening disappeared around a bend and up a hill. Just past the cedar trees, gravel covered the ground, giving traction for cars as they drove up the hill. Wolf had said that she could park at the top of the hill in front of the cottage, but the stones would make a crunchy entrance if she kept going in her truck. Instead, she pulled over and parked in full view of the road. Gundersund would see her truck as he searched for the turn-off and he'd know she was here.

As she climbed the hill, she saw evidence of a vehicle having disturbed the gravel recently. The driver had taken the hill at a high speed, spinning gravel and dirt.

Kala began to have a very bad feeling.

Keeping to the trees along the north side, she walked up the hill and slowed as she reached the crest. The cottage was directly ahead: a rustic one-storey with stained white siding out of the seventies. In Northern Ontario it would have fit in nicely as a camp, not one of the pretentious summer get-aways people owned in the south. At the same time as she took in the details of the structure, she processed the four-door black Nissan parked near the front door and facing downhill. Any hope that Nadirah was here alone vanished.

Kala checked for signs of life before walking over and resting her hand on the hood. The engine was hot. They hadn't arrived long before her.

She scooted around to the side of the cottage and circled down the incline until she was beneath the large deck that jutted out over the cliff. Standing still amongst the beams, she strained for sounds of people above. All was silent except for a bumblebee busily extracting nectar from a bed of clover off to her left and a cardinal holding court from one of the pines farther down the hill. His call was a low whistle repeated over and over, haunting and melodic.

Where could they be?

She moved silently to the steps and stood in their shadow under the deck. All of her senses were on high alert as she scanned the woods and listened for voices in the cottage. Hearing nothing, she climbed the steps and quickly crossed the deck to stand near the wall. The windows were open and she checked the living room and kitchen, but the rooms were empty. Easing open the sliding glass door, she slipped inside.

The interior matched the exterior. In the living room, wood panelling lined the walls. Reading lamps were spaced strategically next to an old plaid couch and well-worn chairs. Bookcases filled with paperbacks, tasselled throw rugs, and an old television with a VCR. A book on local birds lay open and face down on the coffee table. The cottage smelled musty and damp with the peaty aftertaste of a portable toilet. She ducked into the kitchen and saw a coffee cup resting on the drain board. The fridge and stove were ancient. An old yellow table filled most of the room with mismatched wooden chairs. Wide windows looked out over the woods and lake. It was a rustic getaway perched high above the water with a stunning view. She bet the sunsets were spectacular.

She kept going down the short hall and counted three bedrooms, with bunks in two. The last room had a double bed. The sheets and blanket were pulled back. A woman's toiletries filled the bedside table. Kala checked the chest of drawers and found her clothes neatly folded. Her wallet on the dresser confirmed her identity. Nadirah hadn't brought much.

Kala walked back to the sliding door and looked down toward the water. She took one step onto the deck when a scream pierced the silence like a gunshot. One scream and then nothing, but it had been enough for Kala to locate Nadirah and her brother somewhere down at the lake.

She raced across the deck and down the stairs, not caring that the wood creaked under her feet and her steps pounded like hammers. She picked up speed as she ran down the steep path leading to the dock, her arms stretched in front in case she fell. At the bottom of the hill the lake spread out like a gigantic glittering jewel. The land tapered into a rocky flat stretch with the dock at its tip. This bit of the lake was a bay cradled by stretches of thick forest on either side.

Kala stopped and lifted a hand to shield her eyes from the sun. She searched for Nadirah and Ghazi the length of the dock and land in both directions, but they were nowhere to be seen.

Frustration filled her. Nadirah was running out of time, and Kala felt helpless. She started back up the trail, head down, eyes frantically looking for signs in the earth. Steps from the rock landing, she spotted a foot path through the underbrush that she'd missed on her flight down. She squatted and traced an index finger above scuffled footprints. A handful of torn leaves lay scattered on the path. She glanced up. Branches on leafy bushes were bent as if someone had grabbed onto them to stop from being pulled forward.

Kala straightened and thought for a second. She broke a branch on one of the younger trees at the entrance and took out her earring, dangling it from the end that pointed down the path. It wasn't much, but all she had that would mark the way for her partner.

She took off down the narrow trail, avoiding tree roots and branches that stretched across the opening. The air was pea green and lush with foliage and composting vegetation. She felt like she was running through a tunnel of trees and brush with the sun blotted out overhead. A few minutes in, she reached an opening with the blue sky and lake spread before her. She slowed to stay hidden in the trees while she checked out the beach.

Directly ahead, a woman dressed head to toe in a black burka stood framed against the blue horizon. Her back was toward Kala and she was looking out at the lake, her arms flapping up and down as she yelled into the wind. Kala moved a step to look past her and for a split second could not believe what she was seeing. A young man who had to be Ghazi was holding a woman's head under the thigh-high water while her arms flailed and pounded at him, trying to break his hold. Ghazi was laughing, wide-mouthed, toward his mother on the shore. He let Nadirah's head out of the water for half a second and she sputtered water and tried to inhale before he thrust her back under.

It was a sight so grotesque and unthinkable that Kala stood stunned, but only for a moment. Her horror was followed by a rage so intense that it burned through her like wildfire. She kicked out of her shoes and dropped her cellphone as she ran full tilt toward the lake.

The woman in black provided Kala some cover until she got closer. Kala lunged past her before the woman could react and barrelled into the water directly at Ghazi. The woman's screams increased in volume as she warned her son. As Kala rushed into the lake, part of her registered that Nadirah had stopped struggling, but she couldn't stop to think what that meant.

Ghazi's face transformed from gleeful to shocked as he realized what was happening. Kala was on him before he released his hold on Nadirah. She punched him hard between the eyes, hearing the bone in his nose crack. Blood streamed down his face and he grabbed his nose with both hands and screamed in pain. He punched blindly toward Kala's face. One punch made contact with the side of her head and Kala momentarily saw stars. She regained her balance and attacked again, this time thrusting her knee as hard as she could between his legs and punching him in the stomach with her balled up fist. The impact sent him backwards with another shriek of pain. He hit the water with a splash, incapacitated for the time being. The screaming from shore intensified.

Kala turned to search for Nadirah. Fear surged through her at the sight of the girl lying on her stomach, her body bobbing gently in the waves that lapped against her. Kala reached her quickly through the knee-deep water and flipped her onto her back, pulling her under her armpits toward shore. They reached the edge of the water and Kala turned Nadirah onto her side, checking her mouth for obstructions. She rolled her over and onto her back and began performing CPR.

The mother waded out to Ghazi, screeching venom while Kala breathed air in and out of Nadirah's mouth, praying that she wasn't too late. She was aware of the frenetic movements of Ghazi and his mother nearby, but she kept up the CPR. Ghazi had almost reached her when a stream of water spurted out of Nadirah's mouth. She coughed and gasped in air. Kala rolled the girl onto her side, then stood ready to defend herself from the two bearing down on her. They were a frightening sight. The woman was screeching through the veil that covered her face and pounding the air with a fist. Ghazi was covered in scarlet blood streaming from his broken nose. His hands were raised in fists and his eyes were already turning black and blue and bulging with anger.

Kala spread her feet wider. She raised her arms and squeezed her hands into fists. She mentally prepared to withstand a blow. Ghazi came at her like a charging bull, thrusting himself at her and catching her around the waist in a head butt. She was flung backwards into the water, winded by the impact and struggling to breathe. She kicked at him as he scrambled to leap on her and caught him under the chin. His head snapped back but he only took a second to come at her again. Kala got into a sitting position and pushed herself back but not in time. Ghazi flung himself at her and weighted her down, pushing her face under the water.

Kala flailed like Nadirah had done before her but Ghazi was too strong. She tried to gain traction to shove him off balance. Nothing worked and she let herself go limp, willing him to loosen his grip. Darkness and shooting lights filled her brain as she began to black out.

43

GUNDERSUND TOOK EXIT 659 toward Charleston Lake and searched ahead for the gas station and family restaurant that Rouleau had assured him were in plain sight. He'd made record time down Highway 417 once he left the city limits, sticking to the fast lane and managing to avoid being pulled over. Stonechild couldn't be that far ahead unless she'd broken the sound barrier.

He spotted Wolf alone in the parking lot, pacing back and forth like a man waiting on his wife to deliver a baby. Gundersund drew alongside and Wolf jumped into the passenger seat without waiting for an invitation.

"Let's go," Wolf said, slamming the door. His hair was wild and his beard scraggy. Not a look that brokered confidence. He shifted sideways and looked hard at Gundersund as if sensing his reluctance. "I didn't like letting your partner go to the cottage alone and have had a bad feeling."

"Where are the girls?"

"I called a friend, who arrived five minutes ago. Claire will take Dalal and Meeza to her place and we can pick them up when this is over."

Gundersund wasn't liking this change in plans. "I can't take you with me, Wolf. I can't bring you into a potentially dangerous situation."

"I know the risks. We can make better time if I'm along to direct you to the cottage."

The door of the restaurant opened and Gundersund looked over, the ringing of the bell on a chain catching his attention. A pleasant-looking woman in her fifties dressed in pink Lulu Lemon workout gear exited with Meeza and Dalal right behind. Both girls were eating ice cream cones and the younger one was smiling. He watched them cross the parking lot to her SUV and noticed the vanity plate: 4CURLERS. She wouldn't be hard to track down.

"Okay," Gundersund said, "looks like I haven't really got much of a choice if we're going to find them before nightfall. Buckle up." He pulled onto the road heading north. "So what makes you believe Leah hid Nadirah away at this cottage?"

"It's isolated and the first place she would think of. Leah also went away overnight a few weeks back 'to clear her head,' she told me. I thought she was having a night away with her married boyfriend." Wolf stared straight ahead. "I should have trusted her. A Ph.D. in psychology and I couldn't even read my own girlfriend."

"You're only human, buddy. She didn't want you to know and she was acting secretive. I understand a co-worker also stirred the pot."

"Jucinda." He groaned. "I should never have listened to her. Take this turn off."

"Left here?"

"Yeah. It'll take us to the side road that leads to Sand Bay." He slumped back against the seat and folded his arms across his chest.

They travelled in silence past stretches of woods and marshland. The side road to the Sand Bay turnoff came ten minutes in.

Wolf started speaking as if there hadn't been any break in their conversation. "Leah was always helping people. She was soft-hearted and never knew when to say no. She also had this conscience that wouldn't let her do the wrong thing. I know she was trying to protect me from getting involved in helping a caller because we'd both get fired if Mark or Tadesco found out I'd known and said nothing or helped her. The irony was that I quit the night Leah was murdered so it wouldn't have mattered."

Gundersund shot him a glance. "Leah must have known that if Nadirah was in danger, helping her to escape her family would put both of them in danger. Perhaps Leah was keeping you out of it to keep you safe."

"Then we have to protect this person that Leah died trying to help. It's the only thing that makes sense anymore. Helping Nadirah might make up for me doubting Leah, you know?"

"Yeah. I get it." Find meaning out of chaos. Assuage one's own guilt whether real or imagined. When somebody close died violently, family and friends would go searching for answers and try to set things right. Gundersund had seen it play out before.

Wolf suddenly pointed toward the right side of the road. "Is that your partner's truck?"

Gundersund felt the adrenaline start to kick in. "Yeah. She's here."

He cranked the steering wheel sharply to the right and slid in next to her. They both jumped out. Wolf waited for Gundersund to walk around the front of his car. He said, "The cottage isn't far. It's up on a bluff of land overlooking the lake."

They ran up the gravel hill through the trees, Wolf leading the way. He stopped at the top of the incline and pointed at the black Nissan. "Company," he said quietly.

Gundersund's worry meter spiked but he tried not to let it show. "Looks like the Shahans made it here ahead of us." He reached inside his jacket and pulled out his handgun. "Stay behind me, just in case."

They circled the cottage with Gundersund taking the lead. He was relieved not to come across any scenes of carnage but each passing moment began to seem more critical.

"Looks like the cottage is empty," Wolf said, scanning the deck and windows from where he stood near the path down to the water.

"Maybe, but we should go carefully."

They silently climbed the steps to the deck and Gundersund eased his way through the sliding door just as Kala had done earlier. He completed a quick search and returned a minute later to where Wolf stood guard on the deck.

"The good news is that nobody's inside with any injuries. The bad news is that they have to be out there somewhere. You were right about Nadirah staying here. She's set up in the back bedroom. I found her wallet with ID."

Wolf nodded. "It had to be this place. I don't see anybody on the dock from here, but we could go check it out."

Gundersund would have missed Stonechild's clue, pointing them down the path to the beach, if he hadn't had his head down. Smart girl. She'd left one of her turquoise earrings hanging from a broken branch that pointed down an overgrown track between the trees. His admiration for her resourcefulness kept growing.

"Wolf," he said and reached up to take down the earring. He tucked it into his pocket. "This way."

"The path leads to the beach about half a kilometer around the point," Wolf said.

Three minutes running full tilt through the woods felt like a lifetime. When they broke through the green cave of trees into the blinding sunshine, Gundersund's heart was near to bursting in his chest. He struggled to catch his breath, vain enough to try to keep his discomfort from Wolf, who looked unfazed by the run. Gundersund promised himself that he'd get back in the gym when this case was over. No two ways. It took him a second to adjust to the brightness bouncing off the water. He squinted.

"*Merde*," he exclaimed when he'd finally absorbed the horror in front of him. The sight was surreal.

Wolf's voice held equal disbelief. "There's a woman's body lying near shore. He's holding somebody else under water." Wolf began running and so did Gundersund. He remembered his handgun.

"Police!" Gundersund yelled. He stopped and raised the angle of the gun into the air and fired one shot skyward.

The man in the water looked up and raised his hands. Even from this distance, Gundersund could see that Ghazi's face and shirt were smeared with bright-red congealing blood. It was difficult to make out his features under the pulpy gore. He froze for only a moment before turning his back on them and belting it across the beach toward the wood. The woman in black trailed behind him, wailing and screaming at the top of her lungs in a foreign language.

Gundersund and Wolf ignored their flight as they raced toward the two bodies lying on the beach. Gundersund waded into the deeper water and grabbed on to Stonechild by her waist. He flipped her over and dragged her from the water onto the edge of the beach. Laying her down, desperation made his movements feel clumsy and rough.

His initial assessment of her condition had him fear the worst. Her normally glowing skin had a bluish tinge and the pulse in her neck beat faintly under his fingers.

Please, please.

He rolled her onto her back and tilted her head, lifting her chin, putting his ear next to her open mouth. He couldn't see her chest rising and falling; there was no feeling of air on his cheek. *Don't die on me.* He pinched her nose and sealed her mouth with his, giving her a breath big enough to make her chest rise.

Come on. Come on. He repeated several times. *Come on, Stonechild, breathe.* The clock was ticking. He lifted his face to get more air. A sudden movement of her neck where he held her and then she bucked upwards. A frantic struggle for breath and a choking cough. Water began to spew from her open mouth. He managed to lift his face and roll her onto her side before she vomited a stream of water. Her eyes fluttered open, fighting, scared. She rolled back and saw him. The fear in her eyes died away before she closed them and moaned.

Thank Christ. "You're okay, Stonechild," he said, taking hold of her hand. "I've got you." He glanced over at Wolf.

Wolf had found Nadirah lying unconscious on her side in inches of water near shore. He'd hauled her farther onto the beach and had been trying to bring her around. He'd taken off his shirt and wrapped her in it. Wolf met his eyes. "She's alive," he said. "Breathing okay, but unconscious. I want to kill the bastard."

"Join the line."

Gundersund felt the surge of adrenaline that had brought him this far begin to fade. He suddenly felt overwhelmingly tired. He could have stretched out next to Stonechild and slept, but the day was just beginning. He pulled the phone out of his pocket and dialled 911 as he leaned down and said, "Hang on Kala. Nadirah's doing fine. You're both doing fine. They won't get away with this."

44

ROULEAU WAS PICKING up the folder for his meeting when the phone on his desk rang. He glanced at the number before picking up. He heard his voice lighten when he said, "Laney, how are you?"

"Good. I received a message to call you? Was the latest listing not suitable?"

"No, it's actually a great spot, but I've decided to put the house hunting on hold for the time being. My father just had heart surgery and I'm going to stay with him for the next month or so."

"I'm sorry to hear that." She paused and he heard the sharp clicks of a mouse across the telephone wire. "You know, Jacques, a condo has come up in your father's building. Ah, here it is. A two bedroom a few floors down from your father, but it also faces the lake. I could show it to you tomorrow if you have time."

He hadn't considered a condo. When he'd been married to Frances, they'd bought a fixer-upper in Westboro, a neighbourhood in Ottawa, that he'd never gotten around to doing much work on. He still liked the idea of a house though. Maybe one in better condition with a backyard big enough for a barbecue and lawn chair and a place to garden. He liked flowers and figured it was a pastime he could take up.

"Won't hurt to have a look," he said. "Any chance of just renting it for a year?"

"I can check. Meet you there around five tomorrow afternoon? It's number 405."

"Perfect."

He hung up the phone. Renting in his father's building for a year might be the solution for keeping an eye on his dad while giving them both some privacy. He smiled. It also wouldn't hurt to take the opportunity to see Laney again. He might never ask her out, but that wouldn't preclude enjoying her company when their paths crossed.

———

Heath held up a finger and finished his phone conversation while Rouleau waited. He was wearing his full police uniform and his round face beamed with boyish exuberance. After ending his call, he strode around the desk and shook Rouleau's hand, pounding him on the shoulder.

"I'm heading to the downstairs meeting room for the news briefing. I've invited a Queen's professor who's an expert on these honour crime cases and she's arrived. I don't have to tell you how good this looks on the department to have solved this one. We were starting to take a hit in the media for the number of unsolved cases we're carrying. Well done to the team."

"Thank you, sir."

"We've got that Chalmers retirement party Friday night. Will Stonechild be out of the hospital by then?"

"From what I hear, she's out now. Gundersund is driving her back to Kingston. I told him to take her home so she can rest."

Heath's forehead creased. "So soon? How about the other girl?" He looked down at the notes on his desk. "Nadirah Shahan."

"Nadirah will be spending the night in the Brockville Hospital for observation more than anything. She's conscious and stable."

"Well, good that they're making such full recoveries so quickly. Of course, I won't share anything of a medical nature with the press except to say that they are expected to make full recoveries. Privacy laws and all that."

Rouleau checked his watch. "You'll be on the six o'clock news."

"CTV and CBC are covering my news conference. Sure you don't want to be part of it?"

"That's alright. I've got a bit of work to finish up."

"Well, don't burn any midnight oil. Today is a time to celebrate. God knows we get little enough reason most days."

———

Rouleau checked in with Vera to confirm the new hire was starting Monday before he headed back to the office. Woodhouse glanced up from his computer. He raised an arm in the air and motioned Rouleau over.

"I've just come across something odd." Woodhouse's tone and expression were puzzled.

"Oh?"

"This Ghazi Shahan who tried to drown Stonechild and his sister, he's got the same name as the man I saw coming out of Della Munroe's house this morning. Can there be two of them with the same name?"

"How did you get the name of her visitor?"

Woodhouse held up a form. "I had a check run on his licence plate and it came out Ghazi Shahan. I thought I was hallucinating when I heard his name again in relation to Leah Sampson and the attempted drownings today."

Rouleau took the piece of paper and studied it. Then he studied Woodhouse to see if he was trying to get a piece of the day's glory. He had the hopeful look of a man who might have landed on a good idea after a long drought.

"You're sure this fellow was in Della Munroe's house this morning?" Rouleau asked.

"Ghazi Shahan's black Nissan four-door was parked across the street from Della Munroe's house and he definitely came out her backyard and down her driveway. He was at her residence for approximately fifteen minutes."

Rouleau slapped the paper against his hand and smiled. "Brilliant work, Woodhouse. You've just possibly given us the connection that could put Della Munroe away."

Woodhouse grinned and leaned back in his chair with his hands behind his head. He swung his legs onto the desk and crossed them at the ankles. "All in a day's work, boss. All in a day's work."

———

The clock turned over to nine o'clock when Gundersund eased Stonechild's truck into her driveway. The adrenaline rush from the arrests was long gone and Gundersund felt weariness weighing him down. He turned off the engine and looked across at Stonechild. She'd leaned her head against the headrest and hadn't spoken since they left Brockville. In the half darkness, he couldn't tell if she was asleep or unconscious. A flashback to her limp body in the water sent a shudder through him. He reached over and touched her shoulder.

"We're home, Stonechild," he said. "Time to wake up." Relief filled him when she stirred. He slowly let out his breath.

She turned her head sideways and looked at him. Her eyes were black pools in the shadowy light. "Thanks for … everything. I'll see you tomorrow." She pulled the handle and swung the door open.

"You're not getting rid of me that easy." He pushed his door open too. "The doctor would only let you come home if I promised not to leave you alone overnight."

She looked across at him before stepping out of her truck. "I'm releasing you of your promise. I'm fine. All I'm going to do is get some sleep."

"Sorry. That's not on."

He followed her up the driveway and onto the back deck. She stopped at the top of the steps and looked down at him. "Seriously, Gundersund. I don't need a babysitter. Go home and spend some quality time with your wife."

"She's not there, so I'm all yours tonight."

"What about your dog? She must be due for an outing by now."

"Once I get you settled, I'll take Taiku and pick up Minny. The four of us will have a sleepover."

He listened to her grumbling as she unlocked the door. She stepped inside and let the door shut behind her. He caught it before it clicked shut. She was standing a few feet away from the door, watching him and shaking her head.

"I'm too tired to argue with you," she said, bending down to rub Taiku's head. "Could you let him out? He'll walk with you to your place if you call him when you go outside."

She'd disappeared down the hall by the time Gundersund shut the door and he followed her into the living room. The lights were off but he could see the outline of her sitting on the couch from the light through the window. He turned on a lamp, then crouched next to her and undid her shoes, slipping each one off and swinging her legs onto the couch. "Pillow?" he asked.

"Upstairs in my bedroom at the end of the hall."

He returned with a pillow and blanket and helped her to get comfortable. "Are you hungry? I make some mean scrambled eggs."

"You're fussing, Gundersund. I hate when people fuss."

"Actually, I'm hungry. If I make you something, I can make extra for myself."

"Well, you're in luck. I stopped at the store yesterday so you'll find bread, milk, eggs, and cheese. Cook away."

He turned the radio on low and hummed along to golden oldies as he worked. Cooking was something he enjoyed in his downtime even though he joked that he was bad at it. Pasta and seafood dishes were his specialties. Fiona had said the fact he knew his way around the kitchen was one of his better features. He prepared a tray for Stonechild and filled a second plate for himself. As he was about to bring the food to her, he heard a scratching at the door. He let Taiku in and filled his bowl with dry dog food that he'd found in the cupboard, then proceeded to the living room. Stonechild was awake. She propped herself up and accepted the tray.

"It's good," she said with her mouth full. "I didn't think I was hungry, but all of a sudden, I'm starving."

Gundersund sat across from her in the recliner and began eating.

"When will Meeza and Dalal get to see Nadirah?" Stonechild asked.

"Wolf and Claire are taking them over first thing in the morning."

"You trust Wolf with your fancy Mustang?"

"It's just a car. He offered to drive the Shahan girls back tomorrow, and since you insisted on leaving, I took him up on his offer." He smiled at her and speared another forkful of eggs.

She put her fork down and sighed. "Do you ever get weary of it all, Gundersund? All the awful things people do to each other?"

He took his time answering. "I focus on the good we do and don't try to spend much time on the nastiness. For every bad person, there are thousands of people trying to do the right thing. We're making a difference in their lives. That's what gets me through the shit."

"It's just hard to deal with sometimes."

He waited until she met his eyes and kept her gaze. "If we stop feeling, we stop being good at our jobs. You saved a life today, Kala. Maybe three lives, when you count Nadirah's sisters. Wolf says he's going to take them in until they get on their feet. There are details to be worked out, but they're going to do okay. He told me that he can offer counselling in his home, basically a residential setting. He's also taking in Gail Pankhurst when she gets out of the hospital. He's a decent guy. He's one of many decent guys out there."

"Yeah, I guess. Thanks."

He knew she was thanking him for more than his words of wisdom. "You're welcome. Are you done with that?"

She handed over her plate. "I can't eat any more."

He ate the rest of her meal while she watched. Her eyes closed a few times and he knew she was fighting sleep. He stood and picked up the dishes.

"I'm heading over to get Minny but I won't be gone long. See if you can sleep."

She stopped him at the doorway. "Gundersund, I'm not going to stay around Kingston much longer. I haven't told Rouleau yet but thought you should know since you're my partner."

"And I felt like we were just getting started." He said the words lightly to cover his disappointment. "I'll be sorry to see you leave."

"Maybe not too sorry after today." She shot him a quick smile.

He took their dishes into the kitchen. On his way to the back door, he stopped in front of the sliding patio door and looked at his reflection in the glass.

He could still hear the shrill screams of Mrs. Shahan as he chased her down the beach, leaving Wolf with Nadirah and Stonechild once he knew help was on the way. She'd switched to screaming in English when he'd finally caught up with her in the woods. Her burka had slowed her down. He'd tackled her, pinned her arms behind her back, and cuffed her. The evil in her words had shaken him: "My daughters are better off dead than bringing shame on our heads. They do not deserve to live. I wish they had never been born. I should have cut off their heads when I had the chance."

The local police had caught up with Ghazi in his car outside of Brockville.

He heard a cellphone ringing and Stonechild saying hello. He moved back down the hallway and listened in case the call concerned the case. By the time he realized it was a personal call, he'd overheard Stonechild say that she would drop everything to help. Gundersund moved back down the hall and stepped outside onto the deck.

45

ROULEAU BOUGHT TWO pints of Guinness and handed one
to Gundersund. They clinked glasses and wandered over to
the table where Ed Chalmers was holding court. They took
up positions at the ledge nearby. It was Friday night in the
Merchant and the retirement party had moved over from
the dinner and speeches at the hall. A local band was belting
out cover songs on the raised stage in the corner. The place
was crowded with patrons standing in groups around the
bar. The noise level was high.

"Looks like he's having one drink for every year of service," Gundersund observed. The table was filled with empty
glasses, the steady pitchers of beer supplied by the team.

"He's trained for this day his entire career," Rouleau said.

"Any word on Della Munroe?" Gundersund asked.

"The Crown is laying murder charges in the morning.
First degree."

"I thought as much after the Shahan kid admitted to
helping her fake the rape. Why do you think he admitted
to that?"

Rouleau shrugged. "We might have suggested that he
helped her kill her husband. He wanted to make it clear
that he hadn't."

"Do you believe him?"

"I have no doubt he killed Leah Sampson but I don't think he killed Brian Munroe. Della Munroe accomplished that all by herself."

"What about his parents?"

"Their involvement will be harder to prove. The mother was certainly part of the attempted murders. We have nothing on the father."

"Will the daughters move back with him?"

"I doubt it. Nadirah intends to look after her sisters. Even if we can't charge their father, the girls know what went on. They might be convinced to talk."

"Good evening, gentlemen."

Rouleau turned. Heath had appeared at his shoulder and they shook hands. Rouleau looked past him and nodded at Laney Masterson. She was stunning in a cream silk blouse, tight blue jeans, and knee-high boots. The light picked out red highlights in her hair, which tumbled loose on her shoulders. She smiled at him before turning her face and saying something into Heath's ear. Heath nodded and she slipped past him on her way to the washrooms.

"Laney had to work late and missed dinner but was up for a nightcap." Heath looked around. "This place is hopping."

"A typical weekend at the Merchant," Gundersund said, raising his glass.

Heath signalled the waitress and ordered two glasses of wine. He turned back to Rouleau. "So the new man starts Monday? Bennett, is it?"

"Bennett, yes."

"Vera tells me he's from the Ottawa force."

"He is. He was a uniformed officer and helped us with a murder investigation. He wanted to get into Criminal Investigations and applied. He's young and ambitious."

Heath nodded toward Woodhouse, who was sitting next to Chalmers. "That'll make for a nice change. What about Stonechild? Is she staying on?"

"She's taken some time to attend to a personal matter." Rouleau didn't add that she hadn't made any commitment to return.

The wine and Laney arrived at the same time. Heath took her by the arm and nodded toward Chalmers. "We'll just head over and have a word with the man of the hour. See you lads later."

They weaved through the crowd to join those surrounding the Chalmers's table. Rouleau watched as Woodhouse stood and gave Laney his seat. She sat next to Chalmers and angled her chair to watch the band. Rouleau felt like he was nineteen again, watching the pretty girl he liked with another guy.

Gundersund caught his eye. "I thought they were finished. His wife must be out of town."

"Heath's married?"

"Didn't I tell you? His wife comes from a long line of money. They tied the knot about five years ago after a quick courtship. Get you another beer?"

"Yeah." Rouleau watched Heath bend down and say something to Laney. She looked up at him and laughed. "On second thought, I think I'll switch to Scotch. It feels like that kind of night."

Gundersund lifted an arm and signalled for the waitress. "Then I'll join you. It feels like that kind of week."

———

The woman across from Kala shuffled a stack of papers until she found the form she was looking for. Her nails were painted a deep blue, complimenting the streaks in her spiked pink hair. Kala placed her close to forty. She had to be a lifelong smoker judging by the network of lines around her mouth and the stale smell of nicotine around her desk. The hardness in her features was softened by the compassion in her brown eyes. She cleared her throat.

"I've been in touch with social services in Kingston and they'll be assigning a worker for Dawn. You will be living at the address you provided?"

A loaded question. Kala knew this woman wouldn't release Dawn to her care if she knew Kala was between jobs with no fixed address. Deciding whether to keep moving or commit to Rouleau's team was out of her hands if she was to keep her promise to Lily. Such were the mysterious workings of the universe.

"I'll be at that address. As you know, I'm with Criminal Investigations on the Kingston force."

"Her mother asked that she live with you and based on your file, I believe this is the best place for Dawn at this time." The woman stamped and signed the form. She flipped it around to Kala and handed her the pen. "If you agree to being her guardian, sign here."

And if I don't?

"Will I be able to see her mother before we leave?"

The woman shuffled the papers as if buying some time to come up with an answer. She gave a sideways smile that bonded them in some kind of off-colour joke. "The thing is ... she doesn't want to see you."

Lily can't look me in the eye but wants me to take on her kid. The whole set-up was lunacy.

Kala stood with the woman and shook her hand. "I guess I'll be hearing how her trial goes."

"Of course, although I don't expect she'll be out for some time, given it was armed robbery and she was caught on film. She'll be tried in Ottawa where the crime took place. Her partner as well. He'll be arriving from Calgary tomorrow and they'll both be transported to lock up in Ottawa this week sometime."

"My cousin never did things the easy way."

Kala followed the woman down the hallway to collect the twelve-year-old girl who was now her responsibility. Instant substitute parent to an almost-teenager — life was about to get a lot more complicated and she had absolutely no idea if she was up to the challenge.

ACKNOWLEDGEMENTS

MY SINCERE THANKS go to the Dundurn team — in particular, my eagle-eyed editor Jennifer McKnight, who pours hours into making certain I've gotten the story just right, and my publicist Karen McMullin, who is helping to get my books into the hands of a wider audience. Jesse Hooper and Laura Boyle once again created striking cover designs. I am also forever indebted to Dundurn President Kirk Howard and Vice-President Beth Bruder for your ongoing support and belief in Canadian writers, especially of the crime fiction variety!

While *Butterfly Kills* is a complete work of fiction, the issues raised within its pages are not. My communications career in the federal government introduced me to research issues of family violence that sparked the germ of an idea for the overarching storyline. I would like to thank all of my colleagues in the Communications Branch and other sectors at the Department of Justice who have shown such interest in my writing and cheer my successes.

Thank you as well to so many friends and family — your support keeps me writing — and to my growing base of readers. I would like to send special thanks to Janet Bowick for going above and beyond, even as far as Monterey; Dawn Rayner, who always has my back; and to Ottawa City Counsellor

Katherine Hobbs, who never turns down a request to MC an event or promote my work and the work of all of those in our arts community. Finally, thank you to my husband Ted Weagle, who fits my writing obsession into our lives without qualm, and my daughters Julia Weagle and Lisa Weagle and my new son-in-law Robin Guy and his peeps Jane, Bill, and Adam Guy.

Read on for a preview of the next
Stonechild and Rouleau Mystery, *Tumbled Graves*

I

AT FIRST, CATHERINE Lockhart wasn't worried. Perplexed, possibly even annoyed if she was honest, but definitely not worried. It wasn't until she and Sammy stood on the country road in front of Adele Delaney's house that a sense of foreboding rolled slowly upwards like a bad meal from the bottom of her gut. Her shoulders wriggled as a shiver travelled up her back, even as her face was warmed by the late-April sun. *Something doesn't feel right*, she thought. She'd remember that exact moment of trepidation for days afterward.

Sammy tugged at her arm until she looked down into his freckled face. "They're home," he said, pointing a chubby finger toward the rusty Fiat halfway up the long driveway. His blue eyes brightened and his voice rose joyously. "Can I play with Violet?"

She'd meant just to walk by, to assure herself that Adele had been ignoring her phone messages because she'd been called away suddenly. The sight of Adele's car standing unashamedly in the drive felt like a betrayal — as if she were thirteen again and her best friend had just ditched her for the cooler crowd. The bit that didn't feel right, though, was the front door. Wide open, it swung gently back and forth on its hinges in the gusty spring breeze.

Catherine and Sam had moved into the small white house with the blue shutters a kilometre down the road a year and a half ago. She'd wanted Sam to grow up surrounded by trees and space, not in a scuzzy high-rise in the east end of Toronto. Luckily, her freelance writing job meant she could work anywhere. This stretch of land just east of Kingston and north of Highway 2 was close enough to civilization but far enough out of town to feel like they were living in the countryside. They'd met Adele and Violet at a mom-and-me fitness class and their kids had hit it off. Naturally, they'd started meeting up for coffee and playtime during the weekdays when Adele's husband, Ivo, was at work.

Catherine ruffled Sammy's ginger hair, soft and fluffy from his morning bath. The strands felt like warm silk in her fingers. "I'm not sure Violet and her mommy are up for company just now." She checked her wristwatch. "Maybe Violet's having a nap."

"Violet doesn't nap," Sam said, scowling. "She said that napping's for babies."

Before Catherine could stop him, Sam had sprinted across the gravel shoulder of the road and was halfway up the long drive. He stopped long enough to check that she was following before turning and running toward the front steps. A premonition made her call out to him.

"Wait, Sam! Wait for me."

She stepped around the puddles left over from the morning rain. Sam had barrelled through the mud and water in his black rubber boots, not caring about the muck splashing up onto his pants and jacket, but what four-year-old ever cared? She was panting when she reached him. The cigarettes were going to have to go or she would be on a ventilator before she hit forty. For the second time that day, she made a solemn promise to herself to quit. The same promise she made every time she exerted herself beyond a brisk walk. Sam had found a stick and was poking it into an ant hole. She spit onto her fingers and rubbed a smear of mud from his cheek.

"Why's the door open?" Sam looked up at her, his brow creased as he tried to work out what an open door could mean. She glanced up the steps into the shadowy hallway.

"No idea, kiddo, but we shouldn't just rush in. I'll knock and you wait here until Violet's mom tells us to enter."

Sam shrugged and moved over to a mud puddle where he began digging in the muck with his stick. Catherine slowly climbed the steps and grabbed onto the swinging door when she reached the top. She knocked and called down the hallway. The lights were off and gloom thickened towards the kitchen. "Adele! We've just come by to see if everything is okay. Are you home? Adele?"

Catherine kept one hand on the door and listened. The house smelled of cinnamon and apples. Adele must have been baking pies with apples she'd bought during an outing they'd all gone on that Tuesday. She looked back at Sam. He'd made it to the bottom step and looked up at her. "Can we go in?"

She hesitated.

No noise except the normal house sounds — the furnace kicking in, a clock ticking, the shudder of the fridge cycling on. She suddenly felt ridiculous, standing on her friend's steps, imagining the worst inside.

"I'm just going to make sure everything's okay since the door was left open," she said to Sam. "Come wait here in the hall while I have a look."

"I want to come, too," Sam said, stubbornly climbing the steps until he was next to her.

She took his hand and led him into the living room. All looked in order. The furniture was frayed and second hand, but cozy. Sunlight filtered through the white lace curtains. Sam dropped down next to the basket of Lego and started pulling pieces onto the floor. A moment later and he was laying on his stomach, fitting pieces together, their search for Violet forgotten.

She backed out of the room and walked quickly down the hallway into the back of the house, leaving Sam engrossed in building a spaceship. She stood at the entrance to the kitchen and glanced around the large space. The smell of cinnamon and spices was stronger but other smells competed. A container of open milk had been left on the counter, a half-filled glass beside it. A carton of eggs and a block of cheese were next to the stove. Plates of uneaten scrambled eggs and toast sat patiently on the table as if waiting for Violet and Adele to sit down and tuck in. Catherine stepped farther into the room until she was standing beside the kitchen table. A greyish crust had formed on the eggs, which looked the consistency of rubber. She reached a hand out and touched the toast with her fingertips. It was stone cold, unbuttered. She looked around the kitchen, her eyes searching the attached family room for any sign of them. She didn't know whether to be relieved or worried that they weren't anywhere to be seen.

She returned to the doorway to the living room. Sam was still busy with the Lego, so she had time to finish her search. She crossed to the stairs and climbed toward the light coming in from the window halfway up. The carpet was red and frayed but it muffled the sound of her footsteps. The landing was empty except for a laundry hamper at the far end. Catherine took a deep breath and darted the length of the corridor, checking each room as she went. Satisfied that nobody was lying dead on the floor in any of them, she took her time returning with a good look inside the three bedrooms and bathroom. *Nothing. Jesus.* Her overactive imagination was going to kill her before the cigarettes. She laughed out loud at herself before taking the stairs two at a time back to find Sam.

"Let's go, honey bun," she said to him.

He looked up. "Where's Violet?"

"They must have gone out." *In a big hurry.*

"Then why's their car in the driveway?"

Catherine stopped and looked at his scrunched up features, serious eyes so like the father he would never meet. She had no answer to his question or to the others that crowded in alongside. Why had the front door been left unlocked and swinging in the breeze? Why hadn't Adele answered her phone all afternoon? The anxious feeling returned. She reached into her pocket and pulled out her cellphone. She checked if Adele had responded to one of her calls, but no voice mail or text messages. What to do? She didn't feel right just leaving. Ivo worked in a bank downtown on Princess. She knew his direct line because she'd returned his call the summer before when he was organizing a surprise birthday dinner for Adele. She found his number and tapped the screen. He answered on the second ring.

"Catherine," he said as a way of greeting. His voice quavered as it always did when he spoke to her. He'd been a big awkward boy who'd grown into a man without quite recovering from his shyness. "What a pleasant surprise to see your name pop up. Everything okay?"

Now why had he asked that? "I'm not sure. Adele and Violet missed our appointment so I came by to see if they were feeling well. We were supposed to meet at playgroup in the church basement after lunch. The car's in the drive but the front door was open. Nobody's here."

A pause, then, "Are you sure?"

"Yes. Sam and I came in to check on them since the door was open. Their breakfasts are on the table uneaten. Could they have gone out with someone spur of the moment? Maybe in a friend's car?"

"I wouldn't know who. Adele doesn't have any other friends that I know of. I'm going to come home. Can you wait until I get there?"

"Of course." She wanted to say no, but his voice had picked up the worry she'd been trying to ignore for the past half hour.

———

She was sitting on the couch with Sam in her lap, reading a book about trucks, when Ivo clumped into the front hall. She heard the sound of his keys hitting the bowl on the entrance table and something heavier dropping onto the hardwood floor. A moment later and his six-foot-three hulk entered the living room. His shoulders were stooped from trying to hide inside himself and from sitting at a desk all day. His wavy brown hair needed a cut and his glasses were small and round and could use an update. The mystery was why Adele had found him attractive enough to marry. Catherine studied him for hidden depths of character whenever Adele invited her and Sam for supper. They had to be there but so far she hadn't detected anything spectacular. She'd always thought that Adele treated him as an afterthought.

"Any word?" he asked, voice hopeful.

"I'm afraid not," Catherine said.

"Well, I have no idea where they could have gotten to. When I got up this morning, Adele said that she was going to let Violet sleep in and they were going out in the afternoon. What time is it now?"

"Going on four."

"You checked the kitchen?"

Are you thick? "Yeah, and upstairs. Their breakfast is still on the table … uneaten."

She and Sam trailed behind him into the kitchen. He stood looking at the food, then spun around to face her.

"Did you try the basement?"

"No. I couldn't imagine what they'd be doing down there." Even as she said the words, a kind of hysteria began bubbling somewhere around her ribcage. Wild horses couldn't get her to go down there now.

"Well, I'll just run and check. You wait here."

"If you like." She leaned against the kitchen counter and listened to his footsteps clumping down the stairs, fainter as he descended. Sam came over and tugged on her arm.

"I want to go home," he said.

"In a minute. Let's just wait to say goodbye to Ivo." She kept an ear open as he made his way around the basement. What if Violet and Adele were down there? What would that mean? She pulled out her cellphone again and hit Adele's number. Tapping the fingers of her free hand on the counter, she listened to it ring once, twice, three times and then Adele's voice telling her to leave a message. Catherine didn't hide her worry as she had in her last messages, or her growing impatience. "Where are you, Adele? We're worried sick. Call me or Ivo as soon as you can."

She shut her phone and listened for Ivo. Just as she was thinking about calling down to him to make sure he was okay, he reappeared at the top of the stairs, holding Violet's pink knapsack with rabbit ears sticking out the open pouch. Puzzled lines creased the width of his forehead.

"That's odd. Violet never goes anywhere without her rabbit. It looks like she was watching a movie this morning while Adele was making breakfast. The television is still on but the movie is over."

"I wonder if we should call the police."

The words had popped out. They held both of them motionless for a moment. Their meaning had opened a box of fear that neither of them had wanted to acknowledge before now. Ivo looked across to the table where the full plates of food sat untouched. His eyes circled the family room and the mess on the kitchen counter before sweeping back to meet her own.

"You might be right," he said, "because I have absolutely no idea what is going on here. There has to be a logical explanation, but for the life of me, I can't think what it could be."

ABOUT THE AUTHOR

BRENDA CHAPMAN GREW up in Terrace Bay, Ontario, and earned an English degree at Lakehead University and a teaching degree at Queen's University. She spent fifteen years teaching in the field of special education followed by an eighteen-year career in communications with the federal government.

Brenda's first series of middle-grade Jennifer Bannon mysteries garnered critical acclaim, including the Canadian Library Association's nomination for the 2006 Book of the Year for Children Award. In addition to standalones and short stories, she penned the acclaimed Stonechild and Rouleau police procedural series and the Anna Sweet novella series for adult literacy, both nominated for numerous awards, including four Crime Writers of Canada Awards of Excellence. *Blind Date: A Hunter and Tate Mystery*, released in 2022, is the first in an exciting new series.

Brenda, husband Ted Weagle, and daughters Lisa and Julia are all avid curlers in the winter months. Brenda also enjoys working in her garden, travelling, biking, and reading. She is active in the crime-writing community, having served two years as president of Capital Crime Writers and two terms as regional director for Crime Writers of Canada. She and her husband make their home in Ottawa, Ontario.